THE CUSTODIAN

Book #3

Of the

The Moores Hill Thriller Series

By Ray Brown

COPYRIGHT

The Custodian

Published by Human Perimeter Press™
An Imprint of SentriPup Labs, LLC

ISBN: 979-8-9939776-5-2

Cincinnati, Ohio USA

First Edition: April 19, 2026

Chief Editor: Karen Fox, Human Perimeter Press™

Cover design by Human Perimeter Press™

DEDICATION

For Debra Black.

My sister. My biggest cheerleader.

TABLE OF CONTENTS

AUTHOR'S NOTE

The shamanic practices depicted in this novel are inspired by documented indigenous traditions spanning thousands of years across multiple continents.

The ceremonial use of psychedelic plant medicines, from ayahuasca in the Amazon to psilocybin mushrooms among indigenous North American peoples to peyote in Mesoamerica, represents one of humanity's oldest spiritual technologies.

Much of this knowledge was systematically destroyed through colonization and cultural genocide. In North America, the suppression of indigenous spiritual practices was particularly devastating, with sacred sites lost, oral traditions broken, and shamanic lineages forced into hiding or extinction.

The ash circles in this story are fictional. The loss they represent is real.

This novel acknowledges that loss.

~ *Ray Brown*

PROLOGUE

September 15, 2025
Flathead National Forest, Montana

Marcus Chandler found the circle at 2:18 PM on a Tuesday afternoon in mid-September.

He'd been hiking for six hours. Forty-two miles from the nearest road. Deep in wilderness where the maps showed nothing but elevation lines and the occasional creek notation. This was serious backcountry. The kind of terrain that killed three or four unprepared hikers every year.

But Marcus was prepared. Always had been.

Thirty-four years old. Archaeologist by training, wilderness guide by necessity when grant money ran thin. He'd spent three months planning this solo expedition. Mapping routes through Forest Service archives. Studying geological surveys. Cross-referencing Salish oral histories with terrain features that matched sacred site patterns he'd identified in Peru (Nazca Lines) and Rapa Nui (Easter Island).

Pre-Columbian ceremonial sites followed patterns. Geological patterns. Places where limestone bedrock came close to surface. Where electromagnetic readings showed anomalies. Where water ran deep beneath ground. Where indigenous peoples had gathered for thousands of years before European contact.

Marcus had found twelve such sites in five years of research. Published three papers. Built a reputation as someone who could identify sacred locations using scientific methodology combined with respectful attention to indigenous knowledge.

This Montana expedition was his most ambitious yet.

The Forest Service had no record of ceremonial sites in this sector. Too remote. Too difficult to access. But Salish oral histories mentioned a "listening place" in the high country northeast of Kalispell. Where shamans went to hear what the earth remembered. Where vision quests took young people to face themselves.

Marcus had spent two years getting permission from Salish tribal elders to search for it. Had committed to documenting anything he found and sharing discoveries with the tribe before publishing. Had promised to treat any site with appropriate respect.

They'd given him their blessing.

So here he was. Six hours into roadless wilderness. Following geological markers and intuition honed by a decade of fieldwork.

And he'd just found something.

The clearing appeared between two ridges where a natural amphitheater of stone and grass created a space that felt deliberately chosen even though no obvious human construction was visible. Maybe fifty feet across. Surrounded by pine and spruce that had probably stood here for centuries.

Marcus stopped at the clearing's edge and studied the ground with the careful attention that had made his reputation.

Limestone bedrock. Exposed in several places where thin topsoil had eroded over time. Old stone. Very old. Three hundred million years, deposited when this entire region was shallow sea.

He walked into the clearing slowly. Watching his footing. Looking for signs of disturbance or deliberate shaping.

There. Center of the clearing. A flat section of exposed bedrock roughly fifteen feet square where the soil had worn away completely.

Marcus knelt and brushed away a thin layer of pine needles and organic debris with his gloved hand.

And saw the edge of something carved into stone.

His heart rate picked up. This was it. This was what he'd been looking for.

He pulled a small brush from his pack and began carefully clearing the stone surface. Working in a methodical grid pattern. Photographing as he went. Documenting every stage of exposure.

Ten minutes later, the circle was visible.

Carved into bedrock. Ten feet in diameter. Cut to a depth of maybe two inches with remarkable precision. The edge showed tool marks. Deliberate work. Careful work. Old work.

And inside the carved circle, ash.

Not recent ash from any modern fire. This was compressed. Settled into the stone. The kind of ash that had been there for centuries. Maybe millennia.

Marcus sat back on his heels and stared.

This was significant. This was publishable. This was exactly what the Salish elders had described when they spoke of the listening place.

He spent the next hour documenting everything. Photographs from every angle. Measurements with tape and laser range finder. GPS coordinates recorded to seven decimal places. Sketches showing tool mark patterns in the carved edge. Samples of the surrounding soil for later analysis.

Then he noticed the symbols.

Carved around the circle's perimeter. Maybe thirty separate glyphs spaced evenly around the circumference. Not decorative. These were deliberate. Functional.

Marcus pulled out his reference materials. He'd brought printouts of proto-Indo-European symbol sets. Common markings found at sacred sites across multiple continents. The kind of root language that predated written Sanskrit.

He matched the first symbol. Then the second. Then the third.

His hands started shaking.

These were instructions.

Not warnings. Not prayers. Step-by-step instructions for performing a ceremony.

Marcus had seen similar instruction sets at sites in Peru and Rapa Nui. But never this complete. Never this detailed. Never this clearly preserved.

He photographed every symbol. Then started translating using his reference materials and the phonetic reconstruction systems he'd studied at Berkeley.

The ceremony had two parts. Opening and closing. The opening ceremony was relatively simple. Seven steps. Specific words to speak in sequence. A pattern to walk around the circle. The use of specific plant preparations to alter consciousness and enable proper perception.

The closing ceremony was more complex. Required materials Marcus didn't have. Timing he didn't fully understand. But the opening ceremony was clear.

And completely performable.

Marcus checked his watch. 4:15 PM. He had maybe three hours of good daylight left. Enough time to finish documentation. Set up camp. Maybe run some preliminary electromagnetic readings of the site.

He walked the clearing perimeter looking for anything else significant.

And found the mushrooms.

Growing in a dense cluster near the base of a fallen pine log. Twenty feet from the circle. Psilocybin species. Easily identifiable by the blue bruising when he touched the stem. The distinctive cap shape. The spore print pattern.

Psilocybin mushrooms. Growing naturally. Right next to a sacred site with carved instructions specifically mentioning "plant preparations to alter consciousness and enable perception."

This wasn't coincidence.

The ancient peoples who carved these instructions knew about these mushrooms. Knew they grew here. Probably cultivated them. Used them as part of the ceremony. As medicine. As tool for accessing altered states of consciousness that enabled whatever work happened in this circle.

Marcus stood there for a long moment thinking.

He'd come here to document a sacred site. To find what the Salish elders described. To add to human understanding of pre-Columbian religious practices.

And he'd found exactly that. Ceremonial instructions carved in stone. Physical evidence of shamanic practices. Publishable data that would make his career.

But there was another option.

He could document the site academically. Take his measurements and photographs and leave.

Or he could actually perform the ceremony. Experience what the ancients experienced. Understand the practice from the inside rather than just cataloging it from outside.

That was the difference between archaeology and anthropology. Archaeologists studied artifacts. Anthropologists studied experiences. Participated. Engaged. Learned by doing.

Marcus had always been more anthropologist than archaeologist.

He made his decision.

He would perform the opening ceremony. Just once. Just to understand what it did. What the ancients were accessing. Why this location was considered sacred. What kind of consciousness shift the ceremony enabled.

It was academic inquiry. Direct phenomenological research. The kind of first-person data that couldn't be gathered any other way.

And he would be careful. He'd used psilocybin before. Controlled doses in safe settings during graduate school. He understood set and setting. Understood the importance of intention and preparation.

This wouldn't be recreational. This would be research.

Marcus gathered the mushrooms carefully. Approximately two grams dried weight. Enough for a moderate experience. Not heroic dose territory. Just enough to access altered states while maintaining some cognitive function and observational capacity.

He ate them at 5:30 PM. Sitting at the circle's edge. Watching the late afternoon sun angle across the clearing. Autumn light turning everything gold.

While he waited for them to take effect, he reviewed the ceremony instructions one more time. Memorized the sequence. The words. The movements.

Seven steps. Walk the circle perimeter clockwise. Speak specific words at each cardinal direction. Enter the circle at the seventh step. Sit in the ash at the center. Allow consciousness to separate and perceive what the location enables.

Simple. Direct. The kind of ceremony that had probably been performed here hundreds of times over thousands of years.

Marcus felt the first effects around 6:00 PM. Mild euphoria. Visual acuity increasing. Colors becoming more saturated. The standard psilocybin onset he'd experienced before.

He stood and approached the circle.

Began walking the perimeter clockwise.

At north, he spoke the first words. Ancient proto-Indo-European syllables that sounded harsh and guttural in his mouth. He didn't know what they meant. Just that the symbols instructed him to speak them here.

At east, the second words. Smoother. More flowing. His tongue finding the sounds surprisingly easily.

At south, the third words. The psilocybin was building now. Perception shifting. Boundaries becoming more porous.

At west, the fourth words.

The temperature dropped.

Not gradually. Instantly. Marcus felt it like walking through a door into refrigeration. The air went from comfortable September warmth to winter cold in three seconds.

That wasn't normal.

Psilocybin affected visual perception, emotional processing, sense of time. It didn't cause actual temperature changes. It didn't affect thermal sensation in ways that registered as physical cold.

But Marcus was cold. Genuinely cold. He could see his breath condensing in air that had been seventy degrees ten seconds ago.

He looked down at the ash beneath the circle's edge.

It was moving.

Not wind movement. The air was completely still. But the ash was shifting. Swirling in patterns that seemed to respond to his presence. To the words he'd spoken. To something.

Marcus's heart rate increased. This was unexpected. This was outside normal psychedelic parameters.

He should stop. Walk away. Wait for the psilocybin to metabolize. Approach this with more preparation.

But he'd already started the ceremony. Already spoken four of the seven sequences. The instructions were clear about completing what you begin.

Fifth step. Fifth words. The syllables came easier now. Like his mouth remembered them from somewhere deep.

Sixth step. Sixth words.

The pulling sensation began.

Not physical. Not like gravity or magnetism. This was perceptual. Like his awareness was being drawn somewhere. Like there was a direction he could move that wasn't spatial but was somehow real.

Marcus reached the seventh step. Stood directly in front of the circle's carved opening. Spoke the final words.

And stepped into the ash.

His consciousness separated.

Not metaphorically. Not as psychedelic metaphor or altered perception. Marcus had used psilocybin a dozen times. He knew what altered states felt like. This was different.

His awareness detached from his body and moved.

Not through space. Through something else. Through what he could only describe as layers. Like reality had depth he'd never perceived before. Like consciousness could navigate perpendicular to normal dimensions.

Marcus tried to hold onto rational thought. Tried to observe scientifically. Tried to document what was happening so he could write about it later.

But the experience was accelerating beyond his ability to process it analytically.

He was somewhere else now. Nowhere else. Both simultaneously.

His body remained sitting in the ash circle in Montana wilderness. He could still feel it peripherally. Could still sense the cold. Could still sense the clearing around him.

But his awareness was also somewhere that had no physical referent.

A space that wasn't space. Where consciousness existed without substrate. Where awareness operated without neural correlate.

And he wasn't alone there.

Something else was present. Multiple somethings. Awareness without form. Consciousness without body. Perception without perceiver.

They noticed him.

Marcus felt their attention focus and terror spiked through his awareness like electricity.

This was wrong. This wasn't supposed to happen. Psilocybin didn't create encounters with external entities. It altered internal perception. It didn't allow contact with actually separate consciousness.

But these felt separate. Felt other. Felt completely alien to anything Marcus had ever experienced.

They moved closer. Not through space because there was no space. But their attention intensified. Their focus narrowed. They were studying him. Examining him. Trying to understand what he was.

And Marcus realized with horror that they wanted what he had.

A body. Physical form. The ability to act in material reality.

They wanted to cross over. To use him as bridge. To access the world he came from.

Marcus tried to pull back. Tried to return to his body. Tried to reverse whatever he'd done by entering the circle and speaking the words and allowing the separation.

But he didn't know how.

The instructions had been for opening. Not for returning. He'd read about the closing ceremony but hadn't memorized it. Hadn't brought the materials it required. Hadn't understood he would need it.

He was stuck.

And the entities were pressing closer.

Marcus could feel them now. Not physically. But as pressure. As weight. As presence pushing against the boundaries of his awareness trying to find a way in.

They were trying to enter him.

He panicked.

Fought them. Tried to force them away. Tried to build barriers between his consciousness and theirs.

But he didn't know how to do that. Had no framework for defending himself in non-physical space. Had no training in whatever this kind of confrontation required.

The pressure increased.

And Marcus saw something that shattered him completely.

He saw himself.

Not his physical body. His shadow. His capacity for violence. His potential for cruelty. Every dark impulse he'd ever suppressed.

Every selfish desire. Every predatory thought. Every time he'd wanted to hurt someone and chosen not to. Every fantasy of power and domination he'd never acted on.

All of it manifested. Visible. Undeniable.

This was what the ceremony was supposed to show. This was the shadow integration work the ancients had designed these sites for. This was the confrontation with darkness that enabled growth and healing when approached with proper preparation and guidance.

But Marcus had no context for integration. No elder support. No framework for understanding what he was seeing.

He looked at his own darkness and thought it was the entities.

Thought the predatory impulses he was perceiving were external things trying to possess him. Thought the cruelty was them, not him. Thought the violence was invasion, not recognition.

And he fought it.

Fought his own shadow while the entities watched with what felt like curious detachment. Fought what he should have been integrating. Fought himself while thinking he was fighting something else.

Time became meaningless. Marcus didn't know if he'd been in this state for seconds or hours. His body still sat in the ash circle in Montana but his awareness was trapped in this space between dimensions fighting battles that were actually internal while perceiving them as external threats.

He saw terrible things.

Saw himself committing acts of violence. Saw himself hurting people. Saw himself giving in to every dark impulse he'd ever had. Saw himself as predator. As monster. As everything he'd never wanted to be.

Saw what he could become if he made certain choices.

This was the medicine working exactly as designed. Showing him his capacity for darkness so he could integrate it consciously. Choose light while acknowledging shadow. Become whole by accepting all parts of himself.

But Marcus had no framework for that integration.

He just saw himself as monster and couldn't reconcile it with his self-image as good person. Educated person. Respectful researcher. Someone who studied ancient peoples with reverence and care.

He couldn't hold both images simultaneously. Couldn't accept that he contained both light and darkness.

So his consciousness fractured under the pressure.

Part of him still trying to be the rational archaeologist. Part of him convinced he was being invaded by demons. Part of him identifying with the darkness and wanting to give in. Part of him trying to escape. Part of him trying to fight. Part of him trying to die to make it stop.

No integration. Just fragmentation.

And somewhere in that fragmentation, his body started moving.

Marcus wasn't conscious of controlling it. His awareness was still trapped in the space between. But his body stood up. Stumbled out of the circle. Started walking.

The entities weren't controlling him. They weren't possessing him. They had no interest in his physical form. They were just watching with alien curiosity as human consciousness tore itself apart from inability to integrate its own shadow.

Marcus's body walked through wilderness in full psychotic episode.

He was convinced something was chasing him. Something was trying to get in. Something was hunting him through the trees.

But it was all internal. All his own mind fragmenting under the weight of unintegrated shadow perception. All his own darkness trying to be acknowledged and being fought instead.

He ran. Fell. Got up. Ran more. Trees tore at his clothes. Rocks bloodied his hands and knees. He didn't notice. Didn't feel it. Was too deep in psychotic terror to register physical pain.

His body knew it was in danger. Started producing adrenaline in quantities that should have triggered cardiac arrest. Heart rate spiking to 180. 190. 200. Blood pressure critical.

But he kept running.

Kept fighting the thing that was actually himself.

Kept trying to escape what couldn't be escaped because it was internal.

And somewhere in the wilderness, running blind, he fell.

Hit his head on exposed rock. Not hard enough to kill immediately. But hard enough to cause serious damage. Skull fracture. Subdural hematoma. Blood pooling where it shouldn't pool.

Marcus lay on the ground bleeding into his brain while his consciousness remained trapped in the space between fighting battles that didn't exist against enemies that were actually himself.

The psilocybin would metabolize eventually. Would release his consciousness back to normal awareness. Would end the separation and return him to baseline perception.

But by then his brain would have sustained too much damage.

Marcus Chandler died alone in Montana wilderness at approximately 11:47 PM on September 15, 2025.

His body wasn't found for three weeks.

When Forest Service rangers finally located him using search dogs and GPS data from his abandoned vehicle, the cause of death was listed as accidental fall resulting in head trauma.

The coroner noted unusual bruising patterns suggesting extreme physical exertion prior to death. Blood toxicology showed psilocybin metabolites. Death was ruled accidental. Experienced archaeologist took mushrooms in remote wilderness, experienced disorientation, fell, died from injuries.

Case closed.

No one questioned why an experienced researcher would take psychedelics alone in roadless backcountry.

No one noticed the GPS coordinates in his field notebook pointing to a specific location six miles from where his body was found.

No one followed up on the hundreds of photographs on his camera showing an ash circle carved into bedrock with symbols around its perimeter.

No one read his journal entry dated September 15, 2025, 4:30 PM:

Found the site. Instructions intact. Symbols match proto-Indo-European ceremonial language. Planning to perform opening ceremony at sunset. This could revolutionize our understanding of pre-Columbian shamanic practices.

If this works, I'll finally understand what they were accessing. What the medicine was designed to enable.

Academic observation, properly documented.

What could go wrong?

The journal was returned to his parents with his other effects. They never read it. Couldn't bear to look at his research materials. Donated everything to the University of Montana where he'd gotten his doctorate.

The photographs sat in university archives unexamined.

The GPS coordinates were filed with case materials and forgotten.

And in Montana wilderness, forty-two miles from the nearest road, an ash circle remained open.

Unsealed.

Active.

Waiting for the next curious person to find it and make the same mistake Marcus Chandler had made.

The ancient peoples had understood. Had prepared seekers carefully. Had guided integration with months of fasting and meditation and elder support. Had treated the medicine with profound respect.

But that knowledge was gone. Destroyed by colonization. Lost in the gap between indigenous wisdom and modern curiosity.

And the sites remained.

And people kept finding them.

And some knowledge, once lost, kills those who try to recover it without wisdom.

Marcus Chandler learned that lesson.

He just didn't survive it.

DISCOVERY & DUAL THREATS

CHAPTER 1: SEVEN COORDINATES

Owen Mitchell's car pulled into Emma Caldwell's driveway at 10:40 on a Thursday morning in late March.

Emma saw him from the kitchen window of the farmhouse on Oak Street. She set down her coffee and watched him retrieve his laptop bag from the passenger seat, moving with the particular deliberation of someone carrying information that weighed more than hardware.

She had the door open before he reached the porch.

"Morning," Owen said.

"You called an hour ago. You're early."

"Couldn't wait."

Emma stepped back to let him in. Owen had gained weight since the Benefactor investigation ended three months ago. Not much, but enough that his shirt pulled slightly at the shoulders. He'd been spending long hours doing research work for a book about the Aldrich network, sedentary work that kept him at a desk instead of moving through the field investigations that used to keep him lean.

"Coffee?" Emma asked.

"Please."

She poured two cups while Owen set up his laptop on the kitchen table. The farmhouse kitchen still smelled faintly of the eggs she'd made an hour ago. March light came through the windows at an angle that said spring was trying, not quite succeeding. The view from the kitchen included Carnegie Hall's bell tower two blocks south on Main Street, visible above the roofline of the McClanahan house next door.

Owen opened his laptop and waited until Emma sat down across from him.

"I found something in Agent Baker's files," he said. "The cloud backup she gave me access to before she died."

Emma had known this was coming. Owen didn't show up unannounced unless he'd found something that mattered.

"What kind of something?"

"A list." Owen turned the laptop so Emma could see the screen. "Seven GPS coordinates. No context. No notes. No connection to any of the Aldrich network documentation. Just coordinates and a single word attached to each one."

Emma looked at the screen.

Seven lines of latitude and longitude. Seven locations marked with precision. And below each coordinate, in a separate column, the same word repeated:

Custodian.

"When did she create this?" Emma asked.

"File metadata says November 2025. Four months before she died."

Emma studied the coordinates. Numbers meant nothing without context. She pulled the laptop closer, opened a new browser tab, copied the first coordinate into Google Maps.

Montana. Western part of the state. Middle of nowhere, forty-two miles from the nearest town.

She tried the second coordinate.

Peru. The Andes. High altitude location with no visible structures in satellite view.

The third: England. Wiltshire. The satellite image needed no explanation.

The fourth: Turkey. Southern region. Ancient stonework visible even from orbit.

The fifth: Chile. Far out in the Pacific. An island most people only knew from photographs of stone figures.

The sixth: Egypt. The coordinates landed on the Giza plateau with the precision of someone who had been there.

Emma paused before checking the seventh coordinate. Something about the numbers looked familiar. She had seen these specific digits before, but could not place where.

She copied the seventh coordinate into the map.

Moores Hill, Indiana.

The pin dropped on Main Street, directly on top of Carnegie Hall.

Emma stared at the screen for ten seconds.

"You recognize it," Owen said.

"That's here."

"I know. That's why I came over instead of calling."

Emma zoomed in on the Carnegie Hall pin, then zoomed out to see the building's full footprint. She knew every inch of that building. Had attended elementary school there when the historical society still rented classrooms to Moores Hill students. Had walked those halls every day for six years while her mother taught third grade in the west wing and gave historical tours on weekends.

Carnegie Hall wasn't a landmark to Emma. It was muscle memory. The way the main staircase creaked on the third step. The smell of old wood and floor wax in the basement storage rooms. The exact angle of afternoon light through the bell tower windows in March.

"It's not just Carnegie Hall," Emma said. "This coordinate is too precise for that. It's marking a specific location inside the building."

She opened another tab, searched for Carnegie Hall maintenance records. Found the building survey documents from the 2015 renovation. Scrolled through floor plans until she found the basement level, then the sub-basement notation.

There. Maintenance access point. Coordinates listed in the survey documentation.

They matched exactly.

"It's the sub-basement," Emma said. "Under the main floor, below the storage level. Carnegie Hall has a maintenance tunnel that runs underneath the foundation. This coordinate is marking the access point."

Owen leaned forward. "You've been down there?"

"No. But I've seen the maintenance logs. My mother had access to the building records when she was giving tours. She kept copies of the architectural surveys."

"Why would Baker be tracking a maintenance tunnel in Moores Hill?"

Emma didn't answer immediately. She looked at the other six coordinates again. Montana wilderness. Peru mountains. An island lost in the Pacific. Egyptian desert. Turkish highlands. The Wiltshire plain in England.

Seven locations. All remote. All far from major population centers.

Except the seventh.

Moores Hill, Indiana. Population 597. Carnegie Hall, a 118-year-old building on Main Street where the historical society held meetings and elementary school classes took field trips.

"What does custodian mean?" Emma asked.

"I was hoping you could tell me."

"Baker never mentioned this word to you? Never referenced these locations?"

"Not once." Owen pulled the laptop back toward himself, opened a different file. "I've spent two weeks trying to connect these coordinates to the Aldrich network. None of them match known properties. None of them appear in any of the trafficking route documentation. As far as I can tell, Baker never shared this list with anyone. She kept it separate from the main investigation files."

"Was this encrypted?"

"It was. Standard encryption Baker used for sensitive materials. I had her credentials after she died, gave them to the FBI during the investigation cleanup. This list was in a separate folder, isolated from the Aldrich files. She didn't want anyone connecting the two."

Emma stood up and walked to the kitchen window. Carnegie Hall's bell tower was visible above the neighbor's roof. The building looked exactly the way it always looked. Buff brick. White trim. Bell tower rising four stories above Main Street. A landmark. A piece of Moores Hill history.

Her mother had loved that building. Had spent hours there, not just during school hours or tour shifts, but on her own time. Linda Caldwell had photographed every room, documented every architectural detail, kept meticulous records of renovation work and maintenance schedules.

Emma had always assumed her mother's interest in Carnegie Hall was historical. An appreciation for local architecture. A connection to Moores Hill's founding years.

But what if it wasn't?

What if Linda had been watching something?

Emma's phone rang. James McClanahan.

She answered. "Hey."

"Emma, are you home?" James's voice was tight. Controlled. The way he sounded when something was wrong but he was trying not to alarm anyone.

"Yes. Owen's here. What's going on?"

"Town council had an emergency meeting last night. Someone filed a petition to condemn Carnegie Hall. Structural safety concerns. They're claiming the building is dangerous and needs to be demolished."

Emma's stomach dropped. She turned to look at Carnegie Hall's tower through the window. "What kind of safety concerns?"

"Foundation issues. Basement flooding. Electrical problems. The petition cites an engineering report I've never seen before, commissioned by some group called the Moores Hill Safety Coalition. Ever heard of them?"

"No."

"Neither has anyone else. The coalition filed as a nonprofit three months ago. Anonymous donors. No local members that anyone can identify. All correspondence through lawyers in Cincinnati."

"And they want Carnegie Hall demolished."

"Condemned first, then demolished. The engineering report claims the building poses imminent danger to the public. Margaret Hendricks is fighting it, but the coalition has money and lawyers and an official-looking report that most of the town council doesn't have the expertise to evaluate."

Emma looked at the laptop screen. At the seventh coordinate. At the word "Custodian" beneath it.

"When was this petition filed?" she asked.

"Three weeks ago. But it just came to a vote last night. Emergency meeting. I only found out this morning when Margaret called me."

"Why would they call an emergency meeting about a building that's stood for 118 years?"

"That's what I want to know. Something about this feels wrong."

Emma's mind was racing. Baker's encrypted list. Seven coordinates. One pointing to Carnegie Hall's sub-basement. And now, someone trying to condemn the building.

"James, can you come to the farmhouse? Owen found something you need to see."

"Give me twenty minutes."

Emma ended the call and turned back to Owen. "Someone's trying to condemn Carnegie Hall. Petition filed three weeks ago by a group nobody's heard of."

Owen's expression didn't change but his eyes sharpened. "Three weeks ago is when I started finding Baker's encrypted files. When I first saw this list."

"You think it's connected?"

"I think Baker was tracking seven specific locations for a reason. I think she kept this list separate from the Aldrich investigation for a reason. And I think someone filing a condemnation petition against one of those locations three weeks after Baker's encrypted files became accessible is not a coincidence."

Emma sat back down at the table. Looked at the seven coordinates. At the word "Custodian" repeated seven times.

Guardian. Keeper. Someone responsible for maintaining or protecting something.

"We need to see what's in that sub-basement," Emma said.

"I was thinking the same thing."

"Carnegie Hall closes at five. The historical society has a board meeting tonight at seven, so the main floor will be occupied until nine. But the basement levels are restricted access. If we go in after ten, the building should be empty."

"You want to break into Carnegie Hall."

"I want to see what Agent Baker was protecting. And I want to know why someone's trying to condemn a building that happens to sit on top of one of the seven locations she was tracking."

Owen nodded slowly. "We'll need someone who knows the building security."

"James can handle that."

They drank coffee in silence while they waited. Owen scrolled through the coordinates again, cross-referencing with satellite imagery. Emma watched Carnegie Hall's bell tower through the kitchen window and thought about her mother walking through those halls two thousand times without ever mentioning what might be beneath them.

Linda Caldwell had known things. Had tracked things. Had spent twenty years investigating connections that seemed invisible until someone knew where to look.

Emma had always believed her mother's investigation was about the missing women. The disappearances in southeastern Indiana that stretched back decades. The pattern Linda had documented in journals and case files and encrypted drives.

But what if that investigation was connected to something else?

What if the missing women were part of a larger pattern Linda had been tracking all along?

James McClanahan's truck pulled up behind Owen's car at 11:14.

Emma met him at the door. James looked exactly the way he always looked. Jeans, work boots, flannel shirt under a canvas jacket. Red curly hair that needed cutting. The kind of steady competence that came from growing up in a place where you learned to fix your own truck and help your neighbors and not ask unnecessary questions.

He'd quit the Dearborn County Sheriff's Department three months ago. Not because of corruption. Not because of the sheriff's failures during Linda Caldwell's murder investigation. James had quit because he was tired of having his hands tied by budgets, bureaucracy, and the particular politics of rural law enforcement. Ten years as a deputy had been enough.

Now he worked with Emma and Owen at Clue-Minati, the investigation firm they'd founded after Mark Caldwell's trial ended. Better pay than deputy work. His own hours. No sheriff breathing down his neck about jurisdiction and proper procedure.

Emma stepped aside and James came into the kitchen. He nodded to Owen, poured himself coffee without asking, sat down at the table.

"What did you find?" he asked Owen.

Owen turned the laptop around.

James studied the screen for thirty seconds, then looked at Emma. "You know this location."

"Sub-basement access point under Carnegie Hall. The coordinate is exact."

"What's custodian mean?"

"We don't know yet."

James scrolled through the other six coordinates, zoomed in on each satellite image, studied the terrain. "These are all remote. Wilderness. No structures visible except the Carnegie Hall location."

"That's what we're trying to understand," Owen said.

James closed the laptop and looked at Emma. "You want to go down there."

"Tonight. After the historical society meeting ends. Can you get us in?"

"Probably. I'd need to check the building security logs first, see what alarms are active in the basement levels. But Carnegie Hall's security is twenty years old. Basic motion sensors, door contacts. Nothing I can't work around if I have a few hours to prepare."

"Then we go tonight."

James took a long drink of coffee. "Your mother gave tours at Carnegie Hall for fifteen years."

"I know."

"She had keys to that building. Access to every floor. She could have checked the sub-basement anytime she wanted."

"I know."

"If she didn't tell you what was down there, maybe she had a reason."

Emma met his eyes. "Maybe she did. But Agent Baker was tracking this location. She encrypted the coordinates and kept them separate from every other file in her investigation. Whatever's in that sub-basement, it mattered to Baker. It mattered enough that she protected it."

"And Baker died trying to expose the Aldrich network," Owen added quietly.

James was silent for a moment. Then he nodded. "And now someone's trying to condemn the building that sits on top of one of her protected locations. That's not coincidence."

"No," Emma said. "It's not."

James stood up. "I'll go check the building security systems now. Margaret gave me access codes after the Benefactor investigation. I can review the logs remotely, map out the sensor coverage, figure out the best approach route."

"You'll meet us back here?" Emma asked.

"Six PM. I'll have everything mapped by then. We'll go in at ten-fifteen. That gives the board meeting time to end and the building time to clear."

He grabbed his keys and headed for the door. Stopped. Turned back.

"Emma, if there's something under Carnegie Hall that Baker thought was worth protecting, and someone else thinks is worth destroying a 118-year-old building to access, we need to be ready for this to be bigger than we think."

"I know."

James left. Emma heard his truck back out of the driveway and disappear down Oak Street.

Owen closed his laptop. "He's right. This feels bigger than a maintenance tunnel."

Emma walked back to the window. Looked at Carnegie Hall's bell tower. At the building her mother had loved and documented and protected for thirty-five years.

"Baker was FBI," Emma said. "She investigated the Aldrich network for years. Documented human trafficking routes across three states. Built cases that would have brought down fifty people if she'd lived to prosecute them."

"And she kept this list separate from all of that," Owen said. "Which means she thought these seven locations were important enough to protect even from her own agency."

"Why?"

"I don't know. But I think we're about to find out."

Emma checked the time. 11:47 AM. Ten and a half hours until they broke into Carnegie Hall.

Ten and a half hours to prepare for whatever they were going to find twenty feet beneath Main Street.

She turned from the window. "I'm going to review everything my mother kept about Carnegie Hall. Every survey, every maintenance record, every photograph. If there's any indication she knew about the sub-basement, it'll be in her files."

"I'll keep researching the other six coordinates," Owen said. "See if there's any pattern to the locations beyond remoteness. Any historical significance. Any connection to indigenous sites or archaeological features."

They worked in silence for the next six hours. Emma in her mother's old office upstairs, going through boxes of documents Linda had kept about Carnegie Hall. Owen at the kitchen table, searching databases and cross-referencing geographical data.

At 5:30 PM, Emma found something.

A photograph in one of Linda's Carnegie Hall files. Dated 1998. The year Emma's father died. The year everything changed.

The photograph showed the Carnegie Hall basement. Standard documentation photo. But in the background, partially visible behind a shelving unit, Emma could see the edge of a wall that didn't match the others. Different color. Different texture.

Like it had been added later. Like it was covering something.

Emma brought the photograph downstairs. Showed Owen.

"That's the false wall," Owen said immediately. "That's what we're looking for. Your mother documented it twenty-eight years ago."

"She knew," Emma said quietly. "She knew something was down there. She photographed it. She kept the evidence. But she never told me."

"Maybe she was protecting you."

"Or maybe she was protecting whatever's down there."

James arrived at 6 PM exactly. Spread building security diagrams across the kitchen table. Pointed out alarm sensors, motion detectors, camera coverage.

"There's a blind spot," he said. "Rear entrance, east wall. Camera doesn't cover the last six feet of approach. Motion sensor is positioned for the hallway, not the door itself. If we enter there, we can avoid detection until we're already inside."

"And once we're inside?" Emma asked.

"Basement level has motion sensors but they're zoned. If we stay in the storage section, we won't trigger the administrative wing sensors. The sub-basement access isn't on the security grid at all. Whoever installed the system twenty years ago either didn't know about it or deliberately left it off the network."

"So we can access the sub-basement without triggering alarms."

"As long as we're careful."

They reviewed the plan three more times. Entry point. Route through building. Basement access. Emergency exits if something went wrong.

At 9:45 PM, they left the farmhouse.

Drove separately to Carnegie Hall. Parked on different streets. Approached from different directions.

Met at the rear entrance at 10:12 PM.

James had the door open in thirty seconds. They slipped inside. Closed it behind them.

Stood in a maintenance hallway Emma had never seen before.

And began walking toward whatever Agent Karen Baker had died protecting.

CHAPTER 2: THE LIST

The maintenance hallway was exactly what Emma expected from a 118-year-old building. Concrete floor. Cinder block walls painted industrial beige sometime in the 1970s. Fluorescent fixtures overhead, currently dark. The air smelled like old building. Dust and wood and the particular mustiness of spaces that didn't get much ventilation.

James pulled three small LED flashlights from his jacket and handed them out. "Stay close. Don't touch anything you don't need to touch. Security system is offline but I can't guarantee there aren't manual triggers I don't know about."

Emma turned on her flashlight and followed James down the hallway. Twenty feet in, they reached a junction. Left led toward the main building interior. Right led deeper into the maintenance section.

James went right.

The hallway narrowed. The ceiling dropped. Emma could see water stains on the walls where ancient pipes had leaked and been fixed and leaked again. Carnegie Hall was 118 years old. The maintenance infrastructure beneath it had been patched and repaired and jury-rigged by a century of custodians who worked with whatever budget the historical society could scrape together.

They reached a heavy wooden door marked STORAGE. AUTHORIZED ACCESS ONLY. James tried the handle. Locked. He pulled a tension wrench and pick from his jacket pocket. Worked the lock. It gave in fifteen seconds.

The storage room was exactly what Emma expected. Metal shelving units holding cardboard boxes labeled with years and categories. Historical documents. Donation records. Architectural surveys. The accumulated paper trail of a building that had outlived most of the people who built it.

James swept his flashlight across the room, then stopped on the far wall.

"There," he said.

Emma moved closer. At first she didn't see it. The far wall looked like every other wall. Cinder blocks. Beige paint. But when James angled his flashlight at a specific point, Emma caught the line.

A vertical seam. Too straight to be natural. Too deliberate to be coincidence.

The same wall from her mother's photograph. Twenty-eight years later. Still there. Still hiding whatever was behind it.

James walked to the wall and ran his hand along the seam. "False wall. Painted to match. You'd never notice it unless you were looking."

"Can you open it?" Emma asked.

"If I can find the release mechanism." James started at the top of the seam and worked his way down, pressing sections of wall, feeling for anything that moved. Owen kept his flashlight on the door they'd come through, watching for movement.

Emma studied the false wall. Someone had built this. Someone had sealed off whatever was behind it and made it look like solid wall. And someone had documented the coordinates carefully enough that GPS could locate it to within inches.

Baker had known.

And Linda had known.

But neither of them had told Emma what was back there.

James found the mechanism at knee height. A section of baseboard that looked like every other section but gave slightly when pressed. He pushed harder. Something clicked deep in the wall.

The false wall section swung inward on hidden hinges, revealing darkness beyond.

Cold air came through the opening. Not fresh air. Old air. The kind that had been sealed in stone for decades and didn't move unless something disturbed it.

Emma felt the temperature drop five degrees in three seconds.

James shone his flashlight through the opening. "Tunnel. Descending. Stone walls. Looks like original construction, not modern addition."

Emma moved to the opening and looked in. The tunnel was narrow. Four feet wide. Maybe seven feet tall. Cut stone walls that showed chisel marks. Old work. The kind of craftsmanship that didn't exist anymore because nobody needed to hand-carve tunnels beneath buildings when there were machines to do it faster.

But in 1907, when Carnegie Hall was being built, they'd done it by hand.

"We're going down there," Emma said.

"That's why we're here," Owen said from the doorway.

James went first. Emma followed. Owen came last, pulling the false wall section closed behind them but not latching it. If something went wrong, they needed a way out that didn't require finding a hidden mechanism in the dark.

The tunnel descended at a steady angle. Twenty degrees, maybe. Steep enough that Emma had to watch her footing. The floor was stone, worn smooth in the center where generations of feet had walked. The walls stayed four feet apart. The ceiling stayed just above James's head.

Emma counted steps. Thirty. Forty. Fifty. They had to be beneath Main Street by now. Beneath the foundation of Carnegie Hall. Beneath ground that had been undisturbed for thousands of years before someone decided to build a college there in 1856.

At sixty steps, the tunnel leveled out.

At seventy, it widened into a chamber.

James stopped at the threshold and swept his flashlight across the space. Emma stepped up beside him and did the same.

The chamber was circular. Twenty feet across. Fifteen feet tall at the center, domed. The walls were the same cut stone as the tunnel, but here the craftsmanship was different. More deliberate. More careful. The stones fit together with precision that didn't leave gaps.

The floor was flat bedrock. Natural stone that had never been shaped or moved. And carved into that bedrock, perfectly centered in the chamber, was a circle.

Not drawn. Carved. Cut into the stone to a depth of maybe two inches. Ten feet in diameter. And inside that circle, ash.

Pure ash. Gray and black and undisturbed. Ash that looked like it had been placed there deliberately and left alone for longer than Emma could calculate.

Emma stepped into the chamber. The air was colder here. Not the cold of winter air or unheated spaces. This was different. The kind of cold that came from stone that didn't hold warmth. Stone that existed in places where temperature didn't matter because nothing living was supposed to be there.

Owen followed her in. "What is this?"

Emma didn't answer. She was looking at the ash circle. The edges were too perfect. The depth too consistent. Someone had carved this circle into bedrock with precision that required tools and time and knowledge of exactly what they were creating.

But that wasn't what made Emma stop walking.

On the far side of the chamber, carved into the stone wall at eye level, were letters.

R.M. 1907. Sealed.

Emma walked around the ash circle, careful not to step inside it, and moved to the wall. The letters were carved deep. Not scratched. Carved. Each letter two inches tall. The kind of work that took hours with a chisel and mallet.

"R.M.," Owen said, coming up beside her. "Initials?"

"Robert Moore." Emma's voice sounded strange in the chamber. Too flat. Like the stone absorbed sound and didn't let it echo properly. "He founded Moores Hill College in 1856. Built Carnegie Hall in 1907 with Andrew Carnegie's donation. His name is on every building document, every historical record."

"And he sealed this," James said from behind them.

Emma looked back at the ash circle. Sealed. The word implied containment. You sealed something to keep it from spreading. To keep it from escaping. To keep it separate from everything else.

But what had Robert Moore been sealing?

Emma walked back to the circle's edge and knelt down. The ash was undisturbed. No footprints. No marks. No sign that anyone had been in this chamber since Robert Moore carved his initials in 1907.

But Baker had known about this place. Had tracked it with GPS precision. Had labeled it with a single word: Custodian.

Guardian. Keeper. Someone responsible for maintaining something.

Emma stood up and backed away from the circle. The cold was getting worse. Not physically. She could still feel her fingers and toes. But something about the chamber made her skin prickle. Made the hair on the back of her neck stand up. Made every instinct that had kept humans alive for millennia say this is wrong, you shouldn't be here, leave.

"We need to document this," Owen said. He pulled out his phone and started taking photographs. The camera flash lit up the chamber in brief, harsh bursts. Each flash made the ash circle look darker by contrast. Each flash made the carved initials look deeper.

James was examining the tunnel entrance they'd come through. "No other exits. This is the only way in and out."

Emma looked at the chamber again. At the precision of the stone walls. At the ash circle carved into bedrock. At the initials that said someone had found this place and made a decision to seal it.

And then Carnegie Hall had been built on top of it.

And eight years later, Moore Hall had burned down.

And two years after that, the college had closed.

Emma had read the history. Her mother had told her the stories. Moores Hill College, founded in 1856, closed in 1917 and moved to Evansville where it still operated as the University of Evansville. The official reason was financial. The unofficial reason was never quite explained.

But standing here, twenty feet beneath Main Street, looking at an ash circle carved into bedrock that predated written language, Emma thought maybe the unofficial reason was exactly what she was looking at.

Robert Moore had built Carnegie Hall over something he shouldn't have built over.

And consequences had followed.

"Emma." Owen's voice pulled her back. "Look at this."

Emma walked to where Owen stood at the chamber's edge, near the tunnel entrance. He was shining his flashlight on the wall just above the threshold.

More carving. Smaller. Harder to read. But there.

What lies beneath must never be disturbed. What is sealed must remain sealed. Seven sites. Seven families. Seven custodians who know what the ground remembers.

Emma read it twice. Then a third time.

Seven sites.

Seven GPS coordinates in Baker's file.

Seven custodians.

"This isn't the only one," Emma said quietly.

"No," Owen said. "It's not."

James had moved back to the ash circle and was examining the carved perimeter. "The ash is original. Has to be. Nothing's been added or removed in decades, maybe longer. But why carve a circle into bedrock and fill it with ash?"

"I don't know," Emma said.

"Your mother spent thirty-five years working in this building. She had to know this was here."

"She knew." Emma was certain of that. Linda Caldwell had documented everything. Had photographed every corner of Carnegie Hall. Had access to maintenance records and architectural surveys. She would have found the tunnel. Would have found this chamber. Would have read what Robert Moore carved into the wall.

And she had never told Emma.

Because maybe some things weren't meant to be shared. Maybe some knowledge was dangerous. Maybe Linda had been doing exactly what the wall inscription said.

Watching. Guarding. Making sure what was sealed stayed sealed.

Emma looked at the ash circle one more time. At the perfect carved edge. At the ash that had remained undisturbed for more than a century.

Something about this place was wrong in ways Emma couldn't articulate. The cold. The way sound didn't echo. The way her skin kept trying to tell her to leave. All of it added up to a feeling she didn't trust but couldn't ignore.

A sound from above stopped her thoughts completely.

Glass breaking. Distant but distinct. Somewhere in the building above them.

James's flashlight went out immediately. "Off. Lights off now."

Emma killed her flashlight. Owen did the same. Darkness absolute in the chamber.

More sounds from above. Footsteps. Heavy. Multiple people. Moving with purpose through the building.

Not security. Security would have called out. Would have announced themselves. Would have turned on lights.

These people were moving in darkness. Just like Emma's group.

"Someone else is here," Owen whispered.

"They're not being quiet," James said. "They want to be heard."

More sounds. Something being dragged. Metal on concrete. The distinct crack of wood breaking.

"They're destroying something," Emma said.

James moved toward the tunnel entrance. "We need to get out. Now."

They moved quickly but carefully back through the tunnel. Up the incline. Sixty steps to the storage room. James paused at the false wall opening, listening.

The sounds were louder now. Closer. Coming from the main floor directly above the basement.

James opened the false wall carefully. Peered out into the storage room. "Clear."

They slipped through. James pushed the false wall closed behind them. It settled into place with a soft click that sounded too loud in the silence.

The storage room door was still unlocked. James opened it slowly.

The sounds from above had stopped.

Emma's instincts screamed this was wrong. This was a trap. This was deliberate.

But they had to get out.

James led them through the maintenance hallway. Back toward the rear entrance. Moving as quietly as possible.

They reached the main basement corridor.

And saw the damage.

Water was pouring down the stairs from the main floor. Gallons of it. Flooding the basement. The overhead lights were flickering, damaged. And spray-painted across the corridor wall in large red letters: UNSAFE BUILDING.

"They flooded it," Owen said. "Deliberately broke water pipes."

"Not just pipes," James said, shining his flashlight on the electrical panel near the stairs. The cover had been ripped off. Wires were exposed and sparking. "They damaged the electrical system too. Made it look dangerous."

Emma understood immediately. "They're creating evidence. Evidence to support the condemnation petition."

The building alarm started screaming.

Not the security alarm. The fire alarm. Triggered by the water damage or the electrical sparking or both.

"We need to leave," James said. "Right now."

They ran for the rear entrance. Emma's boots splashing through water that was already two inches deep in the corridor. Owen close behind her. James bringing up the rear.

They burst through the rear door into the alley behind Main Street.

The building alarm was deafening from outside. Lights were coming on in nearby houses. People would be calling 911. Police would arrive in minutes.

"Separate," James said. "Meet at Emma's farmhouse. Don't run. Walk normal. If anyone asks, you were home all night."

Emma nodded. Started walking toward where she'd parked her car three blocks away. Forced herself to walk at normal pace. Forced herself to look calm.

Behind her, Carnegie Hall's alarm screamed into the night.

She reached her car. Got in. Started the engine. Drove toward Oak Street at exactly the speed limit.

Her phone buzzed. Text from James: *Police just arrived. Fire department behind them. Building evacuated.*

Another text from Owen: *That wasn't random vandalism. That was professional sabotage.*

Emma pulled into her driveway. Killed the engine. Sat in the dark car for ten seconds trying to process what had just happened.

They'd found the chamber. Found the ash circle. Found Robert Moore's seal from 1907. Found evidence that this was one of seven sites being tracked by Agent Baker.

And while they were underground, someone else had been in Carnegie Hall. Destroying things. Creating evidence of structural failure. Supporting the condemnation petition with deliberate sabotage.

Someone knew about the chamber.

Someone wanted Carnegie Hall destroyed.

And they were willing to commit crimes to make it happen.

Emma got out of the car and went inside. Made coffee. Waited for Owen and James to arrive.

They showed up within ten minutes of each other. James first, then Owen. Both looking grim.

They sat at Emma's kitchen table without speaking for a long moment.

Finally James said, "That was coordinated. Timed perfectly. While we were underground, they were destroying evidence of the building's stability."

"Creating evidence of instability," Owen corrected. "The flooding. The electrical damage. All of it makes the building look dangerous. Makes the condemnation petition look reasonable."

"But why?" Emma asked. "What's worth destroying a 118-year-old building to access?"

"Whatever's in that chamber," James said. "Whatever Robert Moore sealed in 1907. Whatever Agent Baker was tracking. Someone knows about it. And they want it."

Emma looked out the window at Carnegie Hall's bell tower, still visible in the darkness. The alarm had stopped now. The building would be secured. But the damage was done.

More evidence for the condemnation petition.

More pressure to demolish the building.

More danger to whatever was sealed beneath.

"We need to find out what those seven sites are," Emma said. "We need to understand what Baker was protecting. Because someone is coming for Carnegie Hall. And I don't think they're going to stop."

"Agreed," Owen said. "I'll start researching first thing in the morning. Historical records. Archaeological databases. Anything that connects those seven locations."

"I'll talk to Margaret Hendricks," James said. "See what she knows about the condemnation petition. Who's really behind the Safety Coalition. Where their funding is coming from."

Emma nodded. But her mind was still in the chamber. Still seeing the ash circle carved into bedrock. Still reading the words Robert Moore had carved into stone more than a century ago.

What is sealed must remain sealed.

Seven sites. Seven families. Seven custodians.

And someone was trying to unseal one of them.

Emma intended to find out why.

And stop them.

CHAPTER 3: CARNEGIE HALL

Emma didn't sleep.

She sat at her kitchen table until three in the morning searching for everything the internet knew about Robert Moore and Carnegie Hall and Moores Hill College.

There wasn't much.

Robert Moore, born 1848, died 1924. The college was actually founded by his father, Adam Moore, in 1854. Robert had taken over leadership after his father's death in 1889 and served as president until the college closed in 1917.

Carnegie Hall, built 1907 to 1908. Total cost approximately $41,000, with Andrew Carnegie contributing $18,500. Opened January 1908.

Moore Hall, the original building, burned November 13, 1915. Origin of fire undetermined. Total loss. Two years later, the college closed and moved to Evansville.

Emma read everything three times, cross-referenced dates, built a timeline. Then she closed her laptop and sat in the dark kitchen watching Carnegie Hall's bell tower through the window.

Robert Moore had built Carnegie Hall in 1907.

Had carved R.M. 1907. Sealed into the chamber wall beneath it.

Had watched Moore Hall burn eight years later.

Had presided over the college's closure two years after that.

Had died seven years later in 1924.

And somewhere in that timeline, he had documented what he knew. Had written about seven sites and seven custodians and what the ground remembered.

Emma needed to find that documentation.

At six-thirty Friday morning, she made coffee and waited for Carnegie Hall to open.

The Dearborn County Historical Society operated the building on a volunteer schedule. Fridays: 10 AM to 4 PM. Archives access by appointment only.

Emma had an appointment.

She'd called at seven AM and spoken to Margaret Hendricks, the historical society president, who remembered Emma's mother and said of course Emma could access the archives, Linda had loved the Carnegie Hall collection, such a tragedy what happened to her, come anytime.

Emma arrived at 9:52.

The main entrance to Carnegie Hall faced Main Street. Double doors. Original hardware from 1908. The kind of brass handles that had been polished by ten thousand hands over 118 years.

The building looked different in daylight after last night. Police tape still marked the rear entrance. Caution signs warned about water damage. But the historical society was open for business despite the overnight vandalism.

Margaret Hendricks met Emma in the main hall. Seventy-two years old, white hair in a neat bun, cardigan sweater over a floral print dress. The kind of woman who had been volunteering at the historical society since before Emma was born.

"Emma Caldwell." Margaret's smile was warm. "I haven't seen you since your mother's funeral. How are you holding up?"

"I'm alright. Thank you for asking."

"Your mother was a treasure. We still miss her terribly." Margaret gestured toward the stairs. "The archives are in the basement, same as always. You said you were researching Robert Moore?"

"Yes. I'm trying to understand the college's closure. Why it happened when it did."

"Well, you've come to the right place. We have most of Robert Moore's papers. Donated after his death in 1924." Margaret led Emma down the main staircase to the basement level. "Financial records, correspondence, building plans, donation records. It's all cataloged, though I'm afraid the organization is somewhat archaic. Your mother always said we needed to digitize everything, but funding, you know how it is."

The basement smelled like water damage from last night. Wet carpet. Mildew starting. But the archives section was elevated, had escaped the flooding.

Margaret showed Emma to a work table near the shelving units. "Robert Moore's papers are in section C, boxes 1889 through 1924. The collection stops at his death. If you need anything, I'll be upstairs dealing with insurance adjusters. Just come find me."

Emma thanked her and waited until Margaret's footsteps faded up the stairs.

Then she walked to section C and started pulling boxes.

Box 1907 contained building permits and construction records for Carnegie Hall. Architectural drawings. Contractor invoices. Andrew Carnegie's donation letter, dated March 1906, promising $18,500 toward construction of a new academic building.

Emma spread the documents across the work table and studied the architectural drawings. Main floor layout. Second floor classrooms. Third floor administrative offices. Fourth floor bell tower access.

And basement. Single level. Storage and maintenance.

No sub-basement. No tunnel. No chamber.

Emma checked every drawing twice. The basement plans showed a single large room divided into storage sections. No access points to lower levels. No notation of any kind about what lay beneath the foundation.

But Emma had been in that chamber. Had seen the carved stone walls. Had seen the ash circle carved into bedrock. Had read the inscription about seven sites and seven custodians.

Robert Moore had documented everything about Carnegie Hall except the one thing that mattered.

Or he had documented it somewhere else.

Emma returned box 1907 to the shelf and pulled box 1915.

Moore Hall fire investigation. November 13, 1915. Origin of fire undetermined. Total loss. Insurance claim filed. Claim paid. Rebuilding discussed, ultimately abandoned.

And tucked into the back of the fire investigation file, a handwritten note on personal stationery:

The fire was consequence. I knew the risks when I made the decision to disturb what should have remained undisturbed. But I did not know the timing. Eight years. Long enough to believe I had escaped judgment. Long enough to be wrong.

The note wasn't signed. But the handwriting matched Robert Moore's signature on the Carnegie Hall building permits.

Emma read the note three times.

Disturb what should have remained undisturbed.

Not "open the doorway." Not "perform the ceremony."

Disturb.

Across town, James McClanahan sat in his truck outside the Dearborn County Courthouse reviewing public records on his laptop.

The Moores Hill Safety Coalition had filed as a nonprofit organization three months ago. December 2025. The filing listed a Cincinnati address for correspondence. No physical office. No board members named publicly. Just a registered agent, a law firm called Marshall & Associates.

James had looked up Marshall & Associates. Corporate law. Environmental compliance. Real estate development. The kind of firm that helped companies navigate regulations and permits.

Not the kind of firm that typically represented small-town safety advocacy groups.

He dug deeper. Found the engineering report the coalition had submitted with the condemnation petition. Commissioned from a firm called Morrison Technical Services. Based in Louisville.

James searched for Morrison Technical Services. Found a website. Professional. Slick. Portfolio showing dozens of structural assessments for historic buildings across Kentucky, Indiana, and Ohio.

And a pattern.

In the past five years, Morrison Technical had assessed twelve historic buildings. All had been condemned as structurally unsafe. All had been demolished within eighteen months of condemnation.

And all twelve properties had been sold to development companies immediately after demolition.

James made a list. Cross-referenced the properties. Found the connection.

Every building demolished after a Morrison Technical assessment had been located on or near land with indigenous historical significance. Burial grounds. Ceremonial sites. Locations documented in state archaeological databases.

The Safety Coalition wasn't trying to protect public safety.

They were targeting specific sites for demolition.

Back at Carnegie Hall, Emma pulled more boxes. 1916. 1917. The college's final years. Enrollment declining. Funding problems. Faculty leaving.

In box 1917, a folder labeled COLLEGE CLOSURE. FINAL RECORDS.

Inside: financial statements, faculty resignation letters, student transfer records, and a single-page document titled BOARD OF TRUSTEES FINAL RESOLUTION, dated May 1917.

The resolution was dry. Formal. The college would close effective June 30, 1917. Operations would transfer to Evansville. Assets would be sold or donated. The Main Street campus would be maintained by the newly formed Dearborn County Historical Society.

But at the bottom of the resolution, in the margin, someone had written in pencil:

I treated sacred medicine as academic curiosity. I broke what should never have been broken. R.M.

Emma set the document down carefully.

Robert Moore had watched his family's college die because of a decision he made in 1907. Had documented that decision in margins and private notes but never in official records. Had known exactly why the college closed but had never told anyone outside the board of trustees.

And then he had lived seven more years carrying that knowledge before dying in 1924.

Emma checked the time. 11:38. She'd been in the archives for almost two hours.

She returned to section C and pulled box 1924. Robert Moore's death. Estate inventory. Property transfers. Donation records.

The Moores Hill College campus buildings and grounds were transferred to the Dearborn County Historical Society. Carnegie Hall became the society's headquarters. Moore Hall ruins were cleared. The land was sold to a private buyer.

And Robert Moore's personal papers were donated to the Carnegie Hall archives in accordance with his will.

Personal papers. Journals. Documents.

Emma scanned the donation inventory. Seventeen boxes of correspondence. Four boxes of financial records. Two boxes of personal effects.

And one box labeled PRIVATE JOURNALS. SEALED PER TESTAMENTARY INSTRUCTION.

Sealed.

Emma stood up and walked back to the shelving units. Scanned section C. Found box 1924-PJ at the end of the row.

The box was smaller than the others. Wooden, not cardboard. The kind of box made to last. And across the lid, a metal clasp with a small padlock.

Locked.

Emma carried the box back to the work table and examined the padlock. Old. Brass. The kind that had been manufactured before combination locks existed. This needed a physical key.

And Emma didn't have a key.

She looked at the lock more carefully. The mechanism was simple. Single tumbler. Nothing sophisticated. The kind of lock that was meant to keep casual curiosity away, not determined investigation.

Emma pulled a paperclip from the supply drawer at the work table, straightened it, bent the end into a hook, and worked it into the padlock mechanism.

The lock gave in fifteen seconds.

Emma removed the lock and opened the clasp. The box lid lifted on brass hinges that protested with age but didn't resist.

Inside: a single leather-bound journal. Dark brown. Eight inches by ten inches. Maybe two inches thick. The leather was old but well-preserved. No title on the cover. No markings.

Emma lifted the journal out of the box and set it on the work table.

The leather was soft. Worn smooth by hands that had held it many times over many years. Emma opened to the first page.

Robert Moore's handwriting. Dated January 3, 1917.

I am writing this in the final weeks of the college. We will close in June. The students will transfer to other institutions. The faculty will find other positions. And Moores Hill College, founded by my father in 1854, will cease to exist because I made a decision in 1907 that I had no right to make.

I disturbed sacred ground. I treated medicine as curiosity. I broke what the ancients created for healing because I believed my education gave me permission to access knowledge I had not earned.

I was wrong.

***

James called Margaret Hendricks from his truck.

"Margaret, it's James McClanahan. I need to ask you about the Safety Coalition."

"Oh James, isn't it terrible? They're trying to destroy our beautiful building."

"I'm looking at public records. The coalition filed three months ago. Do you know who's actually behind it?"

"Nobody knows. All the correspondence comes through lawyers in Cincinnati. We've never met anyone from the coalition in person."

"And the engineering report they submitted?"

"From Morrison Technical Services. It claims the building is structurally unsound. But James, I've been in this building for forty years. It's solid. That flooding last night was deliberate. Someone cut those pipes."

"I know. I saw the damage. Margaret, I need to tell you something. Morrison Technical has condemned twelve buildings in the past five years. Every single one was demolished. And every single one was located on historically significant indigenous land."

Silence on the other end. Then Margaret's voice, quieter. "You think they're targeting Carnegie Hall because of what's underneath."

"You know about the chamber."

"Of course I know. I've been president of this historical society for twenty years. Your mother knew too, as did Emma's mother. Linda Caldwell. She was very protective of this building. Very particular about who had access to certain areas."

"Did Linda ever tell you what the chamber is?"

"No. Just that it was important. That it had been sealed for good reason. That it should remain sealed."

"And now someone's trying to destroy the building to access it."

"What do we do?"

"Fight the condemnation. I'm gathering evidence that Morrison Technical has a pattern of targeting indigenous sites. That the coalition isn't a legitimate safety organization. That this is coordinated."

"Will that be enough?"

"I don't know. But it's a start."

***

Emma read Robert Moore's journal with hands that started shaking after the first page.

When we excavated the Carnegie Hall foundation in the spring of 1907, we broke through to bedrock at fifteen feet. The stone was ancient. Limestone deposited three hundred million years ago when this entire region lay beneath a shallow sea.

And carved into that bedrock, we found the circle.

Ten feet in diameter. Perfect. The ash was undisturbed, compressed into the stone over what must have been thousands of years. Around the circle's perimeter, symbols. Not random marks. Deliberate carvings. Instructions.

I am an educated man. I studied classical languages at Yale. I recognized elements of proto-Indo-European. Root words that predated written Sanskrit. The symbols were old. Older than any civilization I had studied.

And I could read them.

Two ceremonies documented in those carvings. One to open. One to close.

But the word "open" is misleading. The ancients did not carve these instructions to warn against danger. They carved them for future healers. Future shamans. Future seekers who would come to these sites prepared to face what every human must face: the darkness within themselves.

The ceremony was never meant to "open a doorway to another dimension." It was meant to open the self. To create a sacred space where consciousness could perceive what is always present but normally hidden. Where the shadow could be faced. Where integration could occur.

The ancient peoples who created these sites understood something my civilization has forgotten: that true healing requires facing darkness. That growth demands confronting what we would rather ignore. That wisdom comes only to those willing to see themselves completely, without flinching.

They left these instructions because they wanted future generations to have access to this medicine.

Emma stopped reading. Looked around the empty archive room. Back at the journal.

Medicine. Not evil. Not danger. Medicine.

Robert Moore continued:

They expected the knowledge would be passed down. Elder guidance. Months of preparation. Fasting, meditation, intention-setting. The community support needed to integrate what would be seen.

What they did not expect was that their knowledge would be destroyed. That colonization would break the transmission. That men like me would find these sites with instructions intact but context obliterated.

I performed the opening ceremony alone. Unprepared. Disrespectful of what the ancients had created. I used plant medicine without guidance. I entered the sacred space without intention. I treated profound psychological work as academic experiment.

The ceremony worked exactly as designed.

It showed me my shadow. My capacity for cruelty. My selfishness. My darkness. Everything I could become if I made certain choices.

This is what the medicine does. This is what it has always done. It does not transport consciousness to "another dimension." It reveals dimensions of consciousness that exist within us but remain hidden during normal awareness.

The ancients knew this. They prepared seekers carefully. They guided integration afterward. They understood that seeing one's shadow without framework for integration destroys rather than heals.

I had no framework.

I saw my darkness and it terrified me. I believed I was perceiving something external, something alien, something trying to invade from outside. I did not understand I was seeing myself.

And in my terror and ignorance, I sealed the site.

Emma's phone buzzed. Text from James: *Safety Coalition is front for development company targeting indigenous sites. Found pattern. Twelve buildings condemned and demolished in 5 years. All on ceremonial land.*

She texted back: *Found Robert Moore's journal. The chamber is a healing site. Ancient shamanic medicine. Colonization destroyed the knowledge of proper use.*

James: *So they're trying to destroy sacred medicine sites?*

Emma: *Or access them. I don't know which yet.*

She went back to the journal.

I carved the symbols of closing into the chamber wall. I spoke the words that would prevent future access. I filled the carved letters with iron and salt to bind the closure.

I told myself I was protecting future generations from danger.

But I was protecting myself from truth.

And in doing so, I condemned future generations to the same ignorance that nearly destroyed me. I broke the chain further. I added my own seal to the damage colonization had already done.

The fire that consumed Moore Hall eight years later was not punishment from "the other side." There is no other side. There is only consciousness perceiving itself in states we are not trained to integrate.

The fire was consequence of psychological contamination I created by performing sacred ceremony without preparation, without respect, without guidance. The trauma I experienced radiated outward from the site. The barrier I had weakened through careless use took time to manifest its damage.

By the time Moore Hall burned, I understood what I had done. But it was too late.

Emma turned more pages. Found Robert Moore's documentation of the seven sites. GPS coordinates written in latitude and longitude years before GPS satellites existed. He must have calculated them from astronomical observations and survey data.

Montana. Peru. Rapi Nui. England. Egypt. Turkey.

And Moores Hill, Indiana.

Each site documented carefully. Each location marked. Each custodian family named.

But Robert Moore's tone had changed from his earlier academic writing. This was confession. This was apology.

I have spent months researching the other sites. The Morrison family in Montana. The Valdez family in Peru. The other custodian lineages documented in records that survived colonization's devastation.

What I learned has broken my heart.

These families were not originally "guards" preventing access. They were guides. Shamanic lineages that maintained the sites and prepared seekers for the journey. They understood the medicine. They knew how to support integration afterward.

But colonization destroyed that role. The European powers killed the shamans. Burned the knowledge. Broke the transmission deliberately because they feared what they did not understand.

By the time I found the Carnegie Hall site in 1907, the Morrison family in Montana had been reduced to "guards" keeping people away. The Valdez family in Peru maintained watch but no longer guided seekers. The knowledge of safe use had been lost within living memory.

And now I have made it worse. I have added another seal. Another barrier. Another break in the chain of transmission.

The sites are not dangerous. Unprepared use is dangerous.

The ceremonies are not evil. Approaching them with disrespect and ignorance is evil.

The medicine itself is healing. But medicine without proper dosage, without guidance, without integration support becomes poison.

Emma read faster now, racing through Robert Moore's documentation. His guilt. His understanding of what he'd done. His hope that future generations would understand.

Near the end of the journal, dated November 1917, a final entry:

I have finished documenting what I know. The seven sites. The seven families. The ceremonies and their proper context. Everything a future custodian would need to understand.

I pray someone will read this and see what I failed to see in 1907: these sites are not prisons holding evil at bay. They are hospitals waiting for healers who know how to use them.

The ceremonies are not doorways to other dimensions. They are mirrors showing us ourselves completely. What we perceive as "external entities trying to cross over" is our own shadow seeking recognition and integration.

The ancient peoples understood this. We have forgotten.

Until we remember, we must guard. We must watch. We must prevent unprepared people from accessing medicine they cannot integrate.

But we must also preserve the knowledge. We must document the truth. We must hope that someday, the shamanic wisdom will be recovered and these sites can serve their purpose again.

That is what custodian truly means. Not guard preventing access. But keeper preserving knowledge until it can be properly used.

I am sealing this journal in a box. My will specifies it should remain sealed until someone ready to understand finds it.

May that person have the wisdom I lacked.

May they approach the medicine with respect I failed to give.

May they help restore what colonization destroyed.

The Moore family's responsibility does not end with me. It passes to my children, and their children, and every generation that follows.

We are custodians. We preserve. We protect. We wait.

Someday, perhaps, we will guide again.

Emma closed the journal and sat at the work table for a full minute without moving.

Robert Moore hadn't condemned future generations.

He'd left them instructions to heal what he'd broken.

Her phone buzzed again. James: *Coming to Carnegie Hall. Need to show you something.*

Emma texted back: *Archives. Basement.*

She looked around the empty archive room. Fluorescent lights humming overhead. Metal shelves holding boxes of documents that told only part of the story.

The real story was in this journal.

The real story was about medicine destroyed by colonization and sealed by fear and waiting for someone brave enough to understand it properly.

James appeared in the archives doorway five minutes later. Saw Emma's expression. Saw the journal on the table.

"What did you find?"

Emma gestured at the journal. "Robert Moore's private documentation. He performed a ceremony in the chamber in 1907. Ancient shamanic ritual using plant medicine. It showed him his own capacity for darkness and he panicked. Sealed the site out of fear instead of understanding. The college closed because he broke something he didn't know how to fix."

James sat down across from her. "The sites are shamanic healing locations."

"Yes. The ceremonies use altered consciousness to force confrontation with shadow. With the darkest parts of yourself. The ancients had preparation and guidance to integrate what they saw. But colonization destroyed that knowledge. Now when people find the sites and use them, they see their shadow without framework for integration. And it breaks them."

"That's what the Safety Coalition is afraid of."

"Or that's what they want to access. I don't know which yet."

Emma opened the journal to the section documenting the seven sites. Showed James the coordinates. The custodian families.

"Morrison family in Montana," James read. "Valdez in Peru. Atan on Easter Island. Hassan in Egypt. Yilmaz in Turkey. Whitmore in England. Moore in Moores Hill."

"Seven families guarding seven sites," Emma said. "Preserving knowledge until it can be used properly again. That's what custodian means. That's what Agent Baker was tracking."

"And the Safety Coalition is trying to destroy one of them."

"Or all of them. Carnegie Hall is the only site with a structure built on top of it. Which makes it the only one they can attack through legitimate channels. Condemn the building. Clear the site. Done."

James pulled out his laptop. Opened his research files. Studied the coordinates against archaeological databases.

His expression went dark. "The other six sites are remote. Wilderness. No structures, no permits, no legal mechanism to touch them. But Carnegie Hall sits on Main Street in a town of seven hundred people. They can walk right up to it."

Emma felt ice in her stomach. "So we're the weak point."

"You're the only point. If they take Carnegie Hall, they take the one site they can actually reach."

"Then we need to make sure they don't get it."

Emma looked at the journal. At Robert Moore's careful documentation. At his warnings and hopes and guilt.

"He sealed the Carnegie Hall site because he failed the medicine," Emma said quietly. "He saw his darkness and couldn't integrate it. So he locked it away and hoped nobody else would make his mistake. But he left instructions. Left the truth. Left hope that someday someone would understand what these sites really are."

"And now someone's trying to destroy the one site they can get to."

Emma carefully replaced the journal in the wooden box. Closed the lid. Locked the padlock.

Then she carried it upstairs to Margaret Hendricks.

"Margaret, I need to check out this box. Is that possible?"

Margaret smiled. "Of course, dear. We trust you. Just sign the checkout log."

Emma signed the log. Margaret didn't ask what was in the box.

Emma carried it to her car and set it on the passenger seat.

Robert Moore's journal. The truth about seven sacred sites. Instructions for ceremonies that required preparation destroyed three hundred years ago.

And somewhere, someone was trying to eliminate the one site they could reach.

Emma started the car and called Owen.

"I found Robert Moore's journal. The sites aren't dangerous. They're healing medicine. Ancient shamanic ceremonies for shadow integration. But colonization destroyed the knowledge of how to use them safely."

"So when people access them now..."

"They see their darkness without framework for integration. And it breaks them. That's what kills people. Not the sites themselves. The lack of preparation."

"And the Safety Coalition?"

"James found a pattern. Carnegie Hall is the only one of the seven sites with a structure built on top of it. That makes it the only site they can attack through legal channels. Condemn the building, clear the ground, destroy the site. The other six are remote wilderness. No structures. No permits. No mechanism to touch them."

"So Moores Hill is the target."

"Moores Hill is the only target they can get to. We need to make sure they don't."

"Meet at my house. Bring everything you have on the other six coordinates. We need to understand what we're really dealing with."

Emma ended the call and drove home.

The wooden box sat on the passenger seat. Robert Moore's confession. His guilt. His hope.

Three hundred years of custodian history contained in leather and ink.

And Emma Caldwell, descendent of people who had lived in Moores Hill since before written records, was carrying it home to understand what her mother had spent thirty-five years protecting.

What Agent Baker had died tracking.

What someone was willing to commit crimes to destroy.

Emma pulled into her driveway and picked up the wooden box.

Some medicine heals.

Some medicine destroys.

The difference isn't the medicine.

It's the preparation.

And that preparation had been destroyed before Robert Moore ever found the Carnegie Hall site.

Emma carried the box inside.

Time to learn what Robert Moore had understood too late.

As she entered her house and set the wooden box down, the phone vibrated once on the table.

Unknown number. No caller ID.

She let it ring twice before answering.

"Hello?"

Nothing.

Not silence. Breathing. Faint. Measured. The kind that told her someone was deciding something on the other end.

Then the line went dead.

Emma set the phone down and looked at it for a moment.

Then she went back to work.

CHAPTER 4: FALSE WALL

Emma spread Robert Moore's journal across her kitchen table at 2:18 Friday afternoon.

Owen sat to her left with his laptop open. James sat to her right with coffee. The wooden box sat empty at the end of the table. Carnegie Hall's bell tower was visible through the window behind them, rising above the roofline of the McClanahan house two blocks south.

Emma had called them both from the Carnegie Hall parking lot ninety minutes ago. Come to the farmhouse. I found something. Need you both here now.

They'd arrived within twenty minutes. Owen from his hotel in Cincinnati where he'd been working Baker's files. James from checking building security logs remotely.

Emma opened the journal to the first page and turned it so they could read Robert Moore's opening entry dated January 3, 1917.

I disturbed sacred ground. I treated medicine as curiosity. I broke what the ancients created for healing because I believed my education gave me permission to access knowledge I had not earned.

Owen read it twice. "He performed a ceremony."

"Keep reading," Emma said.

She watched them work through Robert Moore's documentation. The excavation in 1907. The discovery of the ash circle with symbols carved around its perimeter. The instructions for opening and closing ceremonies. The decision to perform the opening ceremony alone, unprepared, treating sacred medicine as academic curiosity.

The experience of seeing his own shadow. His capacity for darkness. His terror at confronting what he could become.

His choice to seal the site instead of integrating what he'd seen.

Moore Hall burning eight years later. The college closing. The guilt Robert Moore carried for seventeen years until his death.

Emma turned pages and found the section she needed them to see. Read aloud:

"Listen to this. When we excavated the Carnegie Hall foundation in the spring of 1907, we broke through to bedrock at fifteen feet. The stone was ancient. Limestone deposited three hundred million years ago. And carved into that bedrock, we found the circle. Ten feet in diameter. Perfect. The ash was undisturbed, compressed into the stone over thousands of years. Around the circle's perimeter, symbols. Instructions. I recognized elements of proto-Indo-European. Root words that predated written Sanskrit."

She paused, looked at them. "The ancients left instructions for healing. For shadow integration work using altered consciousness and plant medicine. They expected the knowledge would be passed down. Elder guidance. Months of preparation. But colonization destroyed the transmission."

"So when Robert Moore found the site in 1907," Owen said slowly, "he had the instructions but not the wisdom."

"Exactly. He performed the ceremony alone. Saw his shadow. Couldn't integrate what he saw. Sealed the site out of terror instead of understanding."

James leaned forward. "And the fire? The college closing?"

Emma found the relevant passage. "He calls it 'psychological contamination.' Says the trauma he experienced radiated outward from the site. The barrier he weakened through careless use took eight years to manifest as Moore Hall burning."

"The site itself isn't dangerous," Owen said. "Unprepared use is dangerous."

"That's what he concluded. The medicine shows you your capacity for darkness. If you're prepared, if you have guidance, you integrate it and grow. If you're not prepared, it breaks you."

Emma turned to the section documenting the seven sites. "He researched the other locations. Found six other families who were guarding similar sites. The Morrison family in Montana. Valdez in Peru. Atan on Easter Island. Hassan in Egypt. Yilmaz in Turkey. Whitmore in England."

She pushed the journal toward Owen. "These are the same coordinates Baker encrypted. The same seven sites. Robert Moore documented them in 1917. Baker was tracking them in 2025."

Owen pulled his laptop closer. "Let me cross-reference the coordinates with current databases. See if there's any recent activity at these locations."

He typed rapidly. FBI missing persons databases. National park incident reports. International archaeological monitoring systems.

Montana coordinates first.

His expression changed. "Emma. Montana. Flathead National Forest. Seven people reported missing since September 2025 in the vicinity of these coordinates."

Emma felt ice in her stomach. "Seven missing in how long?"

"Four months. September through December. Three bodies recovered. Cause of death listed as unknown. Coroner reports show injuries inconsistent with animal attack, accidental fall, or known weapons."

"Someone activated the Montana site."

Owen pulled up more data. "The Morrison family. Robert Moore's journal says they were the Montana custodians." He searched genealogical databases. Property records. "The last Morrison heir died in 2020. Property sold to the state. The site has been unprotected for five years."

"And four months ago, someone found it," James said.

Emma read Robert Moore's notes about the Morrison family. About their role as guides before colonization reduced them to guards. About how the knowledge of proper use had been lost even in their lineage.

Her phone rang. Margaret Hendricks.

Emma answered on speaker. "Margaret?"

"Emma, you need to come back to Carnegie Hall. Now. Something's happened."

Margaret's voice was shaking. Emma stood immediately. "What's wrong?"

"I came back to check the building after the insurance adjusters left. Emma, there's been another attack. More damage. And they left a message."

"We're on our way."

Emma grabbed her keys. Owen closed his laptop. James was already heading for the door.

They drove separately to Carnegie Hall. Arrived to find Margaret standing outside the rear entrance, pale, hands trembling.

"I shouldn't have come back alone," Margaret said. "But I wanted to assess the damage before the town council meeting Monday. The building was unlocked. The alarms were disabled."

"Show us," James said.

Margaret led them through the rear entrance. Down to the basement level where yesterday's flooding had left water stains and damaged carpet.

The damage was worse than last night.

More pipes broken. More water everywhere. The foundation markers Emma had seen in her mother's photographs had been moved, repositioned to make the building appear structurally unstable.

Someone had taken professional demolition assessment tools and made strategic damage that would support the condemnation petition.

But that wasn't what made Emma stop.

Emma stopped walking before she reached the corridor wall.

The dust was wrong.

Not the water damage. Not the broken pipes. Something older than tonight's attack.

The floor near the false wall had been disturbed. Not recently as in weeks. Recently as in days. Maybe hours before the flooding. Someone had been here before the Safety Coalition sent their crew with the pipes and the spray paint.

Someone who had come quietly. Who had not announced themselves with vandalism. Who had come to look at something specific and then left without leaving any other trace.

Emma filed it away. Said nothing. Kept walking.

Then she saw the message.

Spray-painted across the basement corridor wall in large red letters:

THE SITES MUST FALL SEVEN SEALS SEVEN FAILURES

"They know," Owen said quietly. "They know about all seven sites."

James was already photographing the message. The damage. Everything. "This isn't random vandalism. This is a statement. This is someone declaring their intention."

Emma stared at the message. Seven seals. Seven sites. Someone knew exactly what Robert Moore had documented. Knew about the ceremonial locations. Knew about the custodian families.

And wanted them destroyed.

Margaret was looking at Emma with an expression Emma had never seen before. Fear. "What does it mean? Seven seals?"

Emma made a decision. "Margaret, you know about the chamber beneath this building. You've known for twenty years. I need you to tell me everything you know."

Margaret took a breath. "Your mother told me some of it. Not everything. But enough. She said there were seven sacred sites around the world. Ancient ceremonial locations. That the Moore family had been protecting this one for generations. That it had been sealed for good reason and should stay sealed."

"Did she tell you why?"

"She said the sites were powerful. That people who didn't understand them could be hurt. That knowledge had been lost and until it was recovered, the sites needed to be protected."

"Did she say who might want to destroy them?"

Margaret shook her head. "She just said there were people who feared what they didn't understand. Who thought destruction was safer than protection."

Emma looked at the spray-painted message again. *The sites must fall.*

"Someone thinks eliminating the sites is the answer," Emma said. "Instead of preserving them. Instead of recovering the lost knowledge. Just destroy them completely."

"The Safety Coalition," James said. "They're not trying to access the chamber. They're trying to destroy it. Along with the other six sites."

Owen pulled up his research. "I found that pattern earlier. Seven buildings condemned and demolished in the past decade. Each one located near indigenous ceremonial sites. If those sites match Robert Moore's coordinates..."

He cross-referenced rapidly. Checked locations. Compared coordinates.

His face went pale. "Two of them match. Easter Island. Göbekli Tepe, Turkey. Two of the seven sites have already been destroyed."

Emma felt the weight of that information settle in her chest. "Which sites are left?"

"Montana. Peru. Egypt. England. And Carnegie Hall. Five remaining. Two already gone."

Five left. Out of seven sacred ceremonial sites that had existed for thousands of years. Five remained.

And one of them was under direct attack right now.

Emma's mind was racing. "Montana is active. People are dying there. That's the immediate threat. But Carnegie Hall is under coordinated assault. The condemnation petition. The sabotage. The Safety Coalition."

"And we don't know the status of Peru," Owen added. "Or Egypt. Or England."

James looked at Emma. "We can't protect all five. Not with the resources we have."

"No," Emma said. "We can't. Which means we have to make choices."

She looked at the spray-painted message. At the intentional damage throughout the basement. At Margaret's frightened expression.

"James, you stay here. Protect Carnegie Hall. Fight the condemnation. Document the sabotage. Build a case that this is coordinated attack on indigenous sacred sites."

"And you?"

"I go to Montana. Seven people are dead. More will die if that site stays active. Robert Moore left instructions for the closing ceremony in his journal. If I can seal it properly, the deaths stop."

"That's two thousand miles away. In remote wilderness. Where seven people have already died."

"I know. But the Morrison family is gone. There's no one else to seal it. And if I don't, the pattern continues. More deaths. More contamination. Eventually someone uses the Montana deaths as justification to destroy that site too."

Owen looked between them. "And what about Peru, England, and Egypt?"

"You research them. Find out if they're threatened. If there's a custodian family still protecting them. If the Safety Coalition has targeted them yet."

They stood in the damaged basement looking at each other, understanding what they were agreeing to do.

Fight on five fronts. Protect Carnegie Hall. Seal Montana. Monitor Peru, England and Egypt.

Three people. Five sites. All of it critical.

"I'll need time to prepare," Emma said. "Study Robert Moore's closing ceremony instructions. Gather the materials he specifies. Understand exactly what I'm walking into."

"How long?" James asked.

"Days. Not weeks. People are dying in Montana."

"And the town council votes on Carnegie Hall condemnation Monday night," James said. "Four days."

Emma nodded. "Then we have four days to prepare. Four days to build our cases. Four days before both missions launch."

They left Carnegie Hall together. Margaret locked the building behind them, though they all knew locks wouldn't stop whoever was doing this.

Back at Emma's farmhouse, they reviewed the plan.

Owen would research Montana. Pull every database available. Find out who the seven missing people were. What they had in common. Where exactly the deaths occurred. Build intelligence for Emma's approach.

James would investigate the Safety Coalition. Follow the money. Find out who was really funding the condemnation petition. Build evidence for the town council.

Emma would study the closing ceremony. Memorize every word. Every movement. Every material requirement. Prepare to perform a ritual that Robert Moore said required months of preparation but Emma would have days to learn.

At 7:15 PM, Owen and James left to begin their research.

Emma sat alone at the kitchen table with Robert Moore's journal open to the ceremony instructions.

The closing ceremony was complex. Required specific materials: meteorite iron filings, ancient salt deposits, pure silver pieces. Required precise pronunciation of proto-Indo-European words. Required timing calculated to solar position. Required psychological preparation Emma didn't fully understand yet.

But if she could learn it. If she could perform it correctly. She could seal the Montana site. Stop the deaths. Prove the sites could be managed instead of destroyed.

Emma was so focused on the journal she didn't hear the doorbell at first.

When it rang again, she looked up. Checked the time. 7:30 PM. She wasn't expecting anyone.

She walked to the front door and opened it.

Nobody there.

Just a German Shepherd sitting on her porch.

Emma stared. The dog was big. Maybe ninety pounds. Black and tan coloring. Alert dark eyes that looked directly at Emma with unsettling intelligence.

No collar. No tags. Just sitting. Waiting.

"Whose dog are you?" Emma asked.

The dog tilted his head. Didn't move.

Emma looked up and down Oak Street. No one around. No cars. No neighbors looking for a lost dog.

She looked back at the German Shepherd. He was still sitting. Still watching her.

"You lost?"

The dog stood and walked past Emma into the house like he owned the place.

"Hey, wait..."

But the dog was already inside. Moving through the farmhouse with purpose. Checking the living room. The kitchen. Walking down the hallway. Coming back to where Emma stood at the still-open front door.

He sat at her feet. Looked up at her. Tail wagged once.

"Okay," Emma said slowly. "This is weird."

She closed the front door. Pulled out her phone. Called the Dearborn County Animal Control. No reports of missing German Shepherds. Checked the Moores Hill Lost Pets Facebook group. Nothing.

The dog followed her into the kitchen and sat near the table where Robert Moore's journal lay open.

Emma looked at him. He looked back.

"I'm going to call you Rufus until I find your owner," Emma said. "That okay with you?"

The dog barked once. Clear. Definite.

Emma blinked. "Did you just... answer me?"

Tail wag.

"Okay. Rufus. Do you want to stay here?"

One bark.

"Do you want me to take you to the shelter?"

The dog shook his head. Side to side. No.

Emma sat down in her kitchen chair. "You just shook your head no."

Tail wag.

"This is not happening. Dogs don't answer questions."

The dog walked to where Emma sat and put his head on her knee. Looked up at her with those dark intelligent eyes.

Emma put her hand on his head. Scratched behind his ears. The dog's tail wagged.

"You're well-trained. Someone taught you these responses. But who? And why did you come here?"

Rufus didn't answer that. Just stayed close. Head on Emma's knee.

Emma's phone buzzed. Text from James: *Just found out the Safety Coalition hired private security to "protect" Carnegie Hall starting tomorrow. They're not even hiding it anymore.*

Emma texted back: *A dog just showed up at my house. And I think Moores Hill sent him.*

Three dots appeared. Then: *What?*

He communicates. Understands questions. Responds yes or no. Just walked in like he belongs here.

That's weird even for Moores Hill.

I know. But he showed up the same day we discovered the chamber. The same day the second attack happened. The same day I found Robert Moore's journal.

You think it's connected?

I think when a dog shows up who can answer questions on the day I learn I need to go to Montana alone, I don't question it. I accept the help.

Rufus barked once. Like he agreed.

Emma looked at him. "You want to come to Montana with me?"

One bark. Yes.

"It's going to be dangerous."

Rufus didn't respond. Just stayed close. Protective.

Emma made a decision. "Okay then. You're staying. Where I go, you go. We'll figure out who you belong to later."

She stood up. Rufus followed. She walked to the kitchen to make dinner. Rufus stayed three feet away. Always watching. Always alert.

Emma had lived alone in Moores Hill since her mother died. Since Mark's trial ended. Since normal life had tried to return and Emma realized normal life felt empty.

But now there was a German Shepherd in her kitchen who understood questions and had appeared exactly when Emma needed protection most.

She fed Rufus chicken from her dinner. He ate carefully. Politely. Then returned to sitting near her chair.

At 9 PM, Emma's phone rang. Owen.

"I've been researching the Montana missing persons. All seven were experienced outdoorsmen. Hikers. Wilderness guides. People who knew what they were doing. Not tourists who wandered off trails."

"What's the connection?"

"They all disappeared in the same area. Within five miles of the coordinates Robert Moore documented. And Emma, I found something else. One of them, Marcus Chandler, was an archaeologist. Specialized in pre-Columbian ceremonial sites."

Emma felt cold. "He would have known what to look for. How to identify a sacred site."

"Yes. And his body was the first one found. September 15, 2025. Cause of death: head trauma from fall. But the coroner noted unusual patterns. Evidence of extreme physical exertion before death. Like he'd been running in terror through wilderness."

"He found the site. Performed the opening ceremony. Saw his shadow. Couldn't integrate it. Ran until he died."

"That's my theory. And the other six deaths follow the same pattern. People accessing something they don't understand. Experiencing psychological breaks. Dying from exposure or falls or injuries sustained while in altered states."

"How recent was the last disappearance?"

"December 28. Timothy Walsh, 38, solo hiker. Body not found yet. Search called off after two weeks. Assumed dead."

Two weeks ago. The Montana site was still active. Still killing people.

Emma looked at Robert Moore's journal. At the closing ceremony instructions. At the materials she would need to gather. The words she would need to learn.

"I'm going to Montana," she said. "I'm going to seal that site before an eighth person dies."

"When?"

"Soon. I need a few days to prepare. To study the ceremony. To understand what I'm doing. But soon."

"Emma, seven experienced wilderness people have died there in four months. What makes you think you can survive?"

"Because I'll be prepared. Because I know what I'm facing. Because Robert Moore left instructions and I'm going to follow them properly."

"And if you fail?"

"Then James protects Carnegie Hall and you monitor Peru, England and Egypt while someone else figures out how to seal Montana. But I'm not planning to fail."

She ended the call and looked at Rufus. He was watching her with those intelligent eyes.

"You really want to come with me to Montana?"

One bark.

"You understand it's dangerous?"

The dog didn't respond. Just stayed close.

Emma went back to studying the journal. Rufus lay near her chair. Alert. Watchful. A guardian who had appeared exactly when Emma needed one.

Outside the window, Carnegie Hall's bell tower stood against the night sky. Under attack. Under threat. But protected by James while Emma went to seal the site that was actively killing people.

Five sites left. Three missions. Three people fighting to preserve what colonization had broken and the Safety Coalition wanted to destroy completely.

Emma studied Robert Moore's ceremony instructions until midnight. Memorizing words. Understanding movements. Accepting the weight of what she was about to attempt.

At some point, Rufus climbed onto the couch in the living room. Made himself at home. Like he'd always lived there.

Emma went upstairs to bed at 12:30 AM. Rufus followed. Settled on the floor next to her bed. Close enough to reach down and touch. Far enough to be respectful.

"Goodnight, Rufus," Emma said.

One soft woof in response.

Emma lay in darkness thinking about Montana. About seven people dead. About a ceremonial site that had been healing medicine for thousands of years and was now killing people because the knowledge of proper use had been destroyed.

About the choice she was making to go there. To attempt a ceremony Robert Moore said required months of preparation. To face what Marcus Chandler and six others had faced and failed to survive.

But Emma had something they didn't have.

She had Robert Moore's journal. She had the closing ceremony instructions. She had knowledge of what she was walking into.

And she had Rufus. Mysterious guardian. Sent by Moores Hill itself on the exact day Emma discovered she needed to become something her mother had been for thirty-five years.

A custodian.

Someone who stands watch over sacred ground.

Someone who preserves knowledge until it can be used properly.

Someone who seals what needs sealing and protects what needs protecting.

Emma fell asleep with ceremony words circling through her mind and Rufus's steady breathing nearby.

Four days until Montana.

Four days until the town council vote on Carnegie Hall.

Four days to prepare for battles on three fronts.

Emma had spent three months trying to return to normal life after the Benefactor investigation ended.

But normal life was over.

She was a custodian now.

And the work was just beginning.

CHAPTER 5: THE INHERITANCE

Emma woke Saturday morning at 6:56 AM to Rufus licking her face.

"Okay. Okay. I'm up."

The German Shepherd backed away from the bed, tail wagging. Emma sat up and looked at him. He was sitting perfectly still. Alert. Ready for whatever the day required.

"You need to go out?"

One bark. Yes.

Emma pulled on jeans and a sweatshirt and took Rufus downstairs. Let him into the backyard. Watched him work the fence line methodically, checking every corner with the focused attention of an animal who took perimeter security seriously.

She made coffee while Rufus finished his inspection. He came back to the door exactly three minutes later. Emma let him in.

"You're very punctual."

Tail wag.

Emma scrambled eggs for both of them. She still hadn't bought dog food. Rufus ate without complaint, which Emma was beginning to understand was his default setting. He accepted whatever was offered. He complained about nothing. He simply showed up and stayed.

She refilled her coffee and sat at the kitchen table with Robert Moore's journal.

She'd been reading it in sections for three days. The history. The mythology. The ceremony instructions. The documentation of seven sacred sites and the families who protected them. She understood the broad architecture now.

What she hadn't fully worked through was the genealogy section.

This morning, she was going to work through it completely.

***

The genealogy section began on page forty-seven of the journal. Robert Moore's handwriting here was more careful than elsewhere. More deliberate. Like a man who understood he was writing something that needed to survive him.

Emma read slowly.

Robert Moore had founded Moores Hill College in 1854. President from 1889 until 1917. Died 1924. He had documented his own family line forward from himself with the precision of someone who needed his successors to find this information without ambiguity.

He had three children. Two sons, both killed in the Great War. One daughter.

Margaret Moore, born 1895.

Emma made a note.

Margaret Moore had married Thomas Hendricks in 1919. Margaret Moore Hendricks. Two children. David Hendricks, born 1921. And a daughter.

Sarah Hendricks, born 1923.

Emma stopped reading.

She pulled out her phone and opened a genealogy database she'd been using since finding the journal. Searched Moores Hill historical records. Cross-referenced.

Sarah Hendricks married Virgil Ashcraft in 1947. Dearborn County marriage records confirmed it. Sarah Hendricks Ashcraft. Resided in Moores Hill until 1971. Then moved to Lawrenceburg.

Sarah Hendricks Ashcraft had one child.

Linda Ashcraft. Born 1963.

Emma set the phone down on the table.

She picked it back up.

Linda Ashcraft married John Caldwell in 1985. Dearborn County records. Returned to Moores Hill in 1987. Had one child.

Emma Caldwell. Born 1993.

Emma sat very still.

She traced the line again from the beginning. Robert Moore, 1848 to 1924. His daughter Margaret. Margaret's daughter Sarah. Sarah's daughter Linda. Linda's daughter Emma.

Four generations of women carrying the Moore bloodline forward from Robert Moore's death in 1924 to this kitchen table in 2026.

Emma looked at Carnegie Hall's bell tower visible above the neighbor's roofline through the kitchen window.

Her mother had spent thirty-five years at that building. Teaching. Giving tours. Photographing every detail. Documenting every renovation. Every structural assessment. Every contractor who approached with demolition language.

Linda Caldwell had not been preserving local history.

She had been fulfilling custodian responsibility.

Watching. Protecting. Making sure what was sealed beneath Carnegie Hall stayed sealed. Making sure the right people never got close enough to do real damage.

And she had never told Emma. Had never explained why she cared so much. Why the building mattered beyond its historical significance. Why she fought every threat to Carnegie Hall with an intensity that seemed disproportionate to the cause.

She hadn't told Emma because she died before Emma was ready to understand.

Murdered by Mark Caldwell in 2022 while investigating the missing women. Before she could pass the knowledge down. Before she could sit Emma at this kitchen table with this journal and explain what the Moore bloodline carried.

Emma looked at the journal. At Robert Moore's careful handwriting documenting the line he knew would continue after him.

He had built Carnegie Hall over a sealed site in 1907. Had sealed it himself after opening it and failing the medicine. Had spent the rest of his life documenting everything so future custodians would understand what they were protecting and why.

And his great-great-granddaughter was sitting in a farmhouse on Oak Street holding his journal and finally understanding exactly what her mother had been protecting all those years.

***

By noon Emma had cross-referenced the genealogy three times against four different sources. County records. State historical databases. The Moores Hill College archives online. And Robert Moore's journal itself, which confirmed dates and relationships with a precision that suggested he had anticipated someone needing to verify this from a distance of a hundred years.

The conclusion was not ambiguous.

Emma Caldwell was Robert Moore's great-great-granddaughter.

The custodian bloodline had not ended with Robert Moore in 1924. It had passed to Margaret. Then to Sarah. Then to Linda. Then to Emma. Female heirs carried the bloodline forward regardless of the surnames they married into. The custodian inheritance followed the direct line.

Her mother had been the custodian. Had known it. Had fulfilled it.

And now it was Emma's.

She needed to verify it in person. The journal included a detailed map of Oak Hill Cemetery showing the Moore family plot. Section C near the north fence. Robert Moore had documented headstone inscriptions for three generations. Specific language he had requested be carved into stone so future custodians could verify the line without needing to trust documents alone.

Emma decided she would go to the cemetery that afternoon. See the headstones herself. Stand at Robert Moore's grave and understand the full weight of what she had inherited.

She had the rest of the day to prepare for that.

***

Murphy's Bar and Grill sat on the east edge of Moores Hill where Main Street curved into Oak Hill Road. Old brick building, renovated five years ago with a large outdoor patio that overlooked Oak Hill Cemetery across the street.

The cemetery was beautiful. Historic. One of those rare graveyards that looked more like a park than a resting place. Tall oak trees. Manicured grass. White marble monuments scattered across rolling ground. The Moore family plot sat in the northeast corner under the oldest oak tree. The most elaborate section of the entire cemetery. Marble headstones with iron fencing. Visible from Murphy's patio on a clear day.

Saturday afternoon, noon on the dot, the patio was filling up.

Brad Martinez claimed the corner table with his back to the cemetery. Twenty-eight years old. Loud. Already building toward his fourth IPA with the focused dedication of a man who had cleared his entire Saturday for exactly this purpose. College basketball on the outdoor screen above the bar. Purdue and Indiana. Brad had opinions about both.

"I'm telling you," Brad said, gesturing with his beer, "Purdue covered. The refs threw that second half completely."

"You say that about every game," Katie Reynolds said from across the table. Twenty-six. She had her phone out filming Brad for no reason except that Brad's basketball opinions were consistently content gold.

"Because the refs throw every game," Brad said. "This is not a controversial position."

Mike Torres sat to Brad's left. Thirty-one. He had been on the patio since eleven. He was operating at a frequency somewhere between philosophical and profoundly confused. "But what IS a throw? Like conceptually. A throw implies intent. But what if the refs are just bad? Is incompetence the same as corruption?"

"Oh god," Jen Williams muttered. Twenty-nine. Designated adult of the group. Three beers in, which was relatively sober by comparison. "Here we go."

"No seriously," Mike said, leaning forward. "Intent matters. Legally. Ethically. Philosophically."

Brad stared at him. "Dude. What?"

"I'm just asking questions."

"You're just very high."

"Those aren't mutually exclusive."

Katie kept filming. This was going on her Instagram story without question.

The afternoon wore on. More beers. More basketball. More Mike's philosophy. The Murphy's patio filled to capacity. The cemetery across the street sat peaceful and empty in the afternoon sun, its marble headstones catching light through the oak branches.

***

Emma spent the afternoon at the kitchen table with the journal and her phone and three different notebooks filling with cross-referenced dates and names and relationships.

She ate lunch without tasting it. A sandwich she assembled without looking at what she was putting on it. Rufus accepted the crusts she offered and stayed close, his head occasionally appearing at knee level to check on her progress.

By three in the afternoon Emma had compiled a complete documentation of the Moore custodian lineage from 1848 to the present. Seven generations of people who had known about Carnegie Hall and protected it. Some of them understanding the full scope of what lay beneath the building. Others, like Linda, perhaps carrying only partial knowledge. Protecting what they had been told to protect without knowing all the reasons why.

Emma thought about that. About what it meant to carry a responsibility you couldn't fully explain. To stand watch over something without being able to tell anyone what you were watching.

Linda Caldwell had done that for thirty-five years.

Emma had been doing it for three days and already found it nearly unbearable.

She made more coffee. Continued working.

By four-thirty she was ready to go to the cemetery.

***

Rufus was sitting in the kitchen doorway watching her put on her jacket. He had that look he sometimes had. Expectant. Ready. Tail beginning a slow anticipatory wag.

"Not this time," Emma told him.

The tail slowed. Stopped.

"I need to go to the cemetery alone. Quick trip. I'll be back in an hour."

Rufus didn't move from the doorway.

"I need you to stay here. Guard the house." Emma looked at him directly. "Can you do that?"

One beat of silence. Then Rufus walked to his spot near the kitchen table and lay down. Put his head on his paws. Watching her.

"Good boy."

Emma grabbed the journal and her flashlight from the kitchen drawer. The light was already getting long and she didn't know how much time she would need among the headstones.

She locked the front door behind her and drove the five minutes to Oak Hill Cemetery.

***

The Oak Hill Cemetery occupied fourteen acres on the east side of Moores Hill. Graves dating back to 1825. The Moore family plot was in section C near the north fence, exactly where the journal map indicated.

Emma parked near the main entrance at 5:45 PM. The sun was low. Long shadows across the grass. The iron gate stood open. Quiet. No other visitors visible.

She walked through the gate with the journal in her left hand and the flashlight in her right, following the gravel path toward section C.

Murphy's Bar and Grill was visible across Oak Hill Road. The patio was packed. She could hear the noise of it from here. Laughter and the murmur of conversation and the particular energy of a crowd that had been drinking since noon and was now comfortably established in the late afternoon stage of the day.

Emma paid no attention to Murphy's patio.

She was focused on finding the Moore family plot.

***

The Moore family plot announced itself from twenty feet away. Large central monument marking Adam Moore's grave. 1811 to 1889. Founder. Around it, smaller headstones arranged in careful order. Family members. Descendants. The most ornate section of the entire cemetery, exactly as the journal had described.

Emma found Robert Moore's grave to the left of his father's.

ROBERT ALEXANDER MOORE 1848 – 1924 EDUCATOR. BUILDER. PROTECTOR.

She knelt at the grave and traced the final word with her finger.

Protector.

Not president. Not founder. Not college administrator. Robert Moore had chosen that single word above all others to define what he was.

Because he had known what he was protecting. Had understood the weight of it. Had carried the guilt of 1907 for seventeen years until his death and had spent those years documenting everything so whoever came after him would not be starting from nothing.

Emma stood and moved along the plot. Found Margaret Moore Hendricks. 1895 to 1977. Robert's daughter. The woman who had carried the bloodline forward when both sons died in France.

Found Sarah Hendricks Ashcraft. 1923 to 2008. Emma's grandmother. Who had died when Emma was fifteen. Who had known what she was and what Emma would eventually become and had died before Emma was old enough to be told.

Emma was so focused on reading the inscription on Sarah's headstone that she was still moving backward when she ran out of ground.

Her foot came down on empty air.

She had time to think oh no before gravity did the rest.

Emma fell backward into darkness. Instinct took over completely. She tucked the journal tight against her chest with both arms, crossed them over it, protected it the way you protect something irreplaceable. The flashlight flew from her hand.

She hit the bottom hard.

All the air left her lungs simultaneously. Pain detonated through her back and shoulders. The world went sideways for three full seconds.

But the journal was against her chest. Safe.

Emma lay in mud at the bottom of an open grave staring at a rectangle of darkening sky six feet above her and tried to remember how to breathe.

***

It took her approximately forty-five seconds to take stock of the situation.

Open grave. Standard six feet deep. Walls of packed dirt, already muddy from morning groundskeeping. Tarp had been folded back by the crew who had been here earlier. A pile of equipment visible at the edge above. Whoever had been digging this morning had stopped for the day and planned to return Monday.

Emma tried to stand. Her feet slipped in the mud at the bottom. She went down on one knee.

She tried again. Got upright. Looked at the walls. No handholds. No purchase. The dirt was too packed and too wet.

She tried jumping for the edge. Her fingers cleared the rim by two inches. Not enough to grip anything.

Emma pulled out her phone. No signal. The grave was apparently a dead zone for Dearborn County cellular service.

She looked up at the sky.

She yelled.

"Help!"

The wind took her voice immediately. Scattered it into the oak trees.

"HELP! SOMEONE HELP!"

The wind continued not caring.

Emma looked at the journal still pressed against her chest. Still perfectly clean. Not a speck of mud on it.

"Well," she said to no one in particular. "At least you're okay."

She kept yelling. What else could she do.

***

On Murphy's patio, the late afternoon crowd had reached critical mass.

Brad was on his seventh IPA and had moved on from basketball to a comprehensive theory about why Moores Hill needed a second bar. Mike had long since abandoned philosophy and was now simply staring at the sky with the peaceful expression of someone who had made peace with the universe. Katie was filming everything indiscriminately. Jen was trying to calculate how many beers constituted a reasonable Saturday and concluding the number was lower than the current reality.

"We could talk about something else," Jen offered.

"We could talk about this view," Brad said. He had turned his chair around at some point and was now facing the cemetery. "Who puts a bar patio overlooking a graveyard? What is the design logic there?"

"It's atmospheric," Mike said without looking away from the sky.

"It's morbid."

"It's historical," Jen said. "Oak Hill Cemetery is on the National Register. Been here since 1840."

"You're a font of information," Katie said.

"I read the plaque."

Brad was studying the cemetery with the focused attention that seven beers applied to everything. The Moore family plot was visible from where he sat. The elaborate marble monuments catching the last rays of late afternoon sun.

"That's a nice setup over there," he said. "Whoever's in that plot had serious money."

"The Moores," Jen said. "Founded the college. Built Carnegie Hall. Owned most of the town back in the day."

"Old money. Makes sense." Brad squinted. "What's that?"

"What's what?"

"That. Over by the big plot." He pointed. "Near the fence."

The table turned to look.

Near the Moore family plot, something was moving at ground level. Arms. Rising above the grass and dropping back below it. Rising again.

Mike leaned forward. Squinted. "That's coming from the ground."

"From IN the ground," Brad corrected.

A sound carried across the street on the wind. Distant. Rising and falling. Somewhere between a moan and a shout. Lost in the wind half the time. Present the other half.

"What the hell?" Brad said.

"That's a ghost," Mike said with complete certainty. "I have been saying all day this town is haunted. Nobody believed me."

"That's not a ghost," Jen said. But she was looking at the cemetery with the focused attention of someone recalculating.

"What else is IN THE GROUND?" Mike asked.

This stumped the table for a moment.

"It sounds like a woman," Katie said. Her phone was already filming.

"A woman in grief," Mike said. "Mourning her lost love. Drawn back from beyond by the power of unfinished business."

"That's so sad," Brad said.

"That's so haunted," Mike corrected.

The moaning continued. Sometimes louder when the wind shifted. Sometimes fading completely. The arms kept appearing and disappearing. Reaching toward the sky and dropping back.

More people came out of Murphy's. Word traveled fast on a Saturday patio. Ghost in the cemetery. Everyone pulled out their phones.

The footage went on Instagram at 6:04 PM. Facebook at 6:07 PM. TikTok at 6:09 PM.

By 6:15 PM, #MooresHillGhost was trending locally.

By 6:30 PM, someone had called Channel 12 News in Cincinnati.

By 6:45 PM, someone had called the Dearborn County Register.

By 7:00 PM, a news van was pulling into the cemetery parking lot across the street.

***

Inside the grave, Emma had tried everything.

Jumping for the edge. Digging footholds in the muddy walls. Using the journal as a platform. None of it worked. The walls were too slick. The grave was too deep.

She had yelled until her voice went raw. The wind kept taking it.

She found her flashlight in the mud. Dead. The fall had killed it.

She was cold. Her back and shoulders ached from the impact. Mud had worked its way into her shoes and through her jeans and into her jacket. She was thoroughly, comprehensively, unavoidably filthy.

But the journal was still pressed against her chest. Still clean. Still perfect.

Emma sat down in the mud because her legs were tired from trying to climb.

She thought about Rufus at home waiting for her. She had told him an hour. It was well past that now.

She thought about Robert Moore sitting in this same cemetery in 1924 and choosing the word Protector for his headstone.

She thought about Linda teaching tours of Carnegie Hall for thirty-five years knowing what was beneath it.

She thought about Sarah Hendricks Ashcraft who had lived until 2008 carrying knowledge she never passed to anyone because Emma hadn't been old enough to receive it.

Three generations of women who had kept this secret. Who had stood watch over sacred ground without being able to explain to anyone why it mattered so much.

Emma was carrying on a proud tradition.

She was just doing it from inside a grave.

"HELP!" she yelled again. More out of habit than optimism. "JAMES! ANYONE!"

The wind took her voice.

Emma settled in.

***

Eight miles from Oak Hill Cemetery, James McClanahan was watching the Colts lose to Jacksonville.

It was a painful game. Three touchdowns down in the fourth quarter. The kind of loss that wasn't dramatic because it had never been close. James was only still watching out of loyalty, which was the kind of thing you did for teams and people who had given you enough good moments to earn the bad ones.

The game ended. Colts 10, Jacksonville 31. James shook his head and reached for the remote.

The network cut to commercial. When it came back, the local CBS affiliate in Cincinnati had interrupted programming.

"Good evening. I'm Jennifer Martinez. Our top story tonight: Multiple witnesses are reporting possible paranormal activity at historic Oak Hill Cemetery in Moores Hill, Indiana."

James looked up from his phone.

The screen showed cell phone footage. Shaky. Shot from across a street. Arms visible at ground level, reaching toward the sky. An audible sound on the wind. Somewhere between moaning and shouting.

"We go now to our reporter on the scene, David Campbell, at Oak Hill Cemetery in Moores Hill."

The feed cut to a young reporter standing at the cemetery gate. Murphy's Bar and Grill visible in the background. Crowd on the patio pressed against the railing, pointing and filming.

"Jennifer, I'm here at Oak Hill Cemetery where dozens of witnesses report seeing what they're describing as a ghost or paranormal entity. The incident began around six PM when patrons at Murphy's Bar and Grill across the street noticed unusual activity near the historic Moore family plot."

Cut to Brad Martinez. Visibly on his eighth beer. Authoritative expression.

"Man, we saw arms. Coming out of the ground. And moaning. So much moaning. Wind carrying it across the street. I've never seen anything like it and I grew up here. That is definitely a ghost."

Cut to Katie Reynolds. Also visibly several beers deep.

"I got it on video. Look." She held up her phone showing the footage that had already been on Instagram for two hours.

Cut to Mike Torres. Operating at a frequency visible to the naked eye.

"I told them. All day I told them this town was haunted. You can feel it. There's something here. There has always been something here. I felt it the moment we sat down."

James sat forward on his couch.

Oak Hill Cemetery.

Emma had said she was going to Oak Hill Cemetery.

He looked at the footage again. At the arms reaching above ground level. At the movement pattern. At the particular desperate quality of the gesturing.

He looked at the time stamp in the lower corner of the news feed.

Emma had called him at 5:30 to say she was heading to the cemetery. That was two hours and fifteen minutes ago.

James looked at the arms on his television screen.

At the way they moved.

Recognition arrived like cold water.

"That's Emma," he said to his empty living room.

He was already standing up.

"What on earth has she got herself into now."

James grabbed his keys and his jacket and his rope from the truck bed kit and drove eight miles to Oak Hill Cemetery in eleven minutes.

***

The news crew had set up across the street from the cemetery entrance. Reporter doing a live standup with Murphy's patio visible behind him, the crowd still pressed against the railing with phones out.

James parked behind the news van and walked quickly toward the Moore family plot. The reporter broke away from his position and intercepted him.

"Sir, are you here in connection with the paranormal event? Are you a paranormal investigator?"

"I'm her friend," James said without slowing.

"Her? You know the entity?"

"It's not an entity."

"Sir—"

"It's a person."

James didn't slow down. The reporter followed him for fifteen feet and then stopped, apparently deciding that the story happening at the grave was better than the story of a man walking purposefully through a cemetery.

James reached the Moore family plot. Saw the open grave immediately. Walked to the edge. Looked down.

Emma looked back up at him from six feet below.

She was covered in mud from the waist down. Her jacket had significant mud on it. Her hair had escaped whatever she'd put it in when she left home. She was clutching Robert Moore's journal against her chest with both arms like a child protecting a stuffed animal.

Her expression was the precise combination of exhausted and furious that James had seen on her face during exactly two other situations in the time he had known her.

He looked at her for five full seconds.

Then he pulled out his phone and switched to camera mode.

"Don't," Emma said.

"Owen needs to see this."

"James."

"Documentation is important."

"JAMES."

The shutter clicked.

James looked at the photo. It was perfect. He put the phone away.

"How long have you been down there?"

"Two and a half hours."

"Are you hurt?"

"My pride is critically injured. Everything else is fine."

"The journal?"

Emma held it up. Not a speck of mud on it. "The journal is fine."

James almost smiled. He tied the rope to the oak tree nearest the grave, tested the knot, and lowered the other end down to Emma. She grabbed it with both hands, the journal now tucked under one arm.

"Hold on."

James braced his feet against the ground and pulled. Emma used her legs to walk up the muddy wall while James hauled her toward the surface. Hand over hand. Slow and steady.

Emma's head cleared ground level. Then her shoulders. Then James had her by both arms and pulled her up and out onto the grass.

She lay on her back breathing hard. Covered in mud. Grass in her hair. Journal still pressed against her chest.

James sat back and looked at her.

She looked back at him.

Then she punched him in the shoulder. Hard.

"Ow," James said.

"That's for the photo."

"Worth it."

"I could have been stuck all night."

"But you weren't. Because I heroically rescued you after watching you on the news."

"The entire county saw me?"

"Trending locally. Your ghost video has significant engagement."

Emma sat up carefully. Everything ached. The journal was still perfect. She had protected it through two and a half hours of muddy captivity and the thing looked like she had carried it in from the kitchen table.

"At least the journal's okay," she said.

"You protected a three-hundred-year-old book instead of yourself."

"The book is irreplaceable. I'm not."

James stood and offered his hand. She took it. He pulled her to her feet.

The news reporter materialized at their elbow. Camera crew behind him.

"Ma'am, can you tell us about the paranormal activity? What did you experience in there?"

"No paranormal activity," Emma said flatly. "I fell in an open grave. Tarp wasn't secured. Bad luck."

"But witnesses reported..."

"I fell in a hole. That's the story."

James guided her toward his truck. They were halfway across the cemetery when a voice carried from Murphy's patio across the street.

"That's Emma Caldwell! The investigator!"

"She was looking into the ghost!"

"Just like her mom used to look into things!"

Emma and James kept walking. Let them think what they wanted.

James opened the passenger door of his truck. Emma climbed in carefully. Mud transferred to his upholstery immediately.

"Sorry about your truck."

"I've had worse."

***

James drove toward Oak Street. The cemetery disappeared in the rearview mirror. The Murphy's patio crowd was still filming the grave, apparently unwilling to let go of the ghost narrative even after the living person had been extracted from it.

"So," James said. "Find what you were looking for?"

Emma nodded. Her back ached. Her shoulders ached. She smelled like dirt and cold mud and the particular mustiness of ground that had been dug recently.

But she knew what she was now.

"I'm Robert Moore's great-great-granddaughter," she said. "The bloodline passed through his daughter Margaret. Then to Sarah Hendricks. Then to my mother. Now to me. I verified it in the journal, three separate genealogy databases, and county records. And then I went to see the headstones to verify it in stone."

"And confirmed it by falling into a grave for two and a half hours."

"The headstones confirmed it. The grave was just a very painful postscript."

"You could have broken your back."

"Three-hundred-year-old journal versus my back." Emma held it up. Still pristine. "Journal wins every time."

James shook his head. Drove. The town moved past them in the early evening dark.

"Did you hear what they were shouting from the patio?" Emma asked.

"That you were investigating the ghost."

"That I was looking into things. Like my mom."

James was quiet for a moment. "She did look into things."

"Thirty-five years of it. And I never understood why until three days ago." Emma looked at the journal in her hands. "She was a custodian. She knew what was under Carnegie Hall. She knew it was her responsibility to protect it. And she looked after it every single day for thirty-five years without being able to tell anyone why it mattered so much."

"She told people it mattered," James said. "Just not why."

"That's the hardest kind of keeping. Protecting something you can't explain."

They turned onto Oak Street. Emma's farmhouse appeared at the end of the block. The porch light was on.

And in the window beside the front door, a dark shape was visible. Sitting. Watching the street.

Rufus.

He had positioned himself at the window with a sightline to the driveway. He had been there, Emma suspected, since approximately six minutes after she left.

James parked. Emma got out carefully.

Before she reached the front steps the door opened. Rufus came through it and down the steps in three bounds and stood in front of

Emma with his whole back half wagging, looking her over from head to toe, taking inventory.

"I'm okay," Emma told him. "I fell in a hole. It's a long story."

Rufus pressed against her leg. Mud transferred to his fur. He did not appear to care.

Emma put her hand on his head.

They stood in the driveway in the dark for a moment. Emma and Rufus and James and the journal and all the weight of what the day had produced.

Then Emma looked up at Carnegie Hall's bell tower visible against the night sky above the neighbor's roofline.

Twenty feet beneath that building, an ash circle sat sealed.

Robert Moore's great-great-granddaughter was standing in a driveway on Oak Street covered in cemetery mud holding his journal.

Some custodians had dignified origin stories.

Emma Caldwell had become a viral ghost video.

But the bloodline was real. The responsibility was real. The journal in her hands was real.

And the work was just beginning.

"Coffee," James said from behind her. "Then you tell me everything."

Emma nodded and went inside.

CHAPTER 6: THE RECKONING

James made coffee while Emma showered.

She stood under hot water for fifteen minutes and let it work through the cold that had settled into her back and shoulders during two and a half hours at the bottom of a grave. The mud came off in layers. Cemetery dirt. Clay subsoil. The particular gray-brown of ground that had been disturbed recently and not yet settled.

She scrubbed it out of her hair. Watched it spiral down the drain.

By the time she came downstairs in clean clothes and dry socks, James had found her coffee mugs and the good filters and had made a full pot with the focused competence of someone who understood that this conversation required proper preparation.

Rufus was lying near the kitchen table. He had positioned himself exactly halfway between Emma's chair and the back door, which Emma was beginning to understand was his default configuration. Always between her and the most likely point of approach. Always watching. Always within range.

Emma sat down. James set a mug in front of her and sat across the table.

Robert Moore's journal sat between them on a folded dish towel. Still clean. Still perfect. Emma had set it down carefully when she came in and had not touched it since. It seemed like the kind of thing that deserved a moment of respect before being opened again.

"Tell me everything," James said.

Emma told him.

***

She started with the genealogy section of the journal. Walked him through Robert Moore's documentation of the family line. His three children. The two sons lost in France. Margaret Moore surviving and marrying Thomas Hendricks in 1919.

James listened without interrupting. He had that quality Emma had noticed in him over the past weeks. The ability to receive information completely before responding to it. No filling of silences. No performing understanding before it had actually arrived.

"Margaret had Sarah," Emma continued. "Sarah married Virgil Ashcraft. Had one child. My mother."

James nodded slowly.

"And my mother had me." Emma wrapped both hands around her coffee mug. "Robert Moore founded Carnegie Hall in 1854. Built the current structure in 1907 over a sealed ceremonial site. Spent the rest of his life documenting everything he knew about the seven sacred sites and the families who protected them. Died in 1924 knowing that his daughter and her descendants would carry the custodian responsibility forward."

"Did Margaret know?"

"She had to. The journal passed to her. She would have read it." Emma thought about that. A woman in 1924 receiving a journal that explained her father's real life's work. The weight of that. The strangeness of it. "Whether she fully understood it or acted on it in any formal way, I don't know. But she knew."

"And Sarah?"

"Same. The journal passed through the family. Someone kept it. Someone protected it for a hundred years until my mother had it and then until I found it in that farmhouse." Emma looked at the journal on the table between them. "Four generations of women in this family knew what was under Carnegie Hall. Knew they were responsible for it. And none of them told the next generation until it was too late."

"Linda never told you."

"She died before she could. Or she was waiting until I was ready. Or she thought she had more time." Emma shook her head. "I'll never know which one it was."

James was quiet for a moment. The coffee maker had finished its cycle. The kitchen was very still.

"You're sure about the lineage," James said. It wasn't a question. He was checking that she had verified it completely, which was the kind of thing a ten-year deputy did when someone presented him with consequential information.

"Four independent sources. County records. State historical databases. The Moores Hill College archives. And Robert Moore's journal, which documents dates and relationships with the precision of someone who anticipated that future custodians would need to verify this from a distance of a hundred years." Emma held his gaze. "I'm sure."

James nodded. Drank his coffee. Processed.

"Your mother spent thirty-five years at that building," he said.

"Teaching. Giving tours. Photographing every renovation. Attending every town council meeting where Carnegie Hall came up. Fighting every threat to the building's structural integrity with an intensity that never made sense to me until now." Emma set her mug down. "She wasn't a history enthusiast. She was a custodian. She was doing exactly what Robert Moore's journal instructs custodians to do. Watch. Protect. Ensure that what is sealed beneath the building stays sealed."

"And she was murdered before she could pass any of that to you."

"Mark Caldwell killed her last year while she was investigating the missing women. One year before I found the journal. One year before any of this made sense." Emma looked at the window. Carnegie Hall's bell tower was a dark shape against the night sky. "You called me in Nashville the day she died. I drove home and never left. She was gone before I walked through the door. She never got to tell me. And I never got to ask her."

The kitchen held that for a moment.

Rufus shifted position slightly. Resettled. Continued watching.

"So," James said. "What happens now?"

"Now," Emma said, "I figure out how to be what I apparently already am."

***

Emma's phone rang at 8:35 PM.

Margaret Hendricks.

Emma looked at the name on the screen and felt something shift in her chest before she even answered. Margaret Hendricks was the granddaughter of Robert Moore's daughter. Which made her family. Which made this conversation something different from what it had been before.

"Emma, dear." Margaret's voice was its usual careful warmth. But underneath it, something else. Something that had been waiting. "I just saw a very concerning video from the cemetery. Are you alright?"

"I'm fine, Margaret. I fell into an open grave. Twisted my back a little. But I'm okay."

"Were you visiting the family plot?"

Emma paused. Then decided. Margaret deserved the direct answer.

"I was verifying genealogy. I discovered this morning that I'm Robert Moore's great-great-granddaughter. I wanted to see the headstones. Confirm the dates in stone."

Silence on the line.

Not the silence of surprise. The silence of something finally arriving that had been expected for a long time.

"You know," Margaret said quietly.

"I know."

"How much?"

"Everything the journal contains. The seven sites. The custodian families. The ceremony instructions. The history of what Robert Moore did in 1907 and why he sealed the site and what it means that Carnegie Hall sits directly above it." Emma paused. "And the genealogy. All of it."

Another silence. Longer this time.

"Your mother was very careful," Margaret said finally. "About who she told. About what she shared. She protected you specifically. She felt you weren't ready and then she ran out of time to determine when ready would arrive."

"Did you know? About my mother being a custodian?"

"I knew Linda cared about Carnegie Hall with an intensity that went beyond professional interest. I knew she understood things about the building that she never fully explained. And I knew about Robert Moore's journal because my grandmother Margaret told me about it before she died." A pause. "My grandmother knew Robert Moore personally. She was thirty when he died. She told me he was the most burdened man she had ever known. That he carried something he could not put down and could not fully share."

"He opened the site in 1907," Emma said. "Accessed the ceremony without proper preparation. Saw things that broke him. And then sealed it and spent seventeen years documenting everything so future custodians would understand what not to do."

"Yes," Margaret said. "That is what my grandmother told me. Not in those exact words. But yes."

Emma looked at James across the table. He was listening to her side of the conversation with his full attention.

"Did you suspect I was in the custodian lineage?" Emma asked.

"I suspected. But it wasn't my place to say so. That was Linda's responsibility. And when Linda died I didn't know whether to come to you directly or wait for you to find the journal yourself." A long pause. "I'm sorry I waited. I should have come to you sooner."

"You couldn't have known when I'd be ready to receive it."

"No. But I could have given you the option of being ready sooner." Margaret's voice had something in it that had not been there in previous conversations. Weight. Old regret. "I'm sorry, Emma."

"Don't be. I found it. That's what matters."

"Are you planning to go to Montana?"

Emma blinked. "How did you know about Montana?"

"Because that's what custodians do. They protect the sites that still exist. They seal the ones that have been compromised." A pause that felt like a woman choosing her next words precisely. "Your mother would have gone to Montana the moment she learned the Morrison site was active. She would have felt the pull of it the same way you're feeling it now. The responsibility doesn't ask permission."

Emma felt something ease in her chest. Something she hadn't known was tight until it released.

"Seven people have died at that site," Emma said.

"I know."

"I'm not approaching it casually. I'm preparing. Learning the ceremony. Understanding what killed those people and how to avoid the same outcome."

"Good. Robert Moore's journal has the closing ceremony documented in full. It was written by the original site keeper in the sixteen hundreds. Translated and preserved by Robert Moore himself. If you follow it exactly, the ceremony is not dangerous. It's the improvisation that kills people. The hubris of approaching sacred medicine without preparation."

"That's what Marcus Chandler did. And the six others."

"Yes. They felt the pull of the site and approached it without framework. Without ceremony. Without understanding what they were opening." Margaret paused. "You have the framework. You have the ceremony. You have the journal. Don't let urgency replace preparation."

"I won't."

"And Emma." Margaret's voice dropped slightly. "Be careful. Montana has been compromised for some time. The site is not stable. Even with proper preparation you will be facing something that has been open and unguarded for months. That creates variables the journal cannot fully anticipate."

"I understand."

"Come back," Margaret said simply. "Moores Hill needs its custodian."

They ended the call.

Emma set the phone on the table.

James was watching her.

"Margaret knew," Emma said.

"How much?"

"Enough. She suspected I was in the lineage. She knew about the journal. Her grandmother knew Robert Moore personally." Emma picked up her coffee mug and found it had gone cold. She held it anyway. "She confirmed Montana. Said my mother would have gone the moment she knew the Morrison site was active."

"And you're going."

"I'm going." Emma looked at the journal on the table. "As soon as I'm prepared enough to survive it."

James nodded. No argument. No pushback. Just acceptance of the decision and whatever came next.

That was the thing about James McClanahan. He didn't waste energy on the battles that were already decided.

***

James's phone rang at 9:23 PM.

He looked at the screen. His expression changed in the way Emma had learned to read over the past weeks. The slight stillness that arrived before bad news. The professional composure settling into place before he opened his mouth.

He answered. Listened. Asked two questions. Listened more. Said he was on his way.

He set the phone on the table and looked at Emma.

"That was Margaret again," he said. "Someone tried to set fire to the historical records storage at Carnegie Hall last night. Between midnight and two AM. The sprinkler system activated. Significant water damage to the storage room. Some records destroyed. Police are processing the scene now."

Emma felt the cold that had nothing to do with the temperature.

"Last night," she said.

"Between midnight and two AM. While you were at home reading the journal."

"While I was reading about the custodian families and tracing the Moore genealogy." Emma looked at Carnegie Hall's bell tower through the window. "Someone was at Carnegie Hall destroying records."

"The physical evidence of the building's history. The documentation that supports its status on the historical register." James stood and reached for his jacket. "They're not just trying to condemn the building. They're trying to eliminate the paper trail that makes it worth preserving."

"The Safety Coalition."

"Has to be. Same pattern. Create damage. Create evidence of instability. Create justification for condemnation." James was already moving toward the door. "There's more. Margaret said the town council vote has been moved up."

Emma stood. "When?"

"Monday night. Emergency session. The Safety Coalition contacted three council members this afternoon claiming the fire attempt is evidence the building is a public safety hazard. They're using the incident they created to accelerate the process they're driving." James pulled on his jacket. "If the council votes to condemn Monday night, demolition proceedings could begin within weeks."

Emma looked at the journal. At the calendar in her head. At the distance between now and Montana and the gap between what she knew and what she needed to know before she got on a plane.

"Two days," she said.

"Two days until the vote."

"And Montana."

"Seven people dead. More will die if the site stays open." James met her eyes across the kitchen. "You need to leave as soon as you're prepared. But you need to be prepared before you leave. Don't let the council vote push you out the door before you're ready."

"I know."

"Promise me."

"I promise." Emma looked at Carnegie Hall's bell tower. "Go. I'll be here."

"Lock the doors."

"James."

"Lock them anyway."

He left. Emma heard his truck back out of the driveway. Heard it move down Oak Street toward Carnegie Hall and whatever the Safety Coalition had left behind in the historical records storage.

The kitchen was very quiet.

Rufus got up from his position near the table and walked to Emma's side. Pressed against her leg.

Emma put her hand on his head.

"I know," she said. "I know."

***

Owen's text arrived at 9:51 PM.

Peru site status: Valdez family still active. Site protected. No current threats detected. Hassan in Egypt confirmed secure per international network contact. Focusing all research resources on Montana now.

Emma texted back: I need everything. Terrain. Elevation. Weather patterns for the Flathead region this time of year. Access routes. What killed the seven people. Exact locations of all known fatalities relative to the site coordinates. Anything that helps me understand what I'm walking into.

Three dots. Then: Already building the file. You'll have it by morning.

Then: You're really doing this.

Emma typed back: Yes.

A pause. Then: Your mother would be proud of you.

Emma looked at those words for a long time.

She set the phone face down on the table.

Stood up. Walked to the window. Looked at Carnegie Hall's bell tower against the night sky.

Her mother had stood in that building for thirty-five years. Had walked its floors and climbed its stairs and fought its enemies and kept its secret. Had loved it with an intensity that Emma had never fully understood and had never thought to question until it was too late to ask why.

Now Emma understood why.

And her mother was gone. And Carnegie Hall was under attack. And a sacred site in Montana was killing anyone who came near it. And the town council was voting in two days. And Emma Caldwell was standing in a farmhouse kitchen on Oak Street with a journal and a mysterious dog and a former deputy who took photographs of her in graves.

She was, by any objective measure, not ready for any of this.

But she was committed to all of it.

And sometimes that had to be enough.

***

Emma opened the journal to the ceremony section at 10:15 PM.

She had read it before. Multiple times. But reading and learning were different things. Reading was receiving. Learning was absorbing until the knowledge lived in your body rather than just your memory.

The closing ceremony for a compromised sacred site required three things. Correct words spoken in the correct sequence. Correct movement through the site's established perimeter. And correct internal orientation, which Robert Moore's journal described in language that was precise without being reducible to a simple checklist.

You must approach without agenda, Robert Moore had written in 1923. The medicine reads intention more clearly than it reads action. Approach it only as a servant of its purpose, which is to hold what it holds until the ceremony releases it properly.

Emma set the journal down.

Seven people had approached the Montana site in the past year. Each of them with the intention of understanding what it was. Geologists. Researchers. A hiker who had felt something pull at him from forty miles away and followed the feeling until it killed him.

Not one of them had approached it as a servant of its purpose.

That was the difference between them and Emma.

That was the difference between dying in Montana and coming home.

Emma read that paragraph four times.

She thought about Marcus Chandler. A geology professor from the University of Montana. A man who had driven forty-two miles from the nearest town to find an anomaly in the landscape that his instruments had detected. A man who had approached the site with the intention of understanding what it was.

The intention of understanding what it was.

Not the intention of closing it safely.

Emma understood the difference now in a way she had not when she first read the journal three days ago. It was the difference between approaching something as a problem to be solved and approaching it as a responsibility to be fulfilled. The site was not interested in being understood. It was interested in being properly closed by someone who understood why that mattered.

She continued reading.

The Proto-Indo-European words of the ceremony were transcribed phonetically in Robert Moore's careful Victorian handwriting with pronunciation notes in the margins. The original language of the ceremony predated written records. Robert Moore had received it from a Flathead elder in 1906, the year before he opened the Moores Hill site without permission and paid the price for that arrogance.

Emma began speaking the words aloud.

Quietly at first. Testing the sounds. Finding where her mouth wanted to resist the unfamiliar phonemes and training it not to.

Rufus lifted his head from the floor and watched her.

The words were harsh in places. Guttural. Sounds that English had long since abandoned. Her throat worked to produce them correctly. She checked the phonetic notes. Adjusted. Tried again.

Better.

She moved through the opening sequence. Twelve words spoken while standing outside the site's perimeter. Then the movement: three circuits of the perimeter walking counterclockwise. Then the central sequence, twenty-eight words, spoken while facing the site's primary axis, which Robert Moore had documented as running northeast to southwest at the Montana location.

Emma practiced the central sequence until she could speak it without consulting the journal.

Then she practiced it again.

Rufus watched. His head tilted slightly at certain sounds. The very old ones. The ones that the journal indicated were the core of the ceremony, the words that had been spoken over this site and its six counterparts for five thousand years before anyone wrote anything down.

Emma wondered what Rufus heard in those sounds that she could not.

She kept practicing.

***

By midnight, she had the full ceremony committed to memory.

Not just the words. The sequence. The movements. The internal orientation Robert Moore described as approaching without agenda, which she was beginning to understand not as a passive state but as an active one. A deliberate emptying of everything except the purpose of the ceremony itself.

She had practiced it six times in full. Rufus had watched all six. He had not moved from his position on the kitchen floor except once, when Emma had stumbled on a word in the central sequence and stopped and sat down and put her head in her hands for three minutes.

He had come to her then. Had put his head on her knee. Had waited while she collected herself.

Then he had returned to his position and she had started again from the beginning.

That was what Rufus did. He was present for the hard parts and patient through the rest.

Emma closed the journal at 12:23 AM.

She sat at the kitchen table and looked at Carnegie Hall's bell tower through the window. The building was dark at this hour. Quiet. Whatever the Safety Coalition had left behind in the records storage had been processed by the police and James's presence and whatever Margaret Hendricks had done in that efficient and undramatic way she had of getting things done.

Two days until the council vote.

James was protecting Carnegie Hall from the outside. Working through channels. Gathering evidence. Building the case that the condemnation proceedings were manufactured.

Emma's job was to prepare for Montana. To be ready to leave the moment she was confident she would not make the same mistakes that had killed seven people at the Morrison site.

She was not there yet.

But she was closer than she had been this morning.

She thought about what Margaret Hendricks had said. Don't let urgency replace preparation.

She thought about what Owen's text had said. Your mother would be proud.

She thought about Robert Moore's headstone in section C of Oak Hill Cemetery. PROTECTOR.

She thought about Linda Caldwell standing in Carnegie Hall for thirty-five years knowing what was beneath her feet and saying nothing because the time was never right and then running out of time completely.

Emma was not going to run out of time.

She was going to prepare properly. She was going to go to Montana. She was going to close the Morrison site using the ceremony that had been passed through six generations of knowledge keepers before Robert Moore transcribed it in 1923. She was going to come home.

And then she was going to help James save Carnegie Hall.

Because that was what custodians did.

They stood watch.

They sealed what needed sealing.

They protected what their bloodline had always protected.

Whether they had asked for the responsibility or not.

***

Emma's phone buzzed at 12:41 AM. A notification from Instagram.

She had turned off most notifications two hours ago. But this one got through.

The video from the cemetery had been reposted by a paranormal account with four million followers.

Current view count: six million, four hundred thousand.

The caption on the repost read: REAL GHOST FOOTAGE FROM INDIANA CEMETERY. ARMS REACHING FROM GRAVE. MOANING ON WIND. THIS IS NOT STAGED.

The comment section had nine thousand replies.

Emma turned her phone face down on the table.

Rufus looked at her.

"I know," she said. "The legend grows."

One wag. Patient. Philosophical.

"Emma Caldwell," Emma said. "Custodian. Great-great-granddaughter of Robert Alexander Moore. Viral ghost. Protector of sacred ground." She looked at the journal on the table between them. "That's quite a job description."

Rufus put his head on the table edge and looked at her with those dark intelligent eyes that Emma still could not fully account for.

She reached out and scratched behind his ears.

Outside the window, Carnegie Hall's bell tower stood against the midnight sky. Under attack. Under threat. But standing. Still standing.

Two days until the council vote.

Montana waiting beyond that.

The clock running on both.

Emma Caldwell sat at her kitchen table in the farmhouse on Oak Street in Moores Hill, Indiana, and made her peace with what she was and what was coming.

Then she opened the journal again and started from the beginning of the ceremony.

She was not going to let urgency replace preparation.

But she was also not going to sleep when there was work to do.

Rufus settled at her feet.

Guardian. Companion.

Still there at 2 AM when Emma finally closed the journal and went upstairs.

Still there at the foot of the bed when she woke four hours later to start again.

CHAPTER 7: R.M. SEALED

Sunday morning, Emma's back was better. Not healed. But better.

Not good enough for wilderness hiking. But improving.

At 8:15 AM, she called Dr. Patricia Hanson.

Dr. Hanson was a linguistics professor at Miami University in Oxford, Ohio. Emma had found her through academic databases while researching proto-Indo-European languages. Dr. Hanson's specialty was shamanic language reconstruction. Ancient ceremonial texts. The kind of linguistic archaeology that tried to recover how extinct languages sounded when spoken aloud.

Exactly what Emma needed.

The phone rang four times before Dr. Hanson answered.

"Hello?"

"Dr. Hanson, my name is Emma Caldwell. I'm calling about ceremonial language translation. I found your research on proto-Indo-European shamanic texts. I need help with pronunciation."

Silence on the other end. Then: "What kind of ceremonial texts?"

"Ancient. Pre-Columbian possibly. Symbols carved into stone. Instructions for rituals using altered consciousness and plant medicine."

More silence. "Where did you find these symbols?"

Emma made a decision. "Indiana. A sealed chamber beneath a historic building. The symbols are intact. I can read the words but I don't know how to pronounce them correctly."

"Can you send me photographs?"

"I'd rather meet in person. Show you the originals. This is sensitive material."

Dr. Hanson was quiet for a moment. "I'm at my office today. McGuffey Hall, room 312. Can you come to Oxford?"

"Yes. I can be there by eleven."

"I'll see you then."

Emma ended the call and looked at Rufus. "Road trip. You ready?"

One bark. Yes.

The drive from Moores Hill to Oxford was ninety minutes. Emma loaded Rufus into the passenger seat of her car, grabbed Robert Moore's journal wrapped carefully in a protective sleeve, and headed north.

Her lower back protested the drive. The constant pressure on the gas pedal made it throb for some reason. But Emma ignored it. She had bigger problems than a sprained back.

Like learning to pronounce words that could seal a sacred site. Or kill her if she got them wrong.

Rufus sat perfectly in the passenger seat. Alert. Watching the landscape pass. Occasionally looking at Emma like he was checking to make sure she was okay.

"I'm fine," Emma told him. "Just thinking about what I'm about to attempt in Montana."

Rufus's tail wagged once. Encouragement.

Emma drove through southern Indiana countryside. Fields and farms and small towns that looked exactly like Moores Hill. Places where nothing ever happened except births and deaths and the slow passage of seasons.

She reached Oxford at 10:53 AM.

Miami University occupied the center of town. Old campus. Red brick buildings that predated the Civil War. The kind of academic institution that felt permanent, like it had always existed and always would.

Emma parked near McGuffey Hall and studied the building. Three stories. Classical architecture. The linguistics department was housed here, along with several other humanities programs.

She helped Rufus out of the car. Put on the service dog vest James had acquired through contacts Emma still didn't ask about. Rufus wore it perfectly. Looked completely official.

They walked into McGuffey Hall together. Found room 312 on the third floor.

Dr. Patricia Hanson was exactly what Emma expected from a linguistics professor. Mid-fifties, gray hair in a practical cut, reading glasses on a chain around her neck, office filled with books in languages Emma couldn't identify.

She looked up when Emma knocked on the open door. Saw Rufus. Smiled.

"Service dog?"

"Yes. He stays with me."

"No problem. Come in. Close the door, please."

Emma entered and sat in the chair Dr. Hanson indicated. Rufus settled at her feet. Alert but calm.

Dr. Hanson studied Emma for a moment. "You said you found ceremonial symbols carved in stone?"

"Yes. Beneath a historic building in southern Indiana. The site has been sealed since 1907. The person who sealed it left documentation. Including these symbols."

Emma pulled out Robert Moore's journal. Opened to the ceremony instructions. Showed Dr. Hanson the photographs she'd taken of the pages.

Dr. Hanson's expression changed immediately. She pulled her reading glasses on and leaned forward.

"Where did you get this?"

"Private archives. The person who documented these symbols was an educated man. He studied classical languages at Yale. He recognized proto-Indo-European elements."

"He was right to recognize them. These are authentic." Dr. Hanson's finger traced the symbols on the page. "Root words that predate written Sanskrit. Possibly five thousand years old or older. Ceremonial language used by shamanic cultures across multiple continents."

"Can you help me pronounce them?"

Dr. Hanson looked up. "Why do you need pronunciation? These are instructions for ceremonies involving altered consciousness and plant medicine. You're not planning to perform these, are you?"

Emma made another decision. Tell the truth. "Someone already performed the opening ceremony. At a different site. In Montana. Seven people have died in the past four months because that site is now active and uncontained. I need to perform the closing ceremony to seal it properly."

Dr. Hanson set the journal down carefully. "You're serious."

"Completely serious."

"Seven people died?"

"Yes. Missing persons reports. Bodies recovered showing injuries inconsistent with normal wilderness accidents. The site is contaminated. More people will die unless someone seals it."

Dr. Hanson stood up and walked to her office window. Looked out at the campus below. Was quiet for a long moment.

Then she said, "Four months ago, someone else asked me about these exact symbols. A man named Marcus Chandler. Archaeologist from the University of Montana. He showed me photographs of carvings he'd found in Flathead National Forest. Symbols matching what you're showing me now."

Emma felt ice in her stomach. "What did you tell him?"

"I translated the opening ceremony for him. Helped him with pronunciation. Warned him it was dangerous. Told him these ceremonies required preparation, guidance, community support. That accessing altered consciousness without proper framework could cause severe psychological trauma."

"Did he listen?"

"He said he understood the risks. That he would be careful. That this was important academic research." Dr. Hanson turned back to Emma. "He died three weeks later in Montana wilderness. Official cause: accidental fall resulting in head trauma. But I've always wondered if he actually performed that ceremony. If he ignored my warnings. If he's dead because I helped him pronounce words he should never have spoken."

"It wasn't your fault," Emma said quietly. "Marcus Chandler made his own choice. And his death is why I'm here. Someone has to close what he opened. Someone has to seal the Montana site before more people die."

"And you think you're prepared for that?"

"No. I'm not prepared. I have days, not months. I don't have elder guidance or community support or shamanic training. I just have this journal, your expertise, and determination to stop the eighth death."

Dr. Hanson sat back down. "Show me the closing ceremony."

Emma turned pages. Found the instructions Robert Moore had documented. The seventeen sequences. The materials required. The precise movements and timing.

Dr. Hanson studied them carefully. "This is complex. More complex than the opening ceremony. Whoever created these instructions understood deep shamanic practice. This isn't just sealing a physical space. This is closing psychological and spiritual dimensions that the opening ceremony activates."

"Can you help me pronounce the words correctly?"

"Yes. But I need you to understand what you're attempting. The closing ceremony requires being in both states simultaneously. Perceiving both normal consciousness and altered consciousness at the same time. Navigating between dimensions while maintaining enough grounding to complete the ritual properly. If you lose your grounding, if you fall too deep into altered state, you won't be able to finish. And the site stays open."

"I understand."

"Do you? Because Marcus Chandler understood intellectually too. But intellectual understanding and experiential reality are very different things."

Emma met Dr. Hanson's eyes. "Seven people are dead. I can accept the risk or I can let an eighth person die. Those are the only choices. I choose to take the risk."

Dr. Hanson nodded slowly. "Then we'll work on pronunciation. But I'm also going to teach you grounding techniques. Ways to maintain connection to physical reality while experiencing altered consciousness. Emergency protocols for if things go wrong."

"How long will that take?"

"Properly? Months. What we can do today? A few hours."

"Then let's start."

They worked until 4 PM.

Dr. Hanson had Emma repeat each sequence of the closing ceremony dozens of times. Correcting pronunciation. Explaining the meaning behind the words when meaning could be reconstructed. Teaching Emma breathing techniques to maintain grounding. Explaining what altered consciousness felt like and how to navigate it without losing connection to physical reality.

Rufus stayed quiet throughout. Lying near Emma's chair. Occasionally lifting his head when Emma's voice changed. Like he could hear when she got the pronunciation right.

At 3:30, Dr. Hanson recorded the correct pronunciations on her phone. Sent the files to Emma. "Practice these constantly. Every day. Multiple times per day. The words need to become automatic. You can't be thinking about pronunciation while you're experiencing altered consciousness."

"I will. Thank you."

Dr. Hanson walked Emma to the door. Stopped her before she left.

"Emma, can I ask you something?"

"Of course."

"Why you? Why are you the one going to Montana? Why not authorities? Why not someone with actual shamanic training?"

Emma thought about Robert Moore's journal. About the custodian lineage. About being the great-great-granddaughter of the man who sealed Carnegie Hall and carried guilt for seventeen years.

"Because it's my responsibility," Emma said simply. "My family has been protecting these sites for generations. My mother was a custodian. Her grandmother before her. Back to Robert Moore in 1907. This is what we do. We seal what needs sealing. We protect what needs protecting. Even when we're not prepared. Even when it's dangerous. Because if we don't, no one will."

Dr. Hanson nodded. "Your mother would be proud."

"That's what people keep telling me."

Emma left McGuffey Hall with Rufus and the recorded pronunciations and more knowledge than she'd had that morning. Not enough knowledge. But more.

She checked her phone as she reached the car.

Three missed calls from James. Two texts.

Call me when you're done. Important.

Emma called. James answered immediately.

"Where are you?"

"Oxford. Just finished with the linguistics professor. What's wrong?"

"I found something about the Safety Coalition. Emma, they're not a legitimate organization. Morrison Technical Services... the engineering firm that condemned Carnegie Hall... doesn't exist. No professional licensing. No business history. The whole company was created three months ago specifically to target this building."

Emma got into the car. Rufus jumped into the passenger seat. "You're sure?"

"Completely. I traced the corporate registration. Shell company. Fake credentials. The engineer who signed the condemnation report... Dr. Michael Torres... his credentials don't check out either. The professional engineering license number he used belongs to someone who's been dead for two years."

"So the entire condemnation is based on fraudulent evidence."

"Yes. Which means someone with significant resources created a fake safety organization and a fake engineering firm specifically to condemn Carnegie Hall. This isn't about building safety. This is about accessing what's beneath the building."

Emma felt sick. "The chamber."

"Yes. They know about it. They want to reach it. And they're using building condemnation as legal cover to excavate during demolition."

"Can we prove the fraud?"

"I can prove Morrison Technical doesn't exist. I can prove Dr. Torres's credentials are fake. But that doesn't stop the condemnation unless I can get this information to the town council before tomorrow's vote."

"Tomorrow? I thought the vote was Wednesday."

"They moved it up. Emergency meeting tomorrow night at seven. The Safety Coalition is pushing hard. Claiming the gas line damage from last night proves the building is too dangerous to remain standing."

"What do you need from me?"

"Get back here. We need to prepare testimony. Coordinate with Margaret and the historical society. Present evidence that this is fraud, not legitimate safety concern."

"I'm ninety minutes away. I'll be there by six."

"And Montana?"

Emma looked at the recorded pronunciation files on her phone. At the ceremonial instructions she'd spent six hours learning. At Rufus watching her with intelligent eyes.

"I leave Monday night. The vote happens while I'm in Montana. Win or lose on Carnegie Hall, I still need to seal that site before more people die."

"Your back?"

"Better. Not healed. But functional."

"Emma..."

"I know. It's dangerous. Seven people died. I'm not prepared. But someone has to do this and I'm the only person who knows what needs to be done. So I'm doing it."

James was quiet. Then: "Okay. We'll get you ready. Whatever you need."

Emma ended the call and started the car.

Marcus Chandler had consulted Dr. Hanson four months ago. Had learned the opening ceremony pronunciation. Had ignored the warnings. Had performed the ceremony alone in Montana wilderness.

And died three weeks later.

Emma was about to follow the same path. Same location. Same ceremony. Different intentions but similar risks.

Seven people were dead because Marcus Chandler had opened something he couldn't close.

Emma intended to close it. Or die trying.

Those were the only options.

She reached Moores Hill at 5:36 PM. Drove straight to the farmhouse. Found James waiting on her porch with Owen.

They'd been researching. Building the case against the Safety Coalition's fraudulent condemnation.

Emma let them inside. Made coffee. Sat at the kitchen table with Robert Moore's journal open and Dr. Hanson's pronunciation files playing softly from her phone.

"Tell me everything," she said.

James opened his laptop. Showed her what he'd found. Morrison Technical Services registered as an LLC three months ago. No business history before that. No client portfolio. No professional accreditation with engineering oversight bodies.

Dr. Michael Torres, the engineer who signed Carnegie Hall's condemnation report, using a professional engineering license that belonged to someone who died in 2024.

David Werner, the Safety Coalition's lawyer, with no bar association registration in Indiana or any surrounding state.

"They're all fake," James said. "The entire organization was created specifically to condemn Carnegie Hall."

"But why?" Emma asked. "What do they want with the chamber beneath the building?"

"I don't know yet. But they know it exists. They know it's important. And they're willing to commit fraud to access it."

Owen pulled out a map. Marked locations. "Robert Moore documented seven ceremonial sites worldwide. Carnegie Hall is one of them. Montana is another. The other five are scattered across different continents—Peru (Nazca Lines), Egypt (Pyramids of Giza), England (Stonehenge), Rapa Nui (Easter Island) and Turkey (Göbekli Tepe). All remote locations. Most are intact as far as we can determine."

"And they're only targeting Carnegie Hall?"

"As far as I can tell. It's one of three sites with a building constructed over it. The only one vulnerable to building condemnation. The other sites are wilderness or rural locations with no structures or is under a pyramid in Egypt!"

Emma looked at the map. Seven sites. Carnegie Hall. Montana. Five others she'd never heard much of before, other than her history classes in school.

"Thursday night's vote is critical," Emma said. "If we can prove the Safety Coalition is fraudulent, we might stop the condemnation. But we need the town council to listen."

"Margaret is rallying support," James said. "Historical society members. Town residents who value Carnegie Hall. People who don't want to see a 118-year-old building demolished based on questionable evidence."

"What do we have?"

"Proof Morrison Technical doesn't exist. Proof Dr. Torres's credentials are fake. Proof the Safety Coalition was created three months ago specifically for this condemnation. It's strong evidence of fraud. But the council still has to decide whether to believe us or believe the engineering report that looks official."

"We frame it simply," Owen said. "Show them the corporate records. Show them the fake credentials. Ask them one question: Would you condemn a historic building based on a report from an engineer who doesn't exist and a company created three months ago specifically to target this one building?"

"Will that be enough?" Emma asked.

"I don't know. But it's what we have."

Emma's phone buzzed. Text from Dr. Hanson: *I've been thinking about our conversation. The closing ceremony requires materials. Meteorite iron filings. Ancient salt deposits. Pure silver. Do you have access to these?*

Emma texted back: *Not yet. Where can I find them?*

Meteorite iron can be purchased from scientific supply companies. Ancient salt from geological specialty dealers. Pure silver from precious metal suppliers. I can send you sources if you need them.

Please. And thank you.

Within minutes, Dr. Hanson had sent links to suppliers. Emma ordered everything. Rush shipping. Overnight delivery to the farmhouse. The materials would arrive Monday morning. She would pack them before her flight.

Cutting it close.

But doable.

"James left at seven to meet with Margaret and the historical society board. Prepare their strategy for Thursday's town council meeting, build the case for protecting Carnegie Hall."

Owen stayed to help Emma practice pronunciation. Listening carefully. Correcting when needed. Making sure Emma had the words perfect.

Rufus lay nearby. Always watching. Always alert.

Owen left at ten. Emma continued practicing alone.

The proto-Indo-European words sounded harsh and ancient in her mouth. Syllables that predated written language. Sounds that shamans had spoken for thousands of years while guiding seekers through shadow integration work.

Emma wasn't a shaman. Wasn't trained. Wasn't prepared properly.

But she had Robert Moore's journal. Had Dr. Hanson's pronunciation files. Had materials arriving Tuesday. Had three days to become good enough to attempt what seven people had died attempting.

She practiced until midnight. Then fell asleep on the couch with ceremony words circling through her mind.

Rufus climbed onto the couch beside her. Warm. Heavy. Real.

Emma put her hand on his side. "Tomorrow we fight for Carnegie Hall. Tuesday we go to Montana. You ready for all of this?"

One soft bark. Yes.

"Good. Because I need you. I need someone to keep me grounded when I'm performing a ceremony that could break my mind. Someone to bring me back if I go too deep. Someone to protect me if things go wrong."

Rufus put his head on Emma's leg. Looked at her with those dark intelligent eyes that seemed to understand exactly what she was saying.

"You showed up at my door exactly when I needed you," Emma said quietly. "Right when I discovered I was a custodian. Right when I learned about Montana. Right when everything changed. That's not coincidence. Moores Hill sent you. Or the universe sent you. Or something sent you. But you're here. And I'm grateful."

Rufus's tail wagged once. Acknowledgment.

Emma closed her eyes. Listened to Rufus breathing. Let the rhythm calm her racing thoughts.

Tomorrow: town council meeting. Fight for Carnegie Hall. Prove the Safety Coalition was fraudulent.

Tuesday: Montana. Seal the site. Stop the deaths. Perform a ceremony that required months of preparation with only days of practice.

Impossible tasks. Both of them.

But Emma Caldwell was a custodian. Robert Moore's great-great-granddaughter. Inheritor of responsibility that stretched through four generations.

And custodians didn't quit just because the task was impossible.

They did the work anyway.

Protected what needed protecting. Sealed what needed sealing.

Even when they weren't ready. Even when seven people had died trying.

Emma fell asleep with ceremony words in her mind and Rufus beside her and Carnegie Hall's bell tower visible through the window.

Four days until the vote.

One day until Montana.

The clock was ticking.

And Emma Caldwell was committed to both battles.

Win or lose. Live or die.

This was what custodians did.

CHAPTER 8: ASH CIRCLE

Sunday afternoon, Emma's kitchen held the quiet of a house working through something difficult.

She stood at the counter with Robert Moore's journal open to the ceremony instructions, speaking the seventh sequence under her breath. The words came easier now than three days ago, the harsh consonant clusters less foreign in her mouth, the ancient vowel sounds finding their shape with less effort. Three days of practice was doing something. Whether it was enough was a question she couldn't answer yet.

Rufus sat six feet away near the table, watching her.

He'd been there all morning. Not pacing, not seeking attention, just sitting with his head slightly tilted and his dark eyes tracking Emma the way he tracked everything, with a quality of attention that suggested he was filing information away somewhere. When she stumbled over the ninth sequence, the one Dr. Hanson had corrected three times before Emma got the emphasis right, first syllable clipped, second carrying the weight, third releasing rather than holding, his ears shifted slightly.

Emma stopped. Backed up to the beginning of the ninth. Spoke it slowly, the way Dr. Hanson had demonstrated at McGuffey Hall. Said it at practice tempo. Then faster. Then at the speed the full ceremony would require.

Rufus's ears settled.

She kept going. Tenth sequence, eleventh, twelfth. The ancient syllables were becoming familiar the way a new route becomes familiar, no longer requiring conscious navigation, just present in her mouth as she moved through them. The kitchen around her was ordinary: morning light, the smell of coffee she'd made two hours ago and hadn't finished, Carnegie Hall's bell tower visible through the window above the sink. Eighteen thousand years of accumulated indigenous knowledge sitting in a leather journal beside the dish rack.

By the time she reached the seventeenth sequence, the final words, the ones she'd speak standing inside the ash circle, the ceremony was starting to feel like something she owned rather than something she was borrowing.

Dr. Hanson's warning had been unambiguous: you can't be thinking about pronunciation while you're perceiving two states of consciousness simultaneously. The words have to live in muscle memory, not in your attention. Emma ran all seventeen again, slowly, then faster. Third complete run-through. Fourth.

Rufus's tail moved once. Slow, deliberate. Like he was keeping score.

Emma closed the journal. "That's the best they've sounded."

He stood, walked to her, pressed his head briefly against her leg, then moved to the window and looked south toward Carnegie Hall's bell tower, visible above the roofline of the McClanahan house. His tail went still. Something in the set of his posture, the particular stillness that meant he was attending to something she couldn't perceive, made Emma study the tower for a moment herself.

Same building. Same brick. Same bell tower that had been visible from this kitchen since before she was born.

She checked her watch. 3:45 PM. Twenty seven hours until she was in the air.

Emma opened the journal and started again from the beginning.

* * *

Her phone rang at 4:15.

James. She answered on the second ring.

"How's it going?" He was moving, footsteps on concrete, something being set down with a hollow sound.

"Ceremony sequences are solid. You're at Carnegie Hall?"

"Installing the last two cameras. Hidden placement, so if they disable the primaries again tonight, I'll still have footage from angles they won't think to look for." A pause. "Margaret has the board meeting at seven. I'll present everything we have. The pattern documentation, the footage from the three attacks, the fake credentials on Morrison Technical. Build consensus before Thursday's vote."

"You think the board will hold?"

"Most of them. Tom Ashford might be a problem, retired engineer, and the Safety Coalition's report has enough technical language to sound credible to someone who doesn't know the difference between deliberate damage and age-related failure. But Margaret's prepared for him." The sound of a latch clicking. "And after the meeting, I come back here."

His voice was flat. Not anxious, just decided.

"They've hit us three times," he said. "They know Thursday's vote is coming. If they're going to escalate before then, it'll be tonight."

Emma watched Carnegie Hall through the window. "James."

"I've done this before."

"Not with people who have professional gear and no plates on their vehicles."

"No," he agreed. "But I have cameras they don't know about and police on speed dial." A brief pause. "How's the back?"

"Good enough."

"Then go to Montana. I've got Carnegie Hall."

* **

He had the last camera installed by 6:40 PM.

It was positioned behind the electrical panel housing in the maintenance corridor, an angle that covered the false wall and twelve feet of corridor in both directions. Battery powered. Recording to encrypted cloud storage. Invisible unless you knew it was there.

James checked all six primary feeds on his phone, then the four secondaries. Full coverage. He'd disabled the basement fire suppression system while installing cameras and re-enabling it was the last item on his list before leaving for the board meeting.

He was reaching for his phone to pull up the suppression controls when he heard the rear entrance.

Not the alarm. The alarm hadn't triggered. Glass. The specific sound of a pane giving way, clean and deliberate, the way someone breaks glass who has broken it before and knows how to do it quietly.

James went still.

Two seconds. Three.

Footsteps. Two sets. Moving with the particular economy of people who had been in this building before and weren't wasting time orienting themselves.

He called 911 as he moved, keeping his voice low. "James McClanahan. Intruders at Carnegie Hall on Main Street. I'm inside, rear entrance breach, two suspects. Need units now."

"Units dispatched. ETA four minutes. Sir, you need to exit the building and wait for"

He ended the call.

Four minutes. He ran the calculation as he moved. Fire suppression was still offline. Every piece of old wiring, every dry wood beam in a 118-year-old building, was exposed. If they got to the electrical panel and created another arc, four minutes with no automatic response. He needed to get between them and the systems before they reached anything.

James rounded the corner at the base of the stairs and saw them.

Both in dark clothing. Both moving with the practiced efficiency of people who'd done this kind of work before. One carried a bag that clinked with tools. The other was already heading for the maintenance corridor.

"Building's closed," James said. "Police are on their way."

They both turned. A half-second of assessment and then the one with the bag broke left toward the maintenance corridor while the other stepped sideways, positioning between James and the corridor mouth.

Not aggressive. Just placed. The way someone blocks a doorway when they don't want a fight but they need thirty seconds.

"Move," James said.

The person didn't move.

From the maintenance corridor: a pack being unzipped. Tools on concrete. Then the specific mechanical engagement of a pipe cutter finding its grip on metal.

"Stop." James's voice came out harder than he'd planned. "You're cutting a gas line."

The cutting continued. Methodical. Someone who knew exactly what they were doing and exactly how fast they needed to do it.

James tried to push past the blocker, got shoved back, not hard enough to hurt but with the precise, economical force of someone trained to control space without escalating it. Ten years as a deputy had taught him the difference between someone who'd been in fights and someone who'd been taught to fight. He feinted left, got the blocker shifting weight to match, tried to go right, got shoved again. Lost another ten seconds he didn't have.

The hiss started while he was still working for an angle.

The smell hit immediately after. Mercaptan, sharp and chemical, the odorant that makes natural gas detectable, suddenly thick in the corridor air at a concentration that meant the line had been opened cleanly and the gas was moving.

The person from the maintenance corridor emerged at a jog, already past James, already heading for the rear exit. The blocker dropped back and followed without a word between them. James went after them, got through the rear door just as a dark SUV with no plates and an engine already running pulled away from the alley and was gone.

He got the body type of the vehicle. Nothing more.

James called 911 again. "Gas leak at Carnegie Hall, deliberate cut to the main line. Need fire response and gas company immediately." Then the gas company emergency number. Then he walked far enough from the building to be clear of any concentration and stood on the sidewalk watching the windows.

The fire department arrived in six minutes. Gas company behind them. Police third. The block closed down fast, yellow tape, barriers across both ends of the street, neighbors coming onto their porches.

Chief Davis found James in the parking lot. They'd worked together long enough that Davis skipped the preamble. "Deliberate?"

"Pipe cutter. I heard it engaging. Professional grade. They knew exactly where the main line ran."

"Clean cut means criminal sabotage at minimum." Davis looked at the building, at the gas company crew already at the shutoff. "How many incidents now?"

"Four."

James pulled up the secondary camera feeds and advanced the corridor footage. He watched it through once, then again more slowly.

One of them had paused at the false wall.

He hadn't seen it in the moment, he'd been fighting for position with the blocker. But the secondary camera had caught four full seconds of the person with the bag stopping at the false wall, putting a gloved hand flat against the surface, and pressing. Not randomly. Not checking whether the wall was solid. Pressing with the focused intention of someone who knows a release mechanism exists somewhere along a wall and is searching for it methodically, working from one point to the next.

James sat with those four seconds.

He thought about the first attack. The flooding. The carefully broken water pipes staged to look like age-related failure. He thought about the spray-painted message in the basement, the sites must fall, seven seals, seven failures, and what it meant that someone had written that and left it there, not as a threat to the building's occupants but as a statement of intent directed at something far below the foundation. He thought about the engineering report from Morrison Technical, the fake credentials, the Safety Coalition filing as a nonprofit three months ago, all of it constructed with the kind of careful institutional scaffolding that took planning and resources.

None of it was about the building.

It was never about the building.

The condemnation was cover. Legal demolition authority that came with legal excavation rights. Access to whatever lay beneath in the rubble of proceedings that would look, on paper, like routine public safety enforcement. Four attacks designed not to destroy Carnegie Hall but to build a legal case for destroying it, a case that would hold up because the damage was real, carefully calibrated and officially documented and signed off by a structural engineer whose credentials were forged but whose report would survive a cursory check.

James watched those four seconds one more time. The gloved hand pressing the false wall. The methodical search for a mechanism the person already knew was there.

They'd done their homework. They knew about the chamber. And they'd spent three months building a legal pathway to reach it.

He sent Davis the complete footage. All four angles. Everything.

***

Emma's phone rang at 9:23 PM.

"They cut the gas line," James said. "I confronted them, called it in, they ran. Fire marshal is wrapping up now."

Emma sat down at the kitchen table. "Are you okay?"

"Fine. Secondary cameras caught everything." A pause. "Emma. One of them stopped at the false wall. Spent four seconds pressing it, working the surface looking for the release mechanism. They know something is there."

Rufus had come to stand close, not touching, just present.

"They know about the chamber," she said.

"They know something is there. And they've built a legal pathway to reach it." His voice was level but she could hear the weight underneath. "The condemnation isn't about the building. Once they have the order, they can excavate during demolition. It's been the plan from the start."

"Can Davis charge them?"

"He's treating it as criminal sabotage. But criminal charges against unidentified professionals with fake plates and shell company rentals won't stop a legal condemnation order." A pause. "What stops them is what you're going to provide. Proof the sites can be managed. That's the argument that makes destruction unnecessary."

"Then I seal Montana and you use it Thursday."

"Seal it and come home."

"I'll call you from Kalispell."

"Be careful. They know you're going."

"You too."

***

She spent the next two hours moving through the farmhouse with Rufus at her heels.

Her hiking pack sat open on the kitchen floor. Emma went through it once, just once, accounting for the waterproof containers holding the ceremonial materials, the cold weather layers, the emergency supplies, the satellite phone. She knew what was in it. She didn't recount.

Robert Moore's journal was wrapped and secured in her carry-on.

She ran the ceremony sequences three more times while she moved, not stopping at the journal because she didn't need to anymore. All seventeen in order, the timing between them, the emphasis on the ninth. Automatic now. Or close enough to automatic that Montana would tell her whether it was enough.

Rufus followed her from room to room without ranging. He was staying within arm's reach, and the distinction felt deliberate, like something had shifted in how he understood what was coming.

Emma stopped in the doorway of her bedroom.

"You're coming to Montana with me."

He barked once. Clear.

"It's going to be worse than anything we've dealt with here. The contamination has been active for thirty years. Seven people are dead." She watched him. "You understand what we're walking into."

Rufus held her gaze. Didn't bark. Didn't move away. Just stayed in the doorway with the particular stillness that was his version of commitment.

Emma knelt and put both hands on either side of his head. Felt the solidity of him. The warmth. The weight of him being exactly what he was. "Okay. Together."

She went back to the kitchen and sat at the table with the journal closed in front of her.

She thought about what Dr. Hanson had said in the office at McGuffey Hall. That the medicine showed you what you were capable of. Good and evil both. That integration meant acknowledging both while choosing good. That if you weren't prepared, it broke you.

Seven people had gone into that wilderness prepared for a hike and come out broken, or not come out at all. Experienced people. People who knew what they were doing in backcountry terrain. Whatever waited at those coordinates had nothing to do with elevation or weather or navigation. It was something else entirely, something that operated on the inside rather than the outside, and Emma was walking toward it with three days of pronunciation practice and a closing ceremony she'd never performed.

She wasn't ready. She knew that. But ready wasn't the same thing as prepared, and prepared wasn't the same thing as willing, and willing was what she had.

Emma opened the journal one last time and spoke the closing sequence slowly, start to finish. All seventeen. Not reviewing, not drilling, just saying them the way she'd say them in Montana, at pace, in order, in the quiet kitchen with Carnegie Hall's bell tower visible through the window.

Rufus came off the couch while she was on the fourth sequence.

He didn't pace. Didn't investigate. Just walked from the living room to the kitchen doorway and sat down, and stayed there for the remaining thirteen sequences with his head up and his dark eyes on Emma and his ears tracking each word the way they'd tracked the pronunciation drills all morning. Like he was listening for something specific. Like he was checking her work one final time.

When she finished the seventeenth, he held his position for a moment. Then his tail moved twice, slow and deliberate, and he came the rest of the way into the kitchen and settled at her feet.

Emma looked down at him. "Was that good enough?"

He put his chin on her shoe.

She took that as a yes.

Outside, Carnegie Hall's bell tower stood against the dark sky. James was still over there, lights in the building from the fire marshal's crew finishing up. Holding the line tonight so there was still something standing on Thursday.

One day until Montana. Four days until the vote.

Rufus climbed onto the couch and Emma settled beside him.

She put her hand on his back and listened to him breathe.

Tomorrow, both missions launched. James would defend Carnegie Hall through whatever the night brought. Emma would fly to Montana with ceremony words that had finally settled into her body, and a dog who had walked through her door on the exact day she discovered she needed him.

Moores Hill had given her what she needed.

Now she had to be worth it

CHAPTER 9: THE NETWORK

Emma's phone rang before five.

She was already half awake, the way she'd been most of the night, drifting in and out with ceremony words circling through her mind. Rufus lifted his head from the couch cushion when the phone lit up.

Owen. She answered.

"I found something. You need to see it before you leave for Montana."

Emma sat up. "What did you find?"

"Mark Caldwell. I was cross-referencing missing persons databases with the Montana coordinates, looking for any historical pattern that might explain why the site became active in September 2025. Emma, Mark was listed as a missing person in Montana in August 1995. Three weeks. Then he turned up back in Moores Hill with no explanation anyone recorded."

The room was dark. Emma sat with that for a moment.

"Same year the Morrison family died," she said.

"Same month. Samuel Morrison, seventy-two, heart failure. David Morrison, forty-eight, accidental fall. Both deaths within weeks of Mark's disappearance. Emma, I don't think those deaths were natural."

"Where are you?"

"Lawrenceburg. Outside the county evidence storage facility. I called Sheriff Dawson last night. He's meeting me here at six with keys to Mark's storage unit, the one they sealed after the trial. If Mark was in Montana in 1995, if he had contact with that site, we need to know what he did there before you walk into it."

Emma checked her watch. Her flight left Monday evening. She could make Lawrenceburg and back with hours to spare.

"I'll be there," she said.

She dressed fast. Rufus was already at the door by the time she had her jacket on, watching her with the alert patience of a dog who understood that early departures meant something was happening. Emma clipped his lead, loaded her Montana gear into the car, everything packed and ready from the night before, and pulled out of Oak Street in the dark.

The drive to Lawrenceburg was twenty minutes on empty highways. The world was still dark, still asleep, the kind of Monday morning stillness that existed before the day had any shape. Emma drove with the heater running and Rufus in the passenger seat, his head up, watching the road ahead the way he watched everything, like he was navigating alongside her.

She thought about Mark. Not the trial, not the victims, not the particular ugliness that had been laid out over six weeks in a Dearborn County courtroom. She thought about the man she'd known growing up. The fun uncle who'd stepped in after her father died, who'd helped Linda with repairs and shown up for school events and made terrible jokes at Christmas. The man who'd taught Emma to drive in the parking lot behind the old grain elevator and laughed every time she stalled the engine. The man who had sat with her mother through the worst years, steady and present and kind in all the ways a brother-in-law could be kind.

The man who had fooled everyone. Who had hidden something monstrous so completely that not one person in Moores Hill had seen it coming.

The town had spent two years asking itself how. How do you live beside a person for decades and not know? How do you trust someone that completely and be that wrong? Emma had heard it in the diner, in the grocery store, in the careful conversations that people had when they thought they were processing something and were actually still in shock. The question underneath every other question was the one nobody wanted to say directly: did we make him? Did Moores Hill produce this?

She'd never had an answer. Until Owen's call twenty minutes ago.

Rufus put his head on her arm briefly. Then lifted it and went back to watching the road.

"Yeah," Emma said. "I know."

***

Owen's rental car was already in the storage facility lot when Emma arrived. Sheriff Dawson's cruiser pulled in two minutes behind her, headlights cutting across the gravel. Dawson got out looking like a man who'd had four hours of sleep and made peace with it. Civilian clothes, canvas jacket, badge clipped to his belt.

"Emma." He nodded. Then looked at Rufus. "New dog?"

"Long story."

"Owen told me what you found in the databases. The Morrison deaths." Dawson pulled keys from his jacket pocket. "I pulled their files this morning. 1995. Both deaths investigated by Flathead County. Ruled accidental. Case closed." He paused. "But the case agent noted in his supplemental that a person of interest had been identified in the area and couldn't be located for interview. No name in the file. Just a notation."

"Mark was the person of interest," Emma said.

"That's what I think too." Dawson started walking. "Let's see what he kept."

The unit was at the back corner of the facility, away from the road. Dawson worked the padlock and lifted the roll-up door. The smell hit first, dust and old paper and the particular staleness of a sealed space that hadn't been opened since the trial concluded.

Inside: boxes. Dozens of them. Mark's possessions from twenty years of living in Moores Hill, everything that hadn't been kept as evidence or disposed of by the court. The accumulated weight of a life that had looked completely ordinary from the outside.

Owen started on the left wall, working methodically. Dawson took the right. Emma moved toward the back, Rufus staying close at her heel.

She found it twelve minutes in.

A box on the third shelf, labeled in Mark's handwriting. Neat, careful letters. The same handwriting she'd seen on birthday cards as a child, on the note he'd left after fixing her mother's porch railing, on documents introduced at trial.

Personal Journals 1991-2003.

Emma lifted the box down and set it on the concrete floor. Opened it.

Eight leather-bound notebooks inside. The same size, the same dark covers, the same careful documentation she'd come to associate with people who understood that knowledge needed to be preserved. Robert Moore had kept journals like this. Her mother had kept journals like this.

Mark had kept journals like this.

She picked up the first notebook and opened to the first page.

***

January 8, 1991. Mark's handwriting, open and unhurried, the writing of a man with no reason to hide anything.

Robert and I helped Linda move the couch today. The living room looks better with it against the north wall, more space for Emma to spread her things out. She's seven now and she fills a room the way her father does. Same energy. Same way of being completely present in a space.

Emma stopped reading.

Owen had come to stand beside her. She was aware of him there, aware of Dawson somewhere behind her, aware of the cold concrete under her boots and the fluorescent light overhead.

She turned the page.

More entries from 1991. Mark helping with a fence repair. Mark at a cookout. Mark driving Linda to a doctor's appointment when her car was in the shop. The texture of a normal life, written in the voice of a man who was paying attention to it. He wrote about Emma's father occasionally, about missing him, about trying to fill a space that couldn't really be filled.

She read through 1991 and into 1992. Same voice. Same quality of attention. A man who cared about his family, who showed up, who wrote about small moments the way people do when they value small moments.

This was who Mark had been.

Emma turned to the second notebook. 1992 into early 1993. Still the same voice, but something new had appeared alongside the family entries: research notes. Mark had discovered something in the family history and it had caught his attention.

February 14, 1993. Found more of great-uncle Robert's papers in the Carnegie Hall archives, the section Margaret keeps in the restricted storage. He documented something beneath the building during the 1907 excavation. A carved circle in the bedrock. Symbols around the perimeter. He translated some of them: proto-Indo-European ceremonial language. The journal is incomplete but what's there is remarkable. He believed these sites existed worldwide. That they were healing places, not dangerous ones. That colonization had broken the knowledge of how to use them safely. He was deeply guilty about something he'd done there. Something he'd misunderstood.

Emma turned pages.

March 3, 1993. Cross-referenced Robert's coordinates with current geological surveys. The Montana location is accessible. A wilderness area in Flathead National Forest, well off any marked trail. A family called Morrison has maintained custodial responsibility for it since before Robert's time, they were one of the original seven families he documented. I've been trying to reach them through county records but they're private people. I may need to go up there in person. This feels important. Like something our family has been responsible for and walked away from.

He'd gone looking for the Morrison family. Had wanted to meet them, to understand the responsibility his family had abandoned when Robert Moore sealed the Carnegie Hall site and carried his guilt to the grave.

Emma felt something cold moving through her that wasn't the storage unit air.

March 22, 1993. The Morrison family won't engage. Two letters unanswered. Old Samuel Morrison is in his seventies. His son David seems to handle the property now. I drove past the access road, you can't see anything from the road, just Forest Service land going up into the mountains. I've been studying Robert's translation of the opening ceremony. It's not complicated. Seven sequences, specific movements, specific materials. The medicine is described clearly: psilocybin mushrooms, which apparently grow near the site. Robert believed the ceremony was designed to be accessible precisely because it was meant for anyone who came to it properly prepared. I'm thinking about going in August.

Emma set the notebook down carefully. Picked up the third one.

***

The August 1993 entries were the ones she'd been moving toward.

August 12, 1993. Arrived in Kalispell yesterday. Rented a truck. Drove out toward Hungry Horse Reservoir this morning and hiked in from the north, it's rough country, no trails, but Robert's coordinates are precise. I'm camped about four miles from the site. The wilderness up here is extraordinary. I keep thinking about what Robert wrote, about what these sites were designed for, about all the knowledge that was lost. I feel like I'm doing something right. Restoring something. Going back for the family.

Emma read that last line twice. Going back for the family.

He'd gone to Montana because he thought it was the right thing to do. Because Robert Moore had failed his responsibility and Mark had wanted to correct that. He'd gone out of conscience, not darkness.

August 16, 1993. Found the circle this afternoon. Exactly where the coordinates said. Ten feet across, carved into bedrock. The ash is undisturbed, compressed into the stone over what must be centuries, maybe longer. The symbols around the perimeter are exactly what Robert described. I've spent three hours photographing and documenting everything. It's real. All of it is real. I keep thinking about Robert making the same discovery, making the wrong choice. I don't want to make the wrong choice.

He'd been careful. He'd documented before doing anything. He'd thought about Robert's mistake.

August 17, 1993. I've been sitting with this for a full day. The mushrooms are here, exactly where Robert said they'd be, growing near the fallen pine at the clearing's edge. The instructions are clear. The ceremony is designed for exactly this, for a seeker who comes alone to face himself. The ancients built this for individual journeys, not just community ones. Robert was wrong to be afraid of it, wrong to seal it. I'm going to perform the opening ceremony tomorrow at sunset. I feel more ready than I've felt for anything in my life. I'm here for the right reasons. I want to understand what our family has been protecting.

Rufus growled.

Low. Continuous. Not at Emma. At the journal.

Emma kept reading.

August 18, 1993. I don't know how to write what happened.

A long gap on the page. Then:

The ceremony worked. I understood that immediately. It did exactly what Robert described, it opened perception. Showed me dimensions of consciousness that are always present but normally hidden. And then it showed me myself.

I wasn't prepared for what I saw.

I saw my capacity for cruelty. For violence. For predation. Not memories of things I'd done, I haven't done those things. But the capacity. The potential. Every dark impulse I'd ever had and suppressed, all of it present and visible and real. The medicine doesn't lie. That's what Robert meant, I understand it now. The ceremony shows you what you're capable of, completely and without mercy. The ancients designed it that way because they understood that healing requires seeing yourself fully. That you cannot integrate your darkness by pretending it doesn't exist.

But I had no one to guide me through that seeing. No elder. No framework. No preparation for what integration actually meant or how to do it.

I saw what I could become and I had no idea what to do with that seeing.

I'm writing this the next morning. I feel like something is wrong with me. Like a door opened that I don't know how to close.

Emma read that passage three times.

A door opened that I don't know how to close.

He'd gone in good faith. He'd been trying to do the right thing for his family. And the ceremony had shown him his shadow, the same thing it showed everyone who entered it, and he'd been completely alone with what he saw, with no preparation for integration, no elder to tell him that what he was seeing was human potential rather than human destiny.

No one to tell him the darkness was something to be acknowledged and released, not something to be identified with.

She turned pages. More entries from August 1993, from the drive back to Indiana, from the weeks after. Mark trying to make sense of what the ceremony had shown him. Writing about it with the earnest confusion of a good man who'd seen something terrible in himself and didn't know what to do with the seeing.

September 4, 1993. I keep thinking about what I saw. I've been reading everything I can find about shamanic practice, about shadow work, about what the ceremony was actually designed to do. I understand intellectually that what I saw isn't who I am but what I'm capable of. But understanding it intellectually and actually integrating it are different things. I feel like there's something loose inside me that wasn't loose before. Like a weight that shifted.

November 19, 1993. Told Linda I've been having trouble sleeping. She made soup and sat with me for two hours. She's a good person. This town is full of good people. I keep trying to hold onto that.

Rufus pressed harder against Emma's leg.

She kept reading. Into 1994, into 1995. Mark fighting. The entries getting further apart, the handwriting gradually changing, something in his voice shifting by degrees so slow that you couldn't see it move, only notice, looking back, how different he was at the end of a year than at its beginning.

He'd been fighting it. For two years he'd been fighting what Montana had shown him, trying to find his way back to himself, trying to use whatever he'd read and learned to do the integration work without any guidance.

Then September 3, 1995.

Samuel Morrison found me at the site today. I'd gone back. I thought maybe if I could perform the closing ceremony it would undo whatever the opening ceremony had done to me. I've been trying to learn the closing ceremony from Robert's documentation.

Samuel is old but he understood immediately what I'd done. He could see it, I think. He started speaking words I recognized as the closing sequence. He was trying to seal it. And something in me, I have no clean way to say this, something in me refused. Everything the opening ceremony had shown me, all of it, surged up like a tide and I pushed back at what Samuel was trying to do.

His heart stopped.

I didn't touch him. I need to be clear about that. I did not touch Samuel Morrison. But he's dead and it happened because of me and because of what I've become and I don't know how to carry that.

David ran. He saw his father fall. He ran for help. I should have let him go. I know I should have let him go.

The entry stopped there. Incomplete. Like Mark had put the pen down and not known how to finish the sentence.

The next entry was three weeks later.

October 1, 1995. I've been home for three weeks. Nobody knows where I was. The Morrison deaths were ruled accidental. Nobody connected it to me. I keep waiting to feel something about that and I don't feel what I think I should feel. That frightens me more than anything else.

The storage unit was completely silent.

Owen spoke first, his voice quiet and careful. "He went back to try to close it. He went back trying to fix what he'd broken."

"And instead it killed Samuel Morrison," Emma said.

"Because Mark had been carrying two years of unintegrated shadow," Owen said. "His confusion, his terror, all of it deposited in that site every time he went back to try to work through it alone. When Samuel tried to perform the closing ceremony, he ran into everything Mark had left there."

Dawson was very still. "He didn't go back to hurt anyone."

"No," Emma said. "He went back because he was trying to become the person who'd gone in August 1993. Trying to find his way back."

She turned to the fourth notebook. 1996 through 2000. The handwriting continued to change, the entries became sparser, the voice of the man who'd written lovingly about moving a couch and missing his brother almost entirely absent. In its place, something controlled and watchful. The entries from these years didn't describe darkness. They described a man monitoring himself the way you monitor a wound that isn't healing, noting its progress with the detachment of someone who has accepted that the wound is permanent.

She read enough to understand the shape of those years and then she closed the fourth notebook.

The fifth notebook she opened to a single entry, February 2003.

I've been fighting this for ten years. I understand now that I'm not going to win.

She closed it. Put it back in the box. She'd read what she needed to read.

***

Dawson had found the correspondence folder on the right wall, tucked behind a box of financial records. He brought it to Emma without comment.

Three letters. The first dated March 1994, on letterhead that read Friends of Sacred Sites Preservation. The second August 1995. The third October 1995.

She read the first. An organization in Cincinnati reaching out to Mark. They knew about his connection to the Carnegie Hall custodian lineage. They wanted to collaborate. They believed the sites were worth preserving and studying. A Dr. Vincent Aldridge, signing with the particular confidence of someone who had been doing this work for a while.

They'd reached out in March 1994, six months after the ceremony, while Mark was still in his confusion period. Still fighting. Still the man who'd gone to Montana to do the right thing for his family.

He had never responded.

The second letter, August 1995, after the Morrison deaths.

They were disturbed. They'd heard about Samuel and David. They were asking Mark to reconsider collaboration. The tone was still hopeful but something underneath it had changed, a note of alarm below the professional language.

The third letter. October 1995.

Emma read it slowly.

The pivot from preservation to elimination. Aldridge concluding that the sites were too dangerous to exist. The formal declaration that Friends of Sacred Sites Preservation was becoming the Moores Hill Safety Coalition. The language of a man who had looked at two dead custodians and a contaminated site and made a decision that probably felt like the only responsible one available to him.

You bear direct responsibility for this decision.

Emma stood in the storage unit with the letters in her hand and understood the full shape of it.

Mark had gone to Montana in good faith. Had been broken by what he found there, not because of who he was but because he was completely alone with what the medicine showed him, with no framework for integration, no guidance, no community to help him hold what he'd seen. He'd fought it for two years. Had gone back trying to fix it and killed Samuel Morrison not by choice but by contamination. Had spent another two years trying to recover before the Morrison deaths and then another eight years losing ground before the February 2003 entry had closed the door on the man he'd been.

The town of Moores Hill hadn't raised a monster.

Montana had made one. Out of a decent man who'd gone looking for his family's lost responsibility and found something he had no preparation to survive.

"Emma." Owen's voice was quiet. "You understand what this means."

"Moores Hill didn't produce him," Emma said. "They've been asking themselves that for two years. Every person in this town who trusted him, who ate at his table, who bought cars from him and watched him at church and let their kids call him by his first name. They've been asking if they were blind or complicit or just fools." She looked at the letters. "They weren't. He was a good man until Montana."

Dawson exhaled slowly. He'd worked this community for ten years as a deputy, had probably carried his own version of that question. "Nobody could have seen it coming. Because it wasn't there to see until it was already too late."

"Until 2003," Owen said. "Ten years after Montana."

"Ten years of fighting before he lost," Emma said. "The town should know that. They should know what actually happened."

She put the letters back in the folder and handed it to Owen. "Get everything scanned. All of it. James needs the Anti-Custodian origin story for Thursday and I need the journal entries for Montana. But Owen, the entries from 1991 and 1992. The ones where he's just Mark. Where he's helping Linda move the couch and missing my father and being the person everyone knew." She paused. "Those need to be part of the record too."

Owen nodded. "I'll send everything."

Dawson retained the original journals as documentation, thirty-year-old evidence of deaths that would never be prosecuted because the man responsible was already in the ground. He walked Emma and Owen to the parking lot as the first gray light of morning showed above the tree line.

"Be careful in Montana," he said to Emma. "Whatever's out there killed nine people."

"I know what I'm walking into," Emma said. "That's the difference between me and the nine. That and thirty years of compounded wreckage that I intend to finish cleaning up."

She looked at the pale gold beginning to show at the edge of the sky above the tree line.

"Mark went in alone and unprepared because he didn't know what he was walking into," she said. "I know. I have the closing ceremony. I have Dr. Hanson's pronunciation. I have Rufus." She looked at the German Shepherd, who was looking back at her with those dark attentive eyes. "And I know what the medicine is going to show me when I step into that circle. I know it's going to show me what I'm capable of. Same blood as Mark. Same capacity."

She said it plainly, without drama.

"The difference is I know what to do with what I see."

***

She drove back toward Moores Hill on empty morning highways with Rufus in the passenger seat and the full weight of it settled into something she could carry.

She understood Mark now. Understood him in a way that had been impossible before this morning, when he'd been simply the monster the trial had made him. The calculated predator. The man with the careful smile who'd fooled everyone. He was still responsible for what he'd done. Understanding why he'd broken didn't change what the breaking had cost. Twelve women were still dead. Owen still had a scar. Linda Caldwell was still buried in Moores Hill Cemetery.

But now Emma understood that the man who'd done those things hadn't existed until Montana. Had been created by something he'd walked into in good faith, alone, without preparation, in an attempt to honor a family obligation he'd only half understood.

The medicine hadn't created his capacity for darkness. Every person who'd ever stood in that circle had seen their own capacity for darkness. That was the point of the ceremony, the entire design of it. The medicine revealed what was already there. What it was supposed to do, in the hands of a prepared seeker with elder guidance and community support, was help the seeker look at that capacity clearly and then release it. Acknowledge the shadow. Choose the light.

Mark had seen his shadow with no one there to tell him what he was seeing. No one to say: this is human. This is what we all contain. This is what we must acknowledge in order to move past it. No one to guide him through integration.

So the shadow had stayed. Had grown. Had eventually become the thing that the trial had exposed.

Not Moores Hill's fault. Not the town's failure. Not a sign of something broken in the community that had trusted him.

Montana's making. Sacred ground misused. Ancient medicine without the knowledge to use it safely.

Emma pulled into Oak Street as the morning came fully up. Grabbed her pack from the house. Called James from the driveway and gave him the compressed version: Mark, Montana, 1993, the ten-year unraveling, the Morrison deaths, the Anti-Custodian letters. James listened without interrupting. When she finished there was a pause.

"He wasn't always what they convicted," James said. It wasn't a question.

"He was a good man until 1993," Emma said. "The town should know that. After this is over, after Montana is sealed and Carnegie Hall is saved, the town should know what actually happened to Mark Caldwell."

"Yeah," James said quietly. He was silent for a moment. "How's the gear?"

"In the car. How's Carnegie Hall?"

"Standing. Go catch your flight."

Emma ended the call. Looked up at the farmhouse one more time. At the kitchen window where Carnegie Hall's bell tower was visible above the neighbor's roof. Under attack. Still standing. Protected by James while Emma went to close the wound that had started all of it.

She picked up her pack.

Rufus fell into step beside her without being called, walking to the car with the unhurried certainty of a dog who knew exactly where they were going and had already decided he was coming.

Emma loaded the gear. Rufus jumped in.

She started the engine and headed for Indianapolis.

CHAPTER 10: THE MARKING

Owen called while Emma was on the highway, forty minutes outside Indianapolis.

Rufus was in the passenger seat, watching the road with the same alert attention he brought to everything. Indiana farmland moved past on both sides, flat and bare and winter-pale under a clear March sky. Emma had the heater running and the radio off. She'd been running the ceremony sequences in her head for the last twenty miles without meaning to, the words moving through her mind the way music moves through a musician's mind on the day of a performance. Not rehearsal anymore. Just presence. The words had settled somewhere past conscious retrieval into something she trusted would be there when she needed it.

"Walsh's beacon activated again this morning," Owen said. "Strong signal. Stationary. Emma, he's alive. He hasn't moved in weeks but someone is manually triggering that beacon. Someone conscious enough to do that."

Emma's hands tightened slightly on the wheel. "How long has it been?"

"Since December 28. Nearly two months in winter wilderness."

"Where exactly is he?"

"Approximately five miles northeast of the ceremonial site coordinates. Deep in the same sector. I've been cross-referencing terrain maps and there's a creek drainage about half a mile from his beacon position. If he found that drainage early on, if there's a sheltered spot near water, that might explain how he's still alive. But Emma, his window is closing. Whatever reserves he went in with are running out. If he's conscious enough to trigger the beacon he's conscious enough to know he's almost out of time. I think he has forty-eight hours. Maybe less."

She looked at the road ahead. At the mental map she'd been building since she first got Walsh's coordinates. At the terrain between the forest service trailhead and his position, and between his position and the ceremonial site five miles southwest.

"Send me his exact coordinates. I'll route through him first."

"That adds a full day to your approach timeline. Wilderness rescue on top of a closing ceremony, both in terrain that's killed nine people in four months."

"Send me the coordinates, Owen."

He sent them. Emma glanced at the pin on her phone's map at the next stoplight, studied the terrain overlay for thirty seconds, and saw that the route worked. Longer than approaching the site directly but clean. No major elevation problems between the trailhead and Walsh's position. She could reach him by Wednesday afternoon if she set a hard pace, signal for emergency evacuation, and still have enough daylight and energy left to reach the ceremony site by Thursday morning.

She texted one-handed at the light: Got it. Routing through his position first.

"The ceremony is still happening Thursday," she said when Owen picked back up. "Walsh gets pulled out and then the site gets sealed. Both happen or neither happens."

"I know," Owen said. "That's why I called instead of waiting."

Rufus looked at her briefly, the way he did when the conversation in the car shifted in register, and then went back to watching the road ahead.

Emma drove the rest of the way to Indianapolis thinking about Timothy Walsh, alive somewhere in Montana wilderness after two months, still triggering his beacon. Still fighting. She didn't know anything about him beyond what Owen had pulled from the missing persons report. Thirty-eight years old, Kalispell native, solo hiker with ten years of backcountry experience in the Bob Marshall.

The kind of person who knew how to read terrain and manage exposure and navigate without trails. The kind of person the contamination had gotten anyway, just like it had gotten everyone else.

She'd get him out. That had been a decision made in the ten seconds between Owen saying forty-eight hours and her saying send me the coordinates. There hadn't been anything to deliberate about. You didn't leave someone alive in the field because the timing was inconvenient.

She thought about what Walsh had been through. Two months near a contaminated ceremonial site. Two months in winter wilderness with whatever the site had shown him still living in his head. The psychological break the medicine induced without proper preparation wasn't a temporary experience. It didn't end when the psilocybin metabolized. It left something behind. A fracture in how a person understood themselves, in the relationship between what they were and what they were capable of. Walsh had seen his shadow without any framework for integration and he'd been living inside that seeing for two months in a Montana drainage.

She'd need to be careful approaching him. A person in that state, in that terrain, after that long, might not respond to a stranger the way a rational mind would expect.

Rufus, she thought. Walsh would respond to Rufus before he responded to her. That was something.

The Indianapolis skyline appeared ahead, catching the afternoon sun.

Emma moved to the exit lane and thought about Thursday.

***

James spent Monday afternoon at Carnegie Hall with a drill, a ladder, and four battery-powered cameras he'd ordered three days earlier and picked up that morning at the UPS facility in Lawrenceburg.

The primary security system had six cameras. He knew exactly where they were because he'd installed two of them himself after the first attack, and the original four had been in place long enough that their positions were documented in the historical society's maintenance records. That documentation was public. Anyone who'd done basic research on the building could find those positions. And whoever was running these attacks had done considerably more than basic research.

The secondary cameras went somewhere else entirely.

Behind the electrical panel housing in the maintenance corridor, angled to cover the false wall and twelve feet of corridor in both directions. Inside the stairwell housing on the second floor landing, covering the main floor approach from above. Above the metal shelving in the basement storage room, positioned to cover the tunnel entrance and the first eight feet of the passage beyond. And one outside, mounted flush under the eave of the rear entrance overhang, covering the approach from the alley in a low angle that wouldn't be visible from street level.

Battery powered. Recording to encrypted cloud storage through a cellular signal that didn't depend on the building's internal network. No wires connecting them to any system that could be found and disabled from inside.

James worked methodically, testing each camera's angle before committing to the mount, pulling up the cloud feed on his phone to verify the coverage, adjusting twice on the corridor camera before he had the false wall centered in frame the way he wanted it. By the time he finished, Carnegie Hall had secondary coverage from four positions that didn't appear on any maintenance record or security diagram that existed anywhere. Anyone who found and disabled the six primary cameras would have every reason to believe they'd eliminated the recording capability. They'd be wrong.

He checked his watch. The board meeting started in fifty minutes.

Margaret Hendricks had assembled the full historical society board for the occasion: seven people, all volunteers, who'd been showing up for Carnegie Hall for anywhere from two years to four decades. James knew most of them by name and all of them by type. Tom

Ashford, retired structural engineer from the Cincinnati metro who'd moved to Dearborn County for the quiet and stayed for the community. Dorothy Webb, eighty-one, who'd been leading Carnegie Hall tours since 1987 and could tell you the provenance of every photograph in the main hallway. Ruth Holloway, who ran the county historical records office and had been Margaret's closest ally on the board for fifteen years. Four others who ranged from reliable to uncertain depending on the pressure being applied.

James set up his laptop at the head of the conference table and walked them through everything he had.

The security footage first. All three previous attacks laid out in sequence, the footage clean and clearly time-stamped, showing professional two-person teams moving through Carnegie Hall with gear and purpose that bore no resemblance to random vandalism. He paused on the moments that mattered most: the pipe cutter engaging on the gas main, the deliberate targeting of electrical systems, the spray-painted message from the second attack that the police had photographed but hadn't fully understood the significance of. Seven seals. Seven failures. A statement of organizational intent, not a graffiti slogan.

Then the Safety Coalition itself. The fraudulent corporate structure, the anonymous donor network, the law firm in Cincinnati that had filed the petition without a single traceable principal behind it. Morrison Technical Services incorporated eighteen months ago. The engineering credentials on their structural report tracing to a licensed engineer who had died in 2019.

Tom Ashford leaned forward at that. "Let me see the certification numbers."

James turned the laptop toward him.

Ashford looked at the documents for a full thirty seconds. At the signature block. At the PE number in the bottom right corner of the report's certification page. He pulled out his own phone, ran a search, compared what came back to what was on the page.

"This PE number belongs to a man named Gerald Whitfield," Ashford said. "Licensed structural engineer, state of Indiana, 1981 through 2019. He died March 12, 2019. Heart attack." He set his phone down. "Whoever signed this report used a dead man's credentials. That's not an oversight. That's deliberate fraud."

"Yes," James said.

"Then we don't fight the condemnation petition on its merits." Ashford's voice had taken on the focused quality of a man who'd spent forty years identifying exactly where structural problems began. "We invalidate the petition itself. Indiana code requires that structural assessments submitted as the basis for condemnation proceedings be certified by a licensed engineer in good standing. This report bears the credentials of a man who has been dead for seven years. The petition has no valid engineering foundation. It should be dismissed on procedural grounds before the council even considers the substance."

Margaret was already reaching for her notepad. "Tom, can you write that up formally? Something we can put directly in front of the council Thursday evening?"

"I'll have it done by eight tomorrow morning." He closed James's laptop gently. Looked around the table. "James. This is thorough work."

Dorothy Webb, who hadn't spoken since the meeting started, said: "Who are these people really? This Aldridge and his organization?"

"We don't know yet who's ultimately behind them," James said. "What we know is that the Safety Coalition was created specifically to target this building. The engineering firm that produced the structural report didn't exist two years ago. The engineer whose name is on it has been dead since 2019. This entire petition was built on fraud, and that's what we take to the council Thursday."

Dorothy Webb was quiet for a moment. Then she said: "My grandmother's grandmother attended the Moores Hill College. Graduated 1912. She talked about Carnegie Hall her whole life. She's been dead sixty years and I still hear her talking about that building." She looked at James. "Tell me what you need from me Thursday."

The vote was unanimous. Margaret would open with the historical and community significance argument. Ashford would present the petition invalidation motion based on fraudulent credentials. James would walk the council through the security footage from all five attacks, with emphasis on the coordinated nature of the targeting and the footage of the attacker searching the false wall. Ruth Holloway would speak to the county's legal obligation to investigate criminal fraud before acting on any petition derived from it. Owen was compiling additional documentation on the Safety Coalition's fraudulent corporate structure and the fake credentials.

They had a case. Whether it was enough depended on five out of seven council members, and James had been in enough rooms with enough politics to know that evidence was necessary but not always sufficient.

He locked Carnegie Hall after the board members left and settled into the basement security office.

The attacks had come at night. Always night, always the rear entrance, always the same deliberate approach. James had no reason to think tonight would be different, and every reason to think they'd escalate. The condemnation vote was three days away. If they were going to make a move that went beyond the camera-disabling and staged damage of the previous attacks, the window for it was narrowing.

He pulled up all ten camera feeds on his laptop. Made coffee. Settled in.

He thought about the false wall while he waited. About what was behind it. About the sealed chamber twenty feet beneath Main Street that had been there since before Carnegie Hall existed, since before Moores Hill College existed, since before any European had stood on this ground and decided to build something permanent over something ancient. Robert Moore had found it in 1907 and sealed it out of fear and built a building on top of it and spent the rest of his life carrying the guilt of that choice. And now his great-great-granddaughter was in the air over Indiana, headed for Montana, carrying the knowledge Robert Moore had left behind for exactly this moment.

James intended to make sure the building was still standing when she got back.

At eleven-fourteen, the rear camera picked up movement in the alley.

Two figures. Same dark clothing. Same deliberate, economical movement. They went directly to the rear entrance and had the lock picked in under a minute, slightly faster than the last time. Practice made efficient.

James watched them enter on the secondary exterior camera. Watched them work through the basement systematically, disabling the primary cameras one by one. The primaries went dark in under three minutes. Clean and practiced.

The secondaries kept recording.

James called 911. "James McClanahan. Intruders at Carnegie Hall, Main Street, active break-in in progress. I have them on secondary cameras. Send units now."

He watched on his phone while he waited.

They moved to the electrical panel. Created damage that looked, to anyone examining it without context, like the kind of incremental deterioration that an aging building accumulated. James narrated into his phone continuously, time and action and camera angle, building a record that would survive any legal challenge to its admissibility.

Then one of them stopped.

Stood at the maintenance corridor entrance and looked at the false wall. Not a glance. A full stop. The kind of stillness that meant recognition, that meant this is the thing I came for. Three deliberate steps toward it. Both gloved hands against the surface now, working from the left edge toward the center, pressing at intervals of about four inches, feeling for the give that indicated a concealed mechanism.

They knew exactly what they were looking for. They just hadn't found it yet.

James kept his voice level. "Suspect two, eleven twenty-two, at false wall, two-handed search for concealed access mechanism, working left to right across the surface."

The sirens started. Coming up Main Street from two directions.

The figure at the wall pulled back immediately, grabbed the pack from the floor, moved fast for the rear exit. The other one was already ahead. Both of them through the door and across the alley and into a vehicle that was running and moving before James got to the rear entrance.

Dark SUV. No plates. Gone east on the side street before the first police unit turned the corner.

James brought Chief Reeves down to the basement and showed him everything. The new damage at the electrical panel. The disabled primaries. The secondary footage. The moment at the false wall.

Reeves watched the false wall footage twice. "They know something is back there."

"Yes."

"What's back there?"

"Historical artifacts under the historical society's stewardship." James kept his voice level and his face neutral. "Significant enough that someone has been running a thirty-year campaign to access them through legal demolition channels."

Reeves studied the frozen image on the screen for a long moment. The gloved hands against the wall. The methodical search. "Send me all of this. Tonight. Every angle, every incident, everything you have. I want it before I talk to the DA in the morning."

After the police left, James stood alone in the corridor and looked at the false wall.

Five attacks. Ten days. An organization with thirty years of institutional momentum behind it and no apparent intention of stopping. A condemnation vote in three days with a council that was scared of liability and being fed a steady diet of staged evidence by professionals who knew exactly how municipal bureaucracies worked.

And on the other side: Tom Ashford's petition invalidation argument. Ruth Holloway's procedural motion. Five attacks documented from angles they didn't know existed. And Emma, somewhere in the air above the plains right now, carrying everything Robert Moore had left behind.

James called her.

***

She was at the gate when the phone rang, Rufus beside her chair, watching the terminal with the patient attentiveness he brought to every space he occupied. Emma answered on the first ring.

James gave her the report quickly and cleanly. Fifth attack, secondary cameras, the false wall search, Reeves taking it seriously, the board meeting and Ashford's petition invalidation argument. Emma listened without interrupting, asking two precise questions when he finished, and then sat with the information for a moment.

"The petition invalidation is our strongest move," she said. "If Ashford can get that in front of the council before they vote, they can't legally proceed even if they want to. A petition built on fraudulent credentials isn't a petition."

"It depends on whether the council's attorney agrees with Ashford's reading."

"Then make sure the council's attorney has Ashford's written argument in hand before Thursday evening. Give them no room to defer it to a later meeting."

"Already planned." A pause. "Walsh?"

"Routing through his position. I'll reach him Wednesday afternoon. I've been thinking about the approach. Rufus goes to Walsh first, while I'm still outside the contamination radius. Walsh has been out there two months. He's not going to respond well to a stranger walking toward him out of the wilderness. But he'll respond to a dog. Dogs don't carry the psychological weight that people carry when you've been alone for two months with your own shadow."

James was quiet for a moment. "That's a good read."

"I've had time to think on the drive." She paused. "James. You've built a solid case. The board, the cameras, the Ashford argument. You've done what needed doing."

"So have you."

The boarding announcement came over the gate speakers. General boarding.

"Three days," Emma said. "Both missions."

"Both succeed," James said.

"Both succeed."

She ended the call and stood up. Rufus was already on his feet, watching her, vest on and attention fully present the way it was always fully present when movement was imminent.

"Last chance to stay home," Emma said.

He gave her the look that meant this conversation was beneath both of them and began walking toward the gate.

Emma followed.

Rufus settled at her feet when they found their seats, tucking into the space in front of her with the ease of a dog who had done exactly this before, in exactly this kind of space, and had no questions about the procedure. The flight attendant glanced at his documentation, nodded, and moved on. Just another service dog. Unremarkable. Invisible in the specific way that competence is invisible.

The plane pushed back. Indianapolis fell away through the window, the grid of the city giving way to the darker grid of farmland below, the whole southern Indiana landscape laid out flat and clear in the early evening light. Moores Hill was somewhere out there in that grid, south and east, too small to resolve from altitude. 597 people and one historic building and a sealed chamber beneath Main Street and James standing watch in a basement office with ten camera feeds and a determination that had not wavered once in ten days of escalating attacks.

Emma put her hand on Rufus's head and felt him breathe.

"We're going to face something terrible," she said quietly. "Seven people died there. Walsh has been surviving near it for two months and whatever he's experienced has fractured something in him. The contamination is real and it's been building since 1993 and it's going to try to show me exactly what it showed Mark." She paused. "I know what it's going to show me. I know it's going to show me what I'm capable of. Same blood. Same capacity. Same potential for darkness that Mark looked at and decided was his destiny."

Rufus pressed his head against her palm.

"The difference is I know what to do with what I see."

One quiet bark.

Emma leaned back in her seat and let Indiana disappear below her.

Ahead, somewhere beyond Denver and the Rockies and the vast dark of the mountain west, a contaminated ash circle waited in Montana wilderness. Waited for someone who knew what it had done and why and what it would take to end it. Waited for the great-great-granddaughter of the man who had built a building over it in 1907 and carried the guilt of that to his grave. Waited for the custodian who had read every journal, learned every ceremony sequence, understood every consequence.

The plane climbed.

Act Two was beginning.

Both missions active. Both protagonists committed. James holding Carnegie Hall through whatever came at it before Thursday. Emma in the air with ceremony words settled so deep in her memory they'd moved past retrieval into reflex, with a mysterious dog at her feet whose origin she'd stopped questioning because some things didn't need to hold up in any framework she'd ever worked in.

They just needed to be true.

And the clock was ticking on both.

DUAL SIEGE

CHAPTER 11: CONDEMNATION

The plane landed in Kalispell before the mountains were fully visible.

Emma had slept somewhere over Wyoming, not deeply, not restfully, but enough. She woke to the cabin lights coming up and the descent announcement and Rufus already awake at her feet, alert and still in the way he was alert and still when something had shifted in the environment around him. Not agitated. Just attentive. Like a frequency had changed that only he could hear.

Emma looked out the window as the plane banked on approach. The Mission Range came into view first, peaks still heavy with snow in late March, ridgelines sharp against a sky that was clear and very blue and entirely different from Indiana sky. Bigger somehow. More sky per square inch of horizon. The kind of landscape that made the scale of human problems feel appropriately small.

Except the problem Emma was carrying hadn't shrunk on the flight. It had clarified.

She'd used the hours over Wyoming going over the plan one more time. Not the ceremony, that was settled. The logistics. Forest service road from the trailhead, fifteen miles of rough terrain to the end of the navigable road. Then fifteen miles on foot through roadless wilderness to the vicinity of the site. Walsh's position five miles northeast of the site, which meant approaching from the south, hitting Walsh first, getting him stable and signaling for evacuation, then continuing southwest to the ash circle.

Two objectives on the same day in terrain that had killed nine people. The math was tight but it worked if nothing went wrong.

Emma had spent enough time in the field to know that something always went wrong. The variable was whether the thing that went wrong was manageable or fatal. She intended to be in the manageable category.

Rufus stood when the wheels touched down, his balance adjusting automatically to the deceleration. Emma put her hand briefly on his back and felt him breathe.

"Montana," she said.

He looked at the window. At the mountains visible beyond the terminal buildings. His ears moved forward slightly and held there.

Emma gathered her carry-on and waited for the door.

***

The Kalispell airport was small and efficient and full of people who looked like they belonged in serious wilderness. Hunters. Guides. Researchers. The particular demographic of people who came to the Bob Marshall Wilderness in March, which was to say people who knew exactly what March in the Bob Marshall meant and were going anyway.

Emma collected her checked bag at the carousel, verified that the waterproof containers holding the ceremonial materials had survived the flight intact, and moved to the rental car counter.

The agent was a woman in her thirties, efficient and friendly in the way of people who processed a lot of travelers through a small airport and had learned to read them quickly. She looked at Emma's gear. At Rufus in his service dog vest. At the amount of cold weather equipment Emma was checking off on the rental agreement.

"You're heading into backcountry," the agent said. It wasn't a question.

"Bob Marshall Wilderness. North sector."

The agent's hands paused briefly on the keyboard. "That area's had some incidents this past fall. Seven missing persons. Forest Service has advisories posted."

"I know about the incidents," Emma said.

The agent looked at her for a moment. Then finished processing the paperwork. "I'll put you in the Expedition. Four-wheel drive, high clearance. Better for the forest service roads up there." She slid the keys across the counter. "The chains are in the back. Roads should be clear in the valleys but you'll want them if you're going to elevation."

Emma took the keys. "Thank you."

"Be careful out there."

Rufus walked beside Emma to the parking structure with his head slightly raised, testing the air. Montana air. Different from Indiana air in ways that weren't just temperature or altitude. Drier. Cleaner. And underneath those qualities, something else that Emma couldn't name but that Rufus was clearly registering. He wasn't alarmed. Just noting. Filing it away in whatever internal system he used to process the world.

Owen called while Emma was loading gear into the Expedition.

"Landed," she said.

"Good. Walsh's beacon activated twice overnight. Strong signal both times. He's conscious, Emma. Someone is deliberately triggering that beacon on a schedule, roughly every eight hours. He's not just accidentally bumping it. He's maintaining a distress signal."

Emma stopped loading and stood with her hand on the cargo door. "He's been doing that for two months?"

"The beacon records show regular activation going back to early January. Every eight to twelve hours. Someone out there has been methodically signaling for help for nearly two months."

Emma thought about that. About Timothy Walsh in a Montana creek drainage, injured or ill or psychologically fractured by whatever the contaminated site had shown him, but still maintaining a rescue signal every eight hours for two months. Still fighting with whatever part of his mind remained functional.

"He's a survivor," Emma said.

"He is. But Emma, the battery on that beacon isn't infinite. I'm estimating forty-eight hours before it goes dark. Whatever's keeping him going, he's almost out of time."

"I'll reach him Wednesday afternoon. I'm in Whitefish tonight, trailhead Wednesday morning."

"Weather is holding. Clear through Thursday, temperatures in the low thirties overnight and mid-forties by afternoon. You'll have good conditions."

"Send me any updates on the beacon. Anything changes in the signal pattern, I want to know."

"You'll have satellite phone coverage most of the approach. There'll be a dead zone about three miles out from the site, but before that you'll be reachable."

Emma closed the cargo door. Rufus was already in the passenger seat, watching her through the windshield with calm expectation.

"How's James?" Emma asked.

"Holding. He called me this morning. The DA is reviewing the footage from last night. Reeves apparently walked into the DA's office before eight this morning with everything James sent. Tom Ashford's petition invalidation argument is already drafted. Margaret has been calling council members individually since sunrise."

"Good." Emma got in the driver's seat. "I'll meet you in Whitefish," Owen said. "My flight lands in Kalispell two hours behind yours. I'll pick up a rental and head straight up."

Emma paused with her hand on the door. "Owen."

"Don't," he said. "James can't leave Carnegie Hall. Someone has to be with you in that wilderness and it's not going to be Rufus making the navigation decisions."

Emma got in the driver's seat. "Pine Lodge Motel. North side of Whitefish."

"I'll find it."

***

The drive from Kalispell to Whitefish was thirty minutes north on Highway 93, and Emma used every mile of it thinking about Walsh.

Not about the rescue logistics, she'd worked those through on the plane. About the man himself. Two months in the Bob Marshall in winter. Even under normal conditions, without contamination and psychological fracture and the particular horror of the medicine showing you your own shadow without any framework for what you were seeing, two months in that wilderness in winter would have killed most people. The cold alone. The isolation. The physical demands of maintaining any kind of shelter and water source and the minimum caloric intake to keep a body functional.

Walsh had survived all of that. Had kept his hands functional enough to trigger a beacon every eight hours. Had maintained something like a schedule in circumstances that would have destroyed the capacity for schedule in most people.

She thought about what the ceremony had done to him. The pattern was clear now: the opening ceremony without preparation, the shadow presented without framework for integration, the consciousness fracturing under the weight of what it had seen. Marcus Chandler had run through wilderness in terror until his head struck rock. The others had died in versions of the same thing, their own darkness become indistinguishable from external threat.

Walsh was different. Walsh had not run. Walsh had found shelter and stayed put and kept signaling.

Something in Timothy Walsh had held when the others had broken. Emma didn't know what. Maybe stubbornness. Maybe the particular survival instinct of someone who had trained for exactly this kind of emergency and whose training ran deeper than the fracture. Maybe something simpler. Maybe he'd been closer to the drainage when the break happened and the sound of water had kept him anchored to something physical when everything else dissolved.

She'd find out Wednesday. For now it was enough that he was alive.

The mountains pressed closer as she drove north. Whitefish appeared ahead and Emma followed the highway into town, found the Pine Lodge Motel without difficulty, and pulled into the parking lot as the morning was still fresh and cold and clear.

***

The man behind the front desk was in his early sixties, weathered in the specific way of people who'd spent decades in mountain country, the kind of weathering that came from actual outdoor life rather than the cultivated ruggedness of ski resort staff. He processed Emma's reservation with the unhurried efficiency of someone who'd checked in a thousand backcountry travelers and had learned that efficiency was more respectful than conversation.

Then Emma unfolded her map to double-check the approach route, and the motel owner stopped moving.

His eyes went to the sector northeast of Hungry Horse Reservoir. To the area Emma had circled in red pen. To the coordinates she'd marked.

"You're not going in there," he said. It wasn't a question.

"I am," Emma said.

He looked at her for a long moment. At Rufus. At the gear she'd brought. At whatever he read in her face that told him she wasn't a tourist who didn't know what she was walking into.

"Seven people went into that sector between September and December," he said. "Experienced people. People who'd been in the Bob Marshall before. Three bodies recovered. Four still missing." He paused. "Forest Service posted advisories in January. Search and rescue won't go in anymore."

"I know about the seven," Emma said. "There's an eighth. Timothy Walsh. His beacon is still active. He's been signaling every eight hours for two months."

The motel owner's expression changed. Something in it that was more than surprise. Recognition, maybe. The particular expression of a man in a small town who has been watching a family wait for news that doesn't come.

"Walsh. I know that name. Local boy. His family is still hoping." He studied Emma carefully. "Search and rescue tried twice. They couldn't get to his position. Said the terrain in that sector was behaving wrong. Compasses. Navigation. Things that don't work right in there." He paused. "One of the SAR team leaders is a friend of mine. He said it was like the land was lying to them. Like they'd walk north for twenty minutes and end up south of where they started. He's been doing search and rescue in this wilderness for fifteen years and he's never seen anything like it. He won't go back."

"I know what's causing it," Emma said. "And I know how to fix it."

He held her gaze for a long moment. The particular evaluating look of a man who'd seen enough people overestimate themselves in wilderness to know the difference between confidence and foolishness, and who was trying to determine which category Emma fell into.

Whatever he saw made him nod slowly and push the room key across the counter.

"Room 8. Checkout is eleven. If you're not back by Saturday morning, I'm calling the sheriff." He paused. "Walsh's family deserves to know one way or the other."

"I'll bring him out," Emma said.

She meant it the way she'd meant it on the highway when Owen had said forty-eight hours. Not bravado. Just the simple declaration of someone who has assessed the situation and made a decision.

***

Room 8 smelled like pine cleaner and old carpet and the particular clean cold of mountain air coming through a window seal that wasn't quite tight. Two beds, a small bathroom, a table by the window with a view of the parking lot and the tree line beyond it and the mountains above that.

Emma unpacked methodically. Ceremonial materials out of the waterproof containers, each one checked and verified. Meteorite iron filings. Ancient salt. Pure silver pieces. All intact. Robert Moore's journal in its protective sleeve. Dr. Hanson's pronunciation files on her phone, backed up to the satellite phone.

Rufus was not settling.

He'd done a circuit of the room when they first came in, nose working, checking corners and the space under the beds and the bathroom and the narrow gap behind the door. Standard procedure, the way he assessed every new space. But when he finished he didn't find a spot and lie down the way he normally would. He went to the window.

Stood there looking at the mountains.

Emma watched him. His body language was different from the alert watchfulness he'd shown at the airport and on the drive. This was something more focused. His weight was forward slightly. His tail was absolutely still. His ears were tracking something Emma couldn't hear, moving in small precise increments the way ears move when they're trying to isolate a specific sound in a field of competing noise.

"You can feel it from here," Emma said.

Rufus didn't respond. Didn't look at her. Just kept his attention on the mountains with the concentrated stillness of a dog that has located something and is tracking its movements.

The contamination. Forty-plus miles northeast, up in roadless wilderness, an ash circle that had been absorbing Mark Caldwell's darkness for two years before he killed the Morrison family and left it open and festering for thirty more. Seven dead. One survivor running out of time. A search and rescue team that couldn't navigate terrain they'd trained in for fifteen years.

Something was wrong out there in ways that didn't follow normal rules.

Rufus could feel it from a motel parking lot in Whitefish.

Emma turned her attention to the plan.

She spread the topographic map across the bed and went through it in detail. Forest service road northeast from town, passable with the Expedition's clearance, ending at a trailhead that appeared on older maps but not on the current Forest Service database because it had been removed when the access road fell out of maintenance. From the trailhead: fifteen miles on foot, no trails, navigating by GPS and compass through dense forest and steep elevation changes and whatever perceptual distortions the contamination was creating in the surrounding terrain.

She'd need to be methodical. Stay on compass bearing regardless of what the terrain seemed to be doing. Trust the GPS over her instincts if the two disagreed. Keep Rufus close and pay attention to what he was tracking, because what he was tracking would be more reliable than any instrument.

Walsh's position five miles northeast of the site, in what Owen had identified as a creek drainage. Emma's approach from the south would take her to Walsh first, then southwest to the site. Reach Walsh Wednesday afternoon, stabilize him, activate his beacon's SOS mode for helicopter evacuation, leave him as comfortable as possible while she continued to the site.

The ceremony Thursday afternoon. All seventeen sequences, the material placements at the cardinal points, the timing calculated to solar position. Seal the site. Signal for extraction. Hike out Thursday evening or Friday morning.

Clean plan. Tight margins. Every element dependent on the previous one holding.

Emma practiced the ceremony sequences one final time, standing in room 8 with the map spread across the bed and Rufus still at the window and the mountains still visible above the tree line. All seventeen. In order. Without the journal. Without Dr. Hanson's files. From memory alone.

They came without effort. Every syllable in place, every emphasis correct, the timing between sequences natural now rather than counted. The words had settled so completely into her body that they no longer felt like something she'd learned. They felt like something she'd always known and had only recently been reminded of.

She finished the seventeenth sequence and stood in the quiet room.

Rufus turned from the window and looked at her. Something in his posture shifted, the forward-weighted watchfulness easing slightly. Like the ceremony words had changed the quality of the air in the room. Like something that had been out of alignment had moved a fraction of a degree toward correct.

"That's what we're going to do in Montana," Emma said quietly. "Louder. At the site. With the materials in place."

Rufus walked from the window to where Emma stood. Put his head against her leg briefly. Then went back to the window.

Not settled. But present. That was enough.

Emma checked the local news on her phone while she ate the sandwich she'd bought at a gas station outside Kalispell. The top story in the Flathead Beacon was the suspension of search and rescue operations in the northeast sector of the Bob Marshall

Wilderness, the formal declaration that Timothy Walsh was presumed deceased. The statement from the Flathead County Sheriff's Office was careful and sympathetic and final. The area was too dangerous for recovery operations. The family had been notified. A memorial was being planned.

Walsh was triggering his beacon every eight hours and the county had given up on him.

Emma put down the sandwich. Looked at the mountains through the window past Rufus's silhouette.

Walsh had been fighting for two months. Maintaining a signal nobody was coming to answer. Staying alive in contaminated wilderness on whatever reserves of survival instinct and physical toughness had gotten him through January and February and most of March. Whatever the site had shown him, whatever his shadow looked like, whatever he'd been living with in that creek drainage for eight weeks, he'd been fighting anyway.

She was coming.

One more night. Wednesday morning the trailhead. Wednesday afternoon she'd reach him.

She pulled out her phone and called James.

It rang twice before he answered, and in the background Emma could hear Carnegie Hall's particular quality of silence, the way sound moved differently in a space that had been standing since 1907.

"You're in Whitefish," James said.

"Pine Lodge Motel. Room 8. Mountains are visible from the window." She paused. "How's Carnegie Hall?"

***

Later that evening Owen's rental pulled into the Pine Lodge lot at 11:50 PM. Emma was still awake. Of course she was.

CHAPTER 12: SAFETY COALITION

Tuesday morning. The hearing was tonight at seven.

James had been at Carnegie Hall since before sunrise.

He'd slept three hours in the basement security office, upright in the chair with all ten camera feeds running on his laptop, waking every forty minutes or so to check the feeds and the alley and the street out front. The building had been quiet. No movement. No vehicles idling past. Just Carnegie Hall doing what it had been doing for a hundred and eighteen years, which was standing there and refusing to fall down.

At six in the morning he'd made coffee from the supplies Margaret kept in the historical society kitchen and gone through everything one more time. The security footage from all five attacks, organized by date and time and camera angle, exported to three separate encrypted drives. Tom Ashford's petition invalidation argument, printed and formatted and ready for distribution. The corporate fraud documentation: Morrison Technical's fake credentials, the Safety Coalition's anonymous donor structure, the Cincinnati law firm that had filed the petition without a single traceable principal.

He called Margaret at eight.

"Tonight's hearing," he said. "What's the format?"

"Town council chambers. The Safety Coalition's engineer presents first, twenty minutes. Then we respond, twenty minutes. Then public comment, then council deliberation." A pause. "James, their lawyer called this morning. David Werner. He's trying to move the vote to tonight rather than Thursday."

"Can they do that?"

"The council can vote whenever they want. Margaret is pushing back hard. She's arguing that two independent engineering reports can't be meaningfully evaluated in the same session they're presented. She thinks she has enough council members to hold the Thursday timeline."

"She needs to hold it. We need those forty-eight hours."

"I know. She knows. She's been on the phone since seven."

After the gas line attack on Sunday night Reeves had assigned two patrol officers to make regular passes on Carnegie Hall. Every ninety minutes through the night, a unit circling the block, logging the check, visible presence on Main Street. It wasn't a stationed guard but it was something. Reeves had called James Monday morning to tell him, voice carrying the particular careful tone of a man who was doing what he could within budget constraints he didn't control.

"It's not enough," James had said.

"It's what I have right now," Reeves had said. "If there's another incident, I can do more."

There had been another incident. The fifth attack Monday night, two operatives moving through the building while the patrol was on the far side of its rotation, disabling primary cameras, searching the false wall. The patrol had rolled past while they were still inside. The secondary cameras had caught everything. James had called 911 the moment he saw movement and the operatives had cleared out before the unit completed its next pass.

After that, Reeves had put two officers stationed outside. Not rotating. Parked. One at the front entrance on Main Street, one covering the rear alley. Starting at nine PM every night through Thursday's vote.

"It's enough to deter another amateur break-in," James had told Owen on Monday afternoon.

"These aren't amateurs," Owen had said.

James had known that. He'd added it to his list of things to worry about and kept building his case for the hearing.

He called Owen at noon on Tuesday.

"Hearing tonight," James said. "Safety Coalition engineer goes first. Twenty minutes to make the case that Carnegie Hall should be condemned. Then I respond."

"Their engineer is going to present the fraudulent Morrison Technical report," Owen said. "Which Ashford can invalidate on procedural grounds. But James, they know Ashford is coming. Werner has been filing procedural objections since this morning. He's trying to box in the council's options before the hearing even starts."

"What kind of objections?"

"Challenging the admissibility of structural assessments provided by parties with a financial interest in the outcome. He's arguing that since the historical society has an obvious interest in preserving the building, any engineer they bring in is inherently biased."

"That's rich, given that their engineer's credentials belong to a dead man."

"The council doesn't know that yet. Werner is trying to establish the bias framework before Ashford can present the fraud evidence. Make the council predisposed to discount whatever we bring." Owen paused. "James, Werner is good. He knows what he's doing."

"So does Ashford. Send me everything you have on Werner's procedural filings. I want to walk into that hearing knowing exactly what they're going to try."

Owen sent the filings. James read them over lunch, a sandwich he didn't taste, sitting in the basement security office with the camera feeds running and the documents spread across the desk and Carnegie Hall solid and silent around him.

Werner's strategy was clear and professionally constructed. Establish bias. Challenge admissibility. Frame the security footage as evidence of Carnegie Hall attracting criminal elements rather than evidence of organized targeting. Portray the historical society as a sentimental organization prioritizing nostalgia over public safety. Keep the council focused on the engineering question, because on the engineering question the Safety Coalition had a report and the historical society had forty-eight hours to produce a counter-assessment.

It was good strategy. It would work on a council that was scared of liability and inclined to defer to technical expertise.

James intended to change what the council was scared of.

***

The hearing started at seven in the town council chambers, a room that seated about a hundred people and was currently holding closer to a hundred and fifty. Moores Hill turned out for its own. Half the town was there because Carnegie Hall was a landmark and people in small towns do not give up their landmarks without a fight, and the other half was there because a hundred and fifty years of Moores Hill history had taught them that when something strange was happening in this town, you showed up to watch.

The Safety Coalition's engineer went first. A man named Dr. Michael Torres, impeccably credentialed, professionally composed, presenting his findings with the practiced authority of someone who had done this many times before. Foundation compromise. Basement flooding. Electrical deterioration. Each finding illustrated with photographs and measurements and the particular vocabulary of structural engineering deployed in a way that sounded conclusive to anyone who didn't know the field.

James watched the council members' faces while Torres presented. Mayor Patricia Ashcraft, who'd been mayor for three terms and had the controlled expression of someone who wanted to do the right thing and wasn't yet sure what the right thing was. Tom Hargrove, who ran the hardware store and had been on the council for eight years and looked uncomfortable with the engineering testimony in a way that suggested he knew enough to be suspicious of it. Carol

Simmons, who managed the county library and was watching Torres with the particular attentive skepticism of a librarian evaluating a source.

Robert Thornton, who owned the largest farm operation in the county and had the settled calm of someone who'd seen a lot of things over the years and knew that the first version of any story was rarely the complete one.

And Linda Hayes, who was watching David Werner rather than Torres, which James thought was the most interesting thing happening in the room.

Torres finished and sat down.

Werner stood. Addressed the council with the professional warmth of a man who had mastered the art of seeming reasonable while being anything but. He framed his client's petition as a matter of community responsibility. Public safety. The council's obligation to the residents of Moores Hill. He cited three structural failure cases in similar historic buildings across the Midwest, each one resulting in injury or death. He spoke about the volunteer staff who worked in Carnegie Hall every week, the schoolchildren who took field trips there, the elderly residents who attended historical society events in a building that professional engineers had certified as dangerous.

He was smooth and credible and his entire argument rested on a structural report signed by a dead man.

Then it was James's turn.

He'd done this kind of testimony before, in a different context, as a deputy presenting evidence in cases that would be decided by people who needed to understand complicated things quickly and clearly. The skill transferred.

"What you've just seen," James said, "is a structural report produced by an engineering firm that was incorporated eighteen months ago. The credentials on that report belong to a licensed engineer named Gerald Whitfield. Mr. Whitfield died in March

2019. He has been dead for seven years. The person who signed this report used a dead man's identity."

He let that sit for a moment.

Tom Hargrove leaned forward. Mayor Ashcraft's carefully controlled expression shifted by a fraction.

James connected his laptop to the projector. Brought up the Indiana Professional Engineers registry. Gerald Whitfield's license. The date of expiration: March 12, 2019. The notation in the state database: deceased.

"Tom Ashford, who is a licensed structural engineer with forty years of experience and no financial interest in this building, has reviewed the Morrison Technical report. Tom."

Ashford stood. He was a compact man in his sixties who moved with the unhurried certainty of someone who had spent four decades being right about things and had long ago stopped needing to perform the role of authority. He simply was it.

"Indiana code requires that structural assessments submitted as the basis for condemnation proceedings be certified by a licensed professional engineer in good standing," Ashford said. "This report is certified by a man who has been dead for seven years. It is not a valid structural assessment under Indiana law. The condemnation petition resting on this report has no legal foundation. It should be dismissed on procedural grounds before this council considers anything else."

Werner was on his feet immediately. "Mr. Ashford's analysis is itself compromised by his relationship with the historical society and his obvious interest in the outcome."

"I've never met anyone on the historical society board before last night," Ashford said, with the mild patience of a man who has been dealing with bad faith arguments for a long time. "I'm a retired engineer who lives in Dearborn County and was asked to review a document. The document is fraudulent. That's not a conclusion affected by who asked me to look at it."

James moved to the security footage before Werner could file another objection.

He played all five attacks in sequence. Not rushed, not edited down to highlights. The complete footage from each incident, with timestamps, showing professional operatives entering Carnegie Hall, systematically disabling primary cameras, and creating staged damage designed to look like structural deterioration.

"Carnegie Hall is not failing," James said when the footage ended. "It is being attacked. Every piece of damage in Dr. Torres's report was created deliberately, by professionals, to support a condemnation petition that was itself built on fraudulent engineering credentials. This council is being asked to demolish a one-hundred-and-eighteen-year-old historic landmark based on evidence that was manufactured from start to finish."

The chamber was very quiet.

Mayor Ashcraft looked at Werner. "Mr. Werner, your response to the footage?"

"The footage shows vandalism," Werner said. "Serious vandalism, and we condemn it. But vandalism doesn't change the underlying structural reality of an aging building. Carnegie Hall was deteriorating before any alleged sabotage occurred. The alleged vandalism merely exposed vulnerabilities that already existed."

"The alleged vandalism created the vulnerabilities," Ashford said, his voice still carrying that same mild patience. "I've examined the building personally. The damage is recent and deliberate. The foundation is structurally sound. The electrical system is aging but functional. This building does not need to be demolished. It needs its locks changed."

A ripple of laughter moved through the gallery. Small but real.

Werner did not smile.

The deliberation lasted forty minutes. Werner filed three procedural motions, all of which Mayor Ashcraft tabled for later review. The public comment period ran twenty minutes, largely in favor of preservation, with Margaret Hendricks speaking about the building's century of community service, Dorothy Webb speaking about her grandmother's grandmother who had graduated from Moores Hill College in 1912, and two other residents who had prepared careful statements about the building's historical significance.

Two people spoke in favor of condemnation. James suspected both had been coached.

At nine-fourteen, Mayor Ashcraft called for a vote on postponement.

Five to two in favor of postponing the final vote to Thursday evening, giving the historical society forty-eight hours to provide a complete independent structural assessment from an engineer whose credentials were verifiably current.

Werner accepted the postponement without visible reaction. He was already gathering his papers.

***

James was packing up his laptop when Werner fell into step beside him in the corridor outside the chamber. Not confrontational. Just present, the way a man is present when he has something to say and has chosen his moment carefully.

"You did well in there," Werner said.

James didn't respond.

"The Whitfield angle was effective. We should have anticipated it." Werner's voice was professionally neutral, the tone of one competent person acknowledging another's work. "Thursday will be different. We'll be better prepared."

"I'm sure you will be," James said.

"Mr. McClanahan." Werner stopped walking. James stopped too, because Werner had positioned himself in a way that made not stopping awkward, the particular physical chess of a man who knew how to use a corridor. "The historical society is fighting for a building they love. I respect that. But this petition was filed because Carnegie Hall poses a genuine risk to the people who use it. Our engineer's credentialing issue is a procedural problem we'll address. The underlying structural concerns don't go away because of paperwork."

"Your engineer's credentialing issue," James said, "is that he's been dead for seven years and someone used his identity to sign a legal document submitted to a municipal government. That's a felony, not a paperwork problem."

Werner absorbed that without expression. "The DA will make that determination." He paused. "Is there anything that would satisfy the historical society's concerns? Some accommodation that would allow the structural issues to be addressed without full demolition? A compromise that protects the building's historical character while ensuring public safety?"

It was smooth. Professional. The offer of reasonable negotiation from a man who had just watched his fraudulent petition take serious damage in a public hearing and was recalibrating.

"Carnegie Hall doesn't have structural issues," James said. "You manufactured them. So no. There's no accommodation, because there's no genuine safety concern to accommodate."

Werner nodded slowly. Not conceding. Just processing. "Thursday then," he said, and walked away down the corridor with the unhurried confidence of a man who had a plan for Thursday and wasn't worried about it.

James watched him go. Then called Reeves.

"Werner just approached me after the hearing. Mid-forties, around six feet, expensive suit. He's staying somewhere in Cincinnati, probably a hotel. The name David Werner is almost certainly a professional alias. Whatever you can pull."

"I'll run it," Reeves said. "James, the DA is moving on the Whitfield identity fraud angle. That's a felony. If we can connect Werner to the document directly, we have grounds for arrest before Thursday."

"Good. Move as fast as you can."

James sat in his car for a moment. Werner's offer of compromise had been interesting not for what it said but for what it revealed. They were worried about Thursday. The Whitfield exposure had been a genuine problem and they knew it. They were looking for a negotiated outcome that avoided the vote entirely.

Which meant James needed to make sure no one on the historical society's side entertained any compromise before Thursday. Werner would approach Margaret next. Possibly Dorothy Webb. Anyone who might be persuadable.

He sent Margaret a text: Werner may approach you about compromise. Don't engage. Call me first.

Then he drove back to Carnegie Hall.

***

He was back in the basement security office by ten-thirty, coffee made, all ten feeds running.

Officers Daniels and Kowalski were outside. Daniels at the front entrance on Main Street, Kowalski covering the rear alley. Both had checked in with James when he arrived, professional and steady, neither one appearing particularly concerned about another incident. They'd been through two nights of station duty without event. The hearing had gone well for the historical society. The building felt quiet.

James was not feeling particularly calm.

He watched the feeds and thought about Werner. About the smooth way the man had absorbed the Whitfield revelation without flinching, like someone who had anticipated it and had already prepared the next move. About the offer of compromise, which was not generosity but reconnaissance, a way of identifying whether there was a softer target on the historical society's side who might be worked.

They were losing the legal battle. The fraudulent credentials were a real problem. The security footage was a real problem. Ashford's petition invalidation argument was a real problem. Werner was good but he was fighting uphill and he knew it.

What did a thirty-year organization do when it was losing the legal battle?

James was still working through that question at eleven-twenty-two when his phone rang. Not 911. Not a camera alert. Officer Daniels's personal cell number.

He answered immediately.

Silence on the other end. Not complete silence. Ambient sound, outdoor air on a cold night, traffic somewhere distant on Main Street. Then a voice James didn't recognize, calm and professional, speaking quietly.

"Mr. McClanahan. Your officers are safe. They're going to be embarrassed but they're not hurt. We suggest you stay in the building."

The line went dead.

James was already pulling up the exterior camera feeds.

The front entrance camera showed Main Street. Daniels's patrol car was parked at the curb where it had been all evening. The car was there. Daniels was not.

The rear alley camera showed Kowalski's vehicle parked at the alley entrance. Empty.

James switched to the secondary feeds. Scanned every angle. The building's exterior was clear. Whoever had made that call was not visible on any camera.

He called 911. "James McClanahan at Carnegie Hall. Two officers stationed outside, Daniels and Kowalski, have been taken. I don't know where they are. I just received a call saying they're safe but I cannot confirm that. Send units immediately."

Then he called Reeves directly. Told him the same thing in ten seconds flat.

Then he locked himself into the basement security office and watched every feed simultaneously.

They came through the rear entrance four minutes after the call. Not two this time. Four. Moving with the unhurried efficiency of people who had eliminated the obstacle they'd been working around for five nights and were no longer in any particular hurry.

No staged damage. No spray paint. No pretense of anything other than what this was.

Two of them went directly to the false wall. Unpacked bags. The equipment that came out was not the crude pipe cutters and electrical tools of the previous attacks. This was professional geological survey gear. A compact rotary core drill designed for masonry sampling. A ground-penetrating radar unit, handheld, built for subsurface imaging. A sample collection kit with labeled containers. Everything needed to characterize what lay behind a sealed wall without physically breaching it.

The other two spread through the basement, methodical and systematic, photographing the room dimensions and the tunnel entrance and the false wall's position relative to the building's foundation from multiple angles. They moved like people executing a documented procedure, not improvising.

They weren't trying to get through the false wall tonight. They were mapping what was on the other side of it. Building the data set they'd need for the next approach if Thursday failed.

James documented everything from the secondary feeds, narrating quietly into his phone. Time, actions, equipment, camera angles. His voice was steady because that was what the footage needed and it was all he could do from where he was sitting.

The police scanner on his phone crackled. Units responding. Three minutes out.

The four operatives heard the same scanner. They moved immediately and without panic, the practiced efficiency of a withdrawal that had been planned before they entered. Equipment back in bags. Bags shouldered. Two of the four were already through the rear exit before the other two finished packing. The core drill stayed behind. Either it was expendable or the timeline was tighter than expected.

They were gone before the first unit reached Main Street.

Forty seconds later, Reeves's voice came over the scanner, controlled and tight. Officers located. Both in the trunks of their own patrol cars, handcuffed, blindfolded, unharmed. Main Street and the alley behind Carnegie Hall.

James sat in the security office and let that settle.

Daniels and Kowalski had been taken cleanly, without violence, in the middle of a town of 597 people on a Tuesday night, and nobody had seen anything. Professional surveillance on the officers' positions and routines. Professional neutralization. Professional restraint, leaving both men alive and uninjured.

These were not people who were running out of options. These were people who had been patient for two years, for five years, for thirty years, and had simply decided that patience had reached its limit.

James called Emma.

She answered on the second ring. The motel room quiet behind her voice.

"Sixth attack tonight," James said. "They took the two officers stationed outside. Handcuffed them. Locked them in the trunks of their own patrol cars." He kept his voice level because the alternative wasn't useful. "Daniels and Kowalski are fine. Embarrassed and shaken but physically okay. While the officers were neutralized, four operatives came in with geological survey equipment. Ground-penetrating radar. Core drill. They were mapping the chamber, Emma. Building their data set for the next legal approach if Thursday fails."

Emma was very quiet for a moment.

"How did the hearing go?" she asked.

"Vote postponed to Thursday. Ashford's argument landed. Whitfield's dead credentials are a real problem for them and Werner knows it." A pause. "But Emma, they just put two police officers in their own trunks in the middle of Moores Hill. That's not a legal organization running a safety petition. That's something else entirely."

"I know what it is," Emma said. "Thirty years of operation, James. They've been doing this for thirty years and they haven't been doing it gently."

"Can you hold them for forty-eight hours?"

James looked at the false wall. At the secondary camera feeds still recording an empty basement. At the core drill sitting on the floor where they'd left it.

"I can hold this building," he said. "Reeves is going to have every unit in the county outside by morning. Embarrassed police departments respond. But Emma, Thursday's vote matters more now than it did this morning. If Werner walks into that council chamber with his next move already planned, with geological survey data of what's beneath this building, the condemnation becomes one option among several. We need to close Thursday decisively."

"Then we close it decisively," Emma said. Her voice was quiet and certain. "Forty-eight hours. I'm at the trailhead Wednesday morning. I will have sealed the site before your vote."

"I know."

"How's the building?"

"Still standing."

"That's all it needs to be."

They stayed on the line for a moment in the particular silence of two people who have said what needed saying and are simply present with each other across the distance.

"James. Tell Margaret that Dorothy Webb's testimony Thursday will matter more than she thinks. Get Dorothy to talk about her grandmother's grandmother. That's what makes Carnegie Hall real to people who didn't grow up here."

"I'll tell her."

"Get some sleep when you can."

"You too. Trailhead's early."

Emma ended the call.

Outside, James could hear the sound of additional units arriving on Main Street. Voices. Radio traffic. The particular controlled energy of a police department that has just had two of its own humiliated in front of their whole community and is not taking that lightly.

He thought about Daniels and Kowalski, sitting in their trunks in the cold, waiting for someone to find them. Not hurt. But shaken in a way that went deeper than physical harm. The particular violation of having your weapon and your authority and your freedom taken from you by people who were so far ahead of you that you never saw it coming.

That was the message. Not violence. Something worse. We can do whatever we want and there is nothing you can do to stop us.

James put his phone in his pocket and stood in the basement of Carnegie Hall while the building held its silence around him.

Two more days.

He poured the last of the coffee, settled back into the security office chair, pulled up all ten camera feeds, and watched the night.

CHAPTER 13: THE PATTERN

They left the Pine Lodge at six Wednesday morning, the Expedition loaded the night before, the mountains visible in the predawn dark as shapes against a slightly lighter sky. Owen drove the forest service road because he'd studied the topographic maps until midnight and had the route memorized in a way that Emma trusted more than her own tired eyes.

She'd slept four hours. Owen had slept three. Neither of them mentioned it.

The forest service road headed northeast from Whitefish, climbing steadily through lodgepole pine and Douglas fir that pressed close on both sides, the road surface deteriorating from patched asphalt to gravel to something that was technically gravel but felt more like the idea of a road imposed on terrain that had never fully accepted it. Owen drove at the speed the road allowed, which was not fast, his attention moving between the windshield and the GPS unit mounted on the dash.

Rufus was in the back seat, standing rather than lying down, watching the forest through the windows with the same focused attention he'd had since Whitefish. Since the motel. Since somewhere over Wyoming on the flight out, if Emma was honest. He'd been tracking something since before they landed. Whatever it was, they were getting closer to it.

"Beacon check," Emma said.

Owen pulled up the satellite feed on his phone without taking his eyes off the road. "Still active. Same position. He triggered it at two-fourteen this morning, right on his eight-hour schedule." He handed the phone to Emma. "Battery's degrading. Signal strength is down about fifteen percent since yesterday."

Emma studied the position marker. Walsh's beacon, steady and stationary in the creek drainage five miles northeast of the ceremonial site. Two months of eight-hour intervals. Whatever was keeping that man going, it was something that schedule couldn't contain or explain.

"He'll hold until we reach him," Emma said.

Owen nodded. He didn't say it was a fact, and Emma didn't say it was either. They both knew it was what had to be true.

The road ended at eight-nineteen. A Forest Service barrier stood across what had once been a continuation of the road, weathered and partially obscured by growth, a metal sign indicating the trailhead that no longer appeared on current maps. Owen parked on the widest section of road he could find and they sat for a moment in the particular silence of deep wilderness, the kind of silence that wasn't absence of sound but presence of a different kind of sound: wind in high conifers, water somewhere below them, the small purposeful movements of things that lived here.

Emma checked the temperature on her phone. Thirty-one degrees.

Clear sky. Good visibility. Exactly what Owen had said to expect.

She got out and started loading her pack. The ceremonial materials in their waterproof containers, each one settled in the pack's main compartment with padding on all sides. Robert Moore's journal in its protective sleeve. Emergency supplies. Food and water for three days. The satellite phone. Everything accounted for, nothing extra.

Owen shouldered his own pack: navigation equipment, his laptop for remote communication when signal allowed, medical supplies for Walsh, additional emergency gear. He'd thought carefully about what Walsh might need and had packed accordingly. Thermal blankets. Electrolyte packets. High-calorie emergency rations. Splint materials.

Rufus jumped out of the Expedition and stood at the tree line, looking north.

Not at Emma. Not at Owen. At something in the direction they were headed.

"Rufus," Emma said.

He turned. Looked at her. His body language was readable now after weeks together: this is serious, I want you to understand that, but I am with you and we are doing this.

Emma shouldered her pack. "Let's go."

***

The first three miles were hard in the way that roadless wilderness is always hard: no trail to follow, terrain that rose and fell without warning, undergrowth that grabbed at boots and pack straps and required constant attention to navigate without twisting an ankle. Emma's hiking boots were broken in and her ankle had been solid since the cemetery fall two weeks ago, but she felt the demand of the terrain in her calves and her hips within the first hour in ways that reminded her this was not a nature walk.

Owen navigated with the GPS unit and a paper topographic map, cross-referencing constantly, calling out course corrections when the terrain forced them sideways. He was methodical about it, the same quality of attention he brought to everything, and Emma trusted him to hold their bearing.

Rufus ranged ahead, scouting, returning. He stayed within two hundred yards in the dense forest, circling back to Emma every fifteen or twenty minutes to confirm her position before going out again. Emma had come to rely on the pattern. He was checking the ground ahead for things she couldn't detect, and the regularity of his returns was its own kind of information: as long as he came back on schedule, whatever was out there hadn't changed in character.

By ten-thirty they'd covered four miles and Emma was beginning to feel the pace in her shoulders as well as her legs. She called a water break, studied the GPS position, and recalculated the timeline. Walsh's position at seven miles. The ceremonial site at twelve miles from the trailhead. At their current pace they'd reach Walsh by mid-afternoon.

"We're on schedule," Owen said, reading her calculation.

"Barely."

"Barely is fine."

They kept moving.

The strange phenomena started around noon.

The temperature dropped first. Not gradually. Fifteen degrees in the space of five minutes, Emma's breath suddenly condensing in air that had been cool but manageable and was now genuinely cold. No front moving in. The sky above the tree canopy was still clear. No weather explanation for what had just happened.

Emma checked the thermometer on her pack strap. Forty-one degrees to twenty-six in five minutes.

Owen had stopped walking. He was looking at his GPS unit with the expression of a man who trusts instruments and is currently being told not to.

"We're still on course," he said carefully. "But the readings are fluctuating. Signal keeps dropping and reacquiring." He looked up. "It's been doing it for the last twenty minutes but it's getting worse."

"Magnetic anomaly in the geology," Emma said.

"Maybe," Owen said. "Or proximity to the site."

Rufus had come back from his forward position and was standing close to Emma. Not ranging. Not scouting. Close, with his body oriented not forward toward their destination but slightly to their left, toward something in the trees that Emma could not see or hear.

She watched him for a moment. His ears were tracking something. Moving in small precise increments, working to isolate a specific sound in a field of competing inputs.

"Something's out there," Owen said quietly. He wasn't alarmed. Just noting, the way he noted everything.

"The contamination creates perceptual effects," Emma said. "Robert Moore documented them. Things that feel like external presence but are projections of internal state. The medicine activates shadow perception. You start seeing your own darkness as something outside you."

"You really believe that's all this is?"

Emma watched Rufus watch the trees. "I believe the sites affect perception in ways that people interpret as external threat. I believe what feels like something following us is something in us that the proximity of the site is activating." She paused. "I also believe Rufus is detecting something real that I can't detect. Those two things aren't mutually exclusive."

Owen looked at her steadily. "That's a very precise philosophical position to maintain while standing in contaminated wilderness with your compass spinning."

"It's the position that keeps me functional," Emma said. "Let's keep moving."

They pushed on through the afternoon. The terrain got steeper, the elevation changes more dramatic, the forest denser. Progress slowed to less than a mile an hour through sections where they were essentially climbing through undergrowth with their hands as much as their feet.

And the effects intensified.

It was subtle at first, the kind of thing Emma might have dismissed if she hadn't known what to watch for. A persistent sense of being watched from a direction that kept shifting. The feeling that sounds in the forest were slightly delayed from their sources, like an echo that arrived before the original. The particular quality the light had, slanting through the trees at angles that didn't quite match the sun's position.

Emma recognized these for what they were. The medicine wasn't in her system. She hadn't performed any ceremony. But the contamination zone was affecting perception the way Robert Moore had documented, the same way it had affected the SAR team that had come in looking for Walsh and gotten lost. Not hallucination. Something more subtle. Reality slightly misaligned with itself, the volume on the shadow dimension turned up just enough to make the world feel wrong.

She focused on her feet. On the weight of her pack. On Owen's voice calling out course corrections ahead of her. On the physical, the concrete, the real.

Beside her, Rufus stayed close.

Owen was handling it differently. He'd gone quieter over the last hour, more focused on the instruments, checking and rechecking his calculations with the methodical persistence of someone working to stay inside the rational. He hadn't said anything about what he was experiencing but Emma could see it in the way he moved, the slightly too-deliberate quality of each step.

"Owen," Emma said.

He looked at her. His eyes were fine. Present. "I'm okay," he said. "Just need to concentrate on the navigation."

"The site affects perception," Emma said. "What you're feeling is real but it's not external. Don't try to fight it. Just note it and keep moving."

He nodded. Went back to the GPS. Went back to the map. Went back to the methodical work of getting them where they needed to go.

Emma ran the ceremony sequences in her head while she walked. Not practicing. Just keeping them present, keeping the ancient syllables active in her mind as a kind of anchor. Dr. Hanson had talked about grounding techniques, ways of maintaining connection to physical reality while perceiving altered states. Emma had been skeptical at the time. She was less skeptical now.

The words helped. Something in them pushed back against the wrongness in the air around them.

Rufus noticed. He glanced at Emma while she was working through the seventh sequence, a quick flick of his dark eyes, and something in his posture eased slightly. Not settled. But marginally less on edge.

She kept running the sequences.

At two-fifteen they crested a ridge and found a section of relatively open forest, older growth with widely spaced trees, the canopy high enough that light reached the ground. Emma stopped and checked Walsh's beacon position.

One point four miles northeast.

She checked the time. They'd covered nine miles in six hours. Four miles to the site from their current position. Walsh between them and it.

"We'll reach Walsh before dark," she said.

Owen was studying the terrain ahead through a small pair of binoculars. "The drainage should be visible from that next ridgeline. If his position data is accurate, we'll see the creek from there."

Emma looked at Rufus. He was facing northeast. His tail was still. His ears were forward and absolutely fixed.

"He knows Walsh is there," Emma said.

"Or he knows the site is there," Owen said quietly. "They're in the same direction."

Emma shouldered her pack. "One thing at a time. Walsh first."

***

They found the creek drainage at three-forty.

It appeared below the ridgeline as a seam of different vegetation, willows and alders growing along a watercourse that cut through the basin between two slopes. The creek itself was audible before it was visible, the particular sound of water moving over rock in a narrow channel.

Rufus was already heading down the slope toward it.

Emma and Owen followed, moving carefully on ground that was steep and loose. The creek was narrow and fast, snowmelt water running clear and cold over rounded stones. The drainage ran northeast to southwest, exactly as Owen's terrain analysis had predicted. Walsh's beacon position was approximately three hundred yards northeast along the creek.

Rufus had gone ahead. He was moving along the creek bank with his nose working, pausing every thirty feet to check the air, moving on. Searching.

Emma and Owen followed at a distance, letting Rufus work.

They found Walsh's camp at four-oh-seven.

It was built under a rock overhang where the drainage curved around a granite outcropping, a natural shelter that kept the wind off and provided a dry floor of packed earth. Walsh had been thorough and methodical, even in whatever state the site had left him. A debris hut constructed from branches and bark against the rock wall for insulation. A firepit with a significant ash pile that spoke to weeks of use. A water collection system using a folded piece of tarp to channel creek water into a metal cup. Gear organized along the overhang wall with the deliberate system of someone who had decided very early on that organization was survival.

The camp of a man who knew wilderness survival and had been applying that knowledge with the methodical discipline of someone who'd decided to hold on regardless of what was happening inside his head.

Walsh himself was sitting with his back against the rock wall, knees drawn to his chest, eyes open. Watching Rufus approach.

He was alive. Visibly reduced, gaunt in the way of severe caloric deficit, his face weathered to something rawer than the photograph in his missing persons report. His clothing was layered and maintained, no signs of the kind of deterioration that came from passive exposure. He'd been taking care of himself.

His eyes were wrong.

Not vacant. Not absent. Present in a way that was too present, too fixed, the eyes of someone whose attention was aimed at something that only he could see, something that ran alongside the physical world rather than inside it. Emma recognized it from everything she'd read and understood. The shadow, unintegrated, unresolved, sitting alongside his normal perception like a second frequency playing through the same speaker.

He was still in it. Still partially in the state the medicine had opened.

Rufus reached him first.

He approached slowly, head low, tail making small movements. This was different behavior from everything Emma had seen from him in the wilderness. The alert purposeful energy was gone. In its place, the careful deliberate approach of a dog who understood that the person in front of him was fragile in ways that weren't visible.

Walsh looked at Rufus. Something in his expression changed. The too-fixed quality of his eyes shifted, softened, focused on the actual physical presence of the dog rather than whatever was running alongside it.

His hand came out and touched Rufus's head.

Rufus sat down beside him and leaned against his leg.

Walsh closed his eyes for a moment. His breathing changed, deepened, the held quality of someone in sustained vigilance releasing slightly.

Emma and Owen came forward slowly. Walsh heard them and opened his eyes. He looked at Emma with the same assessing quality he'd used with Rufus, checking whether what he was seeing was real or the other kind of seeing.

"Emma Caldwell," she said. Not a question. Just giving him something concrete to orient to. Her name. Her presence. Real.

Walsh looked at her for a long moment. "You know what's out there," he said. His voice was rough from disuse but coherent.

"Yes," Emma said.

"You're going to it."

"Yes."

"Don't go without preparation." He paused. "I wasn't prepared."

"I know," Emma said. "I am."

Walsh looked at Rufus, still leaning against his leg. Then back at Emma. Something in him settled further. Not recovered, not healed, but oriented. Anchored to the present in a way that the contamination had been working for two months to prevent.

Owen was already opening his pack, pulling out the medical supplies, moving with quiet efficiency. He checked Walsh's vital signs, his limbs, his responses. Walsh submitted to it with the cooperative patience of someone who had been waiting a long time to be found and had enough left to understand that being found was the next step in surviving.

"Hypothermic but not dangerously," Owen said quietly to Emma. "Dehydrated. Significant muscle loss. His cognition is intact but he's been through something severe." He looked at Walsh directly. "We're going to get you out of here. Helicopter evacuation is coming. They'll need a landing zone."

"There's a clearing," Walsh said. "Quarter mile south. I found it in January. Marked it." A pause. "I kept thinking someone would come."

"Someone came," Owen said.

Emma activated the emergency SOS function on Walsh's beacon while Owen prepared the thermal blankets and electrolyte solution. The beacon sent its upgraded distress signal with their GPS coordinates. Within minutes Owen's satellite phone showed an acknowledgment: helicopter evacuation team responding, ETA approximately three hours.

Three hours. Emma looked at the sky above the drainage. Still clear. The light was angling lower but there were hours before dark. She looked at Owen.

"I know," he said. He handed her a protein bar and a water bottle. "Eat. We've got time."

Emma sat on a rock beside Walsh and ate without tasting anything, watching Rufus maintain his position against Walsh's leg, watching Walsh's breathing continue to slow and deepen, watching the light move through the drainage.

Four miles southwest, an ash circle carved into bedrock waited in the wilderness.

Tomorrow morning, early, Emma would stand at its edge.

Tonight she sat in a creek drainage and watched a man she'd never met breathe more easily than he had in two months, because a dog had walked over and leaned against him.

She pulled out her satellite phone and called James.

He answered after four rings, his voice carrying the quality of someone who had been awake for a very long time.

"We found Walsh," Emma said. "He's alive. He built a survival camp and maintained it and triggered his beacon every eight hours for two months, James. He held on."

A long pause on the other end.

"How is he?" James said.

"He's going to need time. But he's going to be okay." Emma watched Rufus watching Walsh. "We're four miles from the site. I'll reach it tomorrow morning. Ceremony tomorrow afternoon."

"I know."

"How's Carnegie Hall?"

"Still standing. Every unit Reeves has is outside. They're not getting back in tonight." A pause. "Emma. What they did to Daniels and Kowalski. Moores Hill woke up angry this morning. I think Thursday's vote is going to be different than Werner expects."

Emma thought about that. About a town of 597 people finding out that professionals had handcuffed their police officers and locked them in their own trunks on Main Street.

"Good," she said. "Use it. Let the council feel it."

"I will." A pause. "Emma. You found Walsh."

"Rufus found Walsh," Emma said. "I just followed."

She ended the call and sat in the drainage listening to the creek and the wind in the high conifers and Walsh's steadying breath and the particular silence of Montana wilderness that wasn't silence at all.

Tomorrow morning. The site.

She was ready.

CHAPTER 14: BREAKING SEAL

James had been on the phone since six Wednesday morning and he'd been getting the same answer in different words for four hours.

Unavailable. Fully booked. Not taking new clients. Out of the office until next week. He'd worked through Tom Ashford's list of licensed structural engineers in the region, then Owen's list, then a broader search that pulled in engineers from Cincinnati and Louisville and Indianapolis. Eighteen calls. Eighteen variations of the same answer delivered with the particular careful neutrality of people who had been spoken to already and had made their decisions.

Someone had gotten to them first.

James added this to what he knew about the Safety Coalition: resources, reach, and the foresight to cover contingencies before they became problems. They'd anticipated that the historical society would seek an independent assessment after Tuesday's hearing. They'd spent Wednesday morning making sure that assessment would be difficult to obtain.

He called Owen at ten-fifteen.

"I need a structural engineer with no local ties and no reason to be scared of a well-funded legal organization. Someone outside the normal regional network."

"How far outside?" Owen asked. His voice had the particular quality of a satellite connection, slightly flattened, a half-second delay.

"Far enough that they haven't been contacted yet."

Owen was quiet for a moment, which on a satellite connection meant he was thinking rather than buffering. "Rebecca Thomas. She's a structural engineer out of Louisville, licensed in Kentucky, Indiana, and Tennessee. She's done forensic assessment work, specifically buildings where deliberate damage was disguised as natural deterioration. She testified in an arson case in 2022. She knows the difference between damage that happened and damage that was made to look like it happened."

"Does she take emergency work?"

"I'm going to call her right now."

Owen called back eleven minutes later. Dr. Thomas would drive up from Louisville. She'd arrive by early afternoon. Her rate for emergency forensic assessment was substantial. James said that was fine without hesitating because Ashford had already committed the historical society to covering costs and because the alternative was losing Carnegie Hall by Thursday evening.

He spent the rest of the morning fielding calls from Margaret, from Reeves, from two council members who had questions they weren't comfortable asking in public, and from a reporter at the Dearborn County Register who had gotten wind of the trunk incident and wanted a comment.

James gave the reporter a statement that was factual and brief: two officers had been unlawfully restrained during an attempted break-in at Carnegie Hall, both were unharmed, the incident was under investigation, and the Moores Hill Police Department was taking the situation extremely seriously. He did not mention geological survey equipment. He did not mention the false wall. He did not mention anything that would give Werner useful information about what James knew.

Reeves had called at seven that morning with his voice carrying the particular tone of a man who has been humiliated and is now operating on a different frequency entirely. Three additional officers were being assigned to Carnegie Hall through Thursday's vote. Not patrol passes. Not station duty in patrol cars. Officers inside the building, rotating through the night, with explicit authorization to detain anyone attempting to access the basement or the maintenance corridor.

"They put my people in their own trunks," Reeves had said. "In the middle of Main Street. In my town."

James hadn't said anything to that because nothing needed to be said.

By noon the building had three officers inside and two in the alley, in addition to the squad car that had been sitting in front since Tuesday's patrol cars were found. The Safety Coalition could see this from whatever surveillance positions they'd been using. They knew the access situation had changed.

James was interested to see what they'd do about it.

***

Dr. Rebecca Thomas arrived at one-forty-seven.

She was in her early fifties, compact and efficient, carrying a case of equipment that she'd apparently packed the moment Owen called. She introduced herself to James with the professional brevity of someone who had done a lot of emergency assessments and understood that time was the variable that mattered most.

"Walk me through what happened," she said, and James walked her through it while she set up her equipment. All six attacks, each one described precisely: what was targeted, what damage was created, what the damage was designed to look like.

She listened without interrupting. Took notes on a small pad in handwriting James couldn't read.

"Show me the basement first," she said when he finished.

James led her down. The basement still showed the accumulated damage from six attacks: water staining from the pipe cuts, marks at the electrical panel, the displaced foundation markers that the second attack had repositioned to make the building appear to be settling unevenly. Dr. Thomas moved through it methodically, examining each element with a small flashlight and a device James didn't recognize, kneeling at the foundation walls, checking the electrical panel housing, testing the floor for moisture with an instrument she pulled from her case.

She worked without commentary for forty minutes.

Then she straightened up and looked at James. "The pipes were cut. Clean cuts, recent, the oxidation pattern at the cuts is days old, not months. Corrosion on the surrounding pipe is consistent with age but the cuts themselves are new." She moved to the foundation markers. "These were moved. I can see the original impression in the substrate where they were seated before someone relocated them about eight inches east. Makes it look like differential settling. It's not." She gestured at the electrical panel. "Tampered with. The burn patterns are localized to specific components, not distributed the way you'd expect from age-related failure. Someone applied heat to specific points."

She walked to the far wall, ran her hand along it, tapped in several places. "Sound structure. The foundation is solid. I'd want to do core sampling to be definitive but based on everything I'm seeing, this building is not in imminent danger of anything except continued vandalism."

"Can you present this to the town council tomorrow night?" James asked.

Dr. Thomas looked at him steadily. "Someone paid a significant amount of money for the report that said this building was dangerous. That report is fraudulent, which your engineer already established with the Whitfield credentials. My assessment will contradict it further. Whoever commissioned that report is going to push back hard." She paused. "Yes. I can present tomorrow night. But prepare for pushback."

"I've been preparing for pushback for twelve days," James said. "I'm used to it."

She almost smiled. "Then we're fine."

James spent the afternoon delivering Dr. Thomas's preliminary findings to council members individually, in person, before Werner's office could file more procedural objections. He drove to each of their homes or workplaces with a two-page summary that Ashford had helped him format: the Whitfield credential fraud, Dr.

Thomas's forensic findings, the security footage from six attacks, and the police report from Tuesday night's trunk incident.

He needed five votes Thursday. He was trying to make sure five council members walked into that chamber having already seen the evidence rather than hearing it for the first time under Werner's procedural interference.

Mayor Ashcraft met him at her front door with the expression of someone who had been thinking hard about an unpleasant situation and was grateful to have more information. She read the summary at her kitchen table while James sat across from her, and when she finished she looked up.

"The police incident Tuesday night," she said.

"Daniels and Kowalski were unharmed," James said. "Physically. But yes."

"In my town," Mayor Ashcraft said. Quiet. Not a question.

"Yes."

She set the summary down. "I'll be at the hearing Thursday. I'll read Dr. Thomas's full assessment before then."

Tom Hargrove, at the hardware store, read the summary between customers and then looked at James with the pragmatic expression of a man who has been suspicious of something for a while and has just had his suspicion confirmed. "The Whitfield thing. You proved that already. This just makes it worse for them."

"That's the idea," James said.

Carol Simmons, at the county library, was the most thorough. She asked four specific questions about Dr. Thomas's methodology, two about the Whitfield fraud documentation, and one about the security footage chain of custody. James answered all of them. When he was done she nodded once.

"I'll need to see Dr. Thomas's full report before I vote," she said.

"It'll be on file with the council clerk by nine tomorrow morning," James said.

Robert Thornton read the summary at his kitchen table with the unhurried attention of a man who had been running a large farm operation for thirty years and understood that the difference between a good decision and a bad one often came down to reading the paperwork carefully. He had no questions. When he finished he folded the summary precisely and put it in his breast pocket.

"I'll be there," he said.

Linda Hayes was the only one who mentioned Werner by name. "He came to see me this morning," she said. "Offered a compromise. Said the coalition would withdraw the petition if the historical society agreed to a joint inspection by a mutually agreed engineer."

James kept his expression neutral. Werner had moved fast. "What did you tell him?"

"I told him I'd think about it." She paused. "I'm not going to agree to it. But I wanted you to know he's working the council directly."

James drove back to Carnegie Hall and called Margaret immediately. "Werner is making offers to individual council members. Compromise proposals. Joint inspection arrangement that would effectively give them ongoing access to the building."

"I know," Margaret said. "He called Dorothy Webb this morning too. She told him where to put his joint inspection."

James thought about Dorothy Webb, eighty-one years old, her grandmother's grandmother who had graduated from Moores Hill College in 1912. "She'll be at the hearing tomorrow?"

"Wild horses couldn't keep her away," Margaret said.

James settled into the basement security office as the light outside the high basement windows went from afternoon to evening. Three officers were inside the building, rotating through different positions on a schedule James had worked out with Reeves. Two more were in the alley. The squad car was still on Main Street.

The Safety Coalition knew all of this. Their surveillance positions would have given them a clear picture of Carnegie Hall's current security status. James ran the calculation in his head for the fourth time that day. They could walk away from Wednesday night. The vote was tomorrow. If they lost the vote, they had the geological survey data from Tuesday's mapping operation and a dozen other legal avenues to pursue.

Or they could try again. Push harder. Demonstrate that even a building full of police couldn't stop them.

James knew which option a thirty-year organization with unlimited resources and a specific mission would choose.

He was right.

***

They came at eleven-thirty-eight.

Not through the rear entrance this time. Through the east wall of the building, a section of original brick that backed onto the alley between Carnegie Hall and the building next door. The brick gave way to a cutting tool that James hadn't seen before, a compact hydraulic unit that operated almost silently, creating an opening just large enough for a person to pass through in under four minutes.

Two officers in the basement heard the sound, a low vibration more felt than heard, and moved toward it. The third officer on the main floor heard them moving and followed.

James, in the security office, watched the secondary camera at the east wall pick up the breach and called Reeves before anyone had come through.

"East wall breach. Carnegie Hall. They're cutting through the brick. Units inside are moving toward it."

What followed was not the clean professional withdrawal of the previous attacks.

Three people came through the opening. They had equipment, the same geological survey gear from Tuesday night supplemented with what looked like core sampling tools designed for deeper penetration. They'd planned for the police presence. Had planned to work fast enough that it didn't matter.

What they hadn't planned for was Officer Martinez, who had been a defensive lineman at Indiana University before becoming a cop and who was positioned directly on the other side of the wall when the cutting finished.

The first person through the opening ran directly into Martinez, who did not go backward, and the neat professional operation immediately became something else. Shouting. The sound of equipment hitting the concrete floor. James watched the secondary cameras with the particular focused attention of someone who cannot intervene but needs to document everything precisely.

Two of the three were detained. Martinez had one. Officer Kowalski, who had been in a trunk two nights ago and was not inclined toward patience with the people responsible, had the second pinned against the basement wall with a thoroughness that James suspected fell outside standard procedure but that he was not going to comment on.

The third ran. Back through the breach, into the alley, toward a vehicle that James couldn't see from his camera angle. He heard the engine. Then Reeves's voice on the scanner, calm and controlled: suspect vehicle heading east on Oak Street, units in pursuit.

They lost the vehicle three minutes later in the residential streets east of Main Street. It was fast and the driver knew the area, or had studied it well enough that it amounted to the same thing.

But two of them were in handcuffs in the Carnegie Hall basement, which had not happened before.

And in the confusion of the retreat through the breach, someone had dropped a laptop.

James found it on the basement floor near the east wall opening, partially under a section of displaced brick. Consumer grade. Nothing that looked like field equipment. The kind of thing someone carries for communication and coordination rather than survey work.

He photographed it in place before touching it. Then bagged it and called Reeves.

"Evidence," he said. "Laptop dropped during the retreat. I'm preserving it."

"Don't turn it on," Reeves said.

"I know," James said. He also knew that what was on that laptop was more important to him than what was in it for Reeves's criminal case, and that the two interests might not align perfectly, and that he needed to be careful about how he handled the next few hours.

He sat with the bagged laptop in the security office and thought about it for ten minutes. Then he called Owen.

Owen's satellite connection was worse than it had been that afternoon, the signal degrading in the way that signals degraded in mountain wilderness at night.

"I have a laptop," James said. "Dropped by one of theirs during the seventh attack. I need to know what's on it. But I can't turn it on without breaking Reeves's evidence protocol. And I can't give it to Reeves tonight without losing access to it."

Owen was quiet for a moment. "Photograph every surface. Every label, every port, every identifier. Then open it and photograph the keyboard, the screen while it's off, the battery indicator, everything you can see without powering it. Send me the photos. I can tell you what we're dealing with from the hardware."

James did this while he and Owen stayed on the line, photographing systematically, sending images through his phone. Owen studied them on the other end.

"It's not encrypted," Owen said. "Standard consumer security. If you power it on there's a fair chance it boots to a desktop. But you'd be creating a chain of custody problem for Reeves."

"What I need to know is whether there's anything on it that tells us who these people are and what they're actually after," James said. "Before Reeves seizes it and it disappears into an evidence room for six months while the lawyers argue."

A long pause. "Open it," Owen said. "Power it on. Document the time. Document that you did it in the course of assessing the scene for security purposes. If it boots, photograph whatever's visible immediately, then close it and hand it to Reeves."

James opened the laptop. It booted. The screen came up without a password prompt, which James documented with a photo and a timestamp notation. The desktop was sparse. A few folders. An open browser window that had been left running.

He photographed the screen immediately.

The browser showed an email client, still logged in, messages visible without opening anything. James photographed every visible message header before touching anything else. Then he photographed the folder structure on the desktop. Then he closed the laptop and placed it back in the evidence bag.

He sent all the photographs to Owen.

Owen was quiet for four minutes. James sat in the security office and listened to the sounds of two arrested individuals being processed in the basement above him and waited.

"James." Owen's voice was careful in the specific way it got when he'd found something significant. "The email headers. Three messages visible. Subject lines. The first one reads 'Site 7 assessment updated.' The second reads 'Unsealing prevention protocol.' The third one." A pause. "The third one reads 'Convergence timeline: all seven must fall before the window closes.'"

James sat very still.

"What's convergence?" he said.

James thought about the Montana site. About Emma four miles from the ash circle. About what sealing the Montana site would mean in the context of what Owen had just read him.

"Owen," James said. "Is Emma right there with you?"

"She's next to me," Owen said. "Hold on."

A brief rustling. Then Emma's voice, the same thin satellite connection, the same mountain wilderness at night.

"James." She'd been listening. He could hear it in the way she said his name, already partially caught up.

"Seventh attack tonight," James said. "They cut through the east wall. Martinez detained two of them. The third got away. And they left a laptop behind. Owen read the visible emails from the photos I sent." He paused. "They're targeting all seven sites on a timeline. They have something called a convergence protocol. All seven sites must fall before a specific window closes."

The connection held for a moment of static.

"Convergence," Emma said. She was thinking through it, he could hear the quality of her silence.

"Robert Moore's journal," James said. "Did it mention what happens if all seven sites are sealed? Or if they're all destroyed?"

"It mentioned the sites are connected," Emma said slowly. "That they were designed as a network. Seven sites, seven families, functioning together as a system for healing. But he didn't describe what the network was capable of when it operated as a whole." A pause. "If the Anti-Custodians believe that sealing the sites restores the network, that restoring the network enables something they're calling convergence, then destroying the sites isn't just about preventing individual ceremonies. It's about preventing the whole system from coming back online."

"Can you seal Montana tomorrow and still have it matter?" James asked. "If they destroy Carnegie Hall Thursday night regardless of the vote?"

"I seal Montana because it's killing people," Emma said. "That's reason enough regardless of what it means for the network." A pause. "But James. Don't let them have Carnegie Hall. Whatever convergence means to them, whatever they're afraid the network will do if it's restored, they've been running a thirty-year campaign to prevent it. They've destroyed four sites. They've falsified legal documents, attacked police, cut through building walls. That level of effort means they believe the stakes are very high."

"Which means the stakes are very high," James said.

"Yes," Emma said. "Win Thursday. I'll seal Montana. We'll figure out what convergence means after."

James ended the call and sat in the basement of Carnegie Hall with the bagged laptop on the desk in front of him and the sound of Reeves arriving upstairs with more units.

Seven sites. A network. A convergence that an organization was willing to commit serious federal crimes to prevent.

And tomorrow night, a town council in Moores Hill, Indiana was going to vote on whether to condemn a building.

James picked up the evidence bag and went upstairs to meet Reeves.

Whatever convergence meant, it was going to have to wait until Thursday was decided.

One thing at a time.

CHAPTER 15: FLOODED GROUND

The helicopter had come at nine-forty Wednesday night.

Emma had heard it before she saw it, the particular thrum of rotors in mountain air, different from the wind and the creek and the sounds the wilderness made on its own. She'd been sitting by the fire Owen had built near Walsh's camp, not sleeping, running ceremony sequences in her head the way she'd been running them for two weeks, and when she heard the rotors she'd stood and activated the signal light Owen had left at the marked clearing a quarter mile south.

The evacuation team had been efficient and careful. Two paramedics who knew wilderness medicine and who had clearly been briefed that the patient's condition involved psychological as well as physical crisis. They'd assessed Walsh, stabilized him for transport, asked Emma three direct questions about how long he'd been exposed and what she knew about the cause. She'd answered the physical questions and deflected the others. Walsh had looked at her from the stretcher as they carried him to the clearing.

"Don't go in without preparation," he'd said again. The same words. Like they were the most important thing he knew.

"I'm prepared," Emma had said.

He'd held her gaze for a moment. Then he'd closed his eyes and let the paramedics do their work, and the helicopter had lifted into the Montana night and taken Timothy Walsh home.

Emma and Owen had made camp in the drainage after that, close to the creek, and Emma had slept four hours in her sleeping bag with Rufus pressed against her back. Not the restless fractured sleep of the past week but something cleaner, the sleep of someone who has completed one thing and not yet begun the next. When she woke before dawn Thursday the fire had burned to coals and Owen was already up, sitting with his pack between his knees, studying the topographic map by headlamp.

"Four miles," he said without looking up. "The terrain gets worse between here and the site. Elevation change of about eight hundred feet. Rocky. Dense undergrowth on the lower section, then it opens as we get into the higher ground."

Emma pulled on her boots. "Walsh's camp was here," she said, looking at the map. "The site is southwest. We circle the drainage and head up."

"That's the cleanest approach." Owen folded the map. "Coffee's hot."

She drank it standing, looking at the creek in the predawn gray. The water was the same clear cold snowmelt it had been yesterday. The trees were the same trees. But something had shifted in the night, some quality of the air or the light or the particular weight of this place, and Emma felt it in her chest the way you feel a change in atmospheric pressure before a storm.

They were inside the contamination zone. Had been since yesterday afternoon. But they were closer now, and the site knew it.

"How do you feel?" she asked Owen.

He considered it. "Like something is watching. Constantly. From a direction I can't identify." He paused. "I know what it is. That doesn't make it less persistent."

"Keep talking to me if it gets worse," Emma said. "External voice helps."

"I know. I read Moore's documentation too." He shouldered his pack. "Rufus hasn't settled since the helicopter left."

Emma looked at the dog. He was standing at the edge of the firelight, facing southwest. Toward the site. His hackles were not raised but his body had that forward-weighted quality she'd come to recognize as sustained alert attention. Not fear. Assessment.

"He's ready," Emma said. "Let's go."

***

The first mile was manageable in the gray predawn light, moving along the creek drainage before turning southwest and beginning to climb. The undergrowth was dense and wet with overnight condensation, grabbing at their boots and pants legs, requiring the kind of careful high-stepping progress that ate time and energy without producing proportional distance.

Owen navigated. Emma carried the ceremony materials and ran sequences in her head.

The psychological effects were present from the moment they left camp, not the subtle misalignment of Wednesday afternoon but something more direct. The sense of being watched had the quality of something close rather than distant. Sounds arrived from the wrong directions. Twice Emma stopped because she'd heard what sounded like her name spoken in a voice she didn't recognize, and both times the forest was silent when she turned.

"You're hearing things," Owen said, not a question.

"Yes."

"So am I." He kept moving. "What are you hearing?"

"My name. A voice I don't know."

Owen was quiet for a moment. "I'm hearing footsteps. Parallel to us. Keeping pace. About thirty feet to the left." He paused. "There's nothing there. I checked twice."

"The contamination creates auditory effects," Emma said. "Robert Moore documented it. Sound that seems to originate outside when it's actually internal. The boundary between perception and projection gets thin."

"You're very calm about this."

"I've been preparing for this for two weeks," Emma said. "Being calm is part of the preparation."

The terrain steepened after the first mile, the ground changing from soft forest floor to rocky slope as they climbed out of the drainage toward higher ground. The undergrowth thinned and gave way to exposed granite, ancient and lichen-covered, the kind of rock that had been here before the trees and would be here after them. Emma's hands found holds without being directed, her body reading the terrain in the way it does when you've been moving through wilderness long enough that it becomes instinct rather than calculation.

Rufus picked his way up the rock face ahead of them, surefooted and deliberate, pausing on ledges to look back and confirm they were following.

The temperature at the top of the first rise was noticeably colder than the drainage below. Emma checked her thermometer. Thirty-eight degrees. It had been forty-three when they left camp. The elevation explained part of it. The rest was the same temperature phenomenon they'd experienced Wednesday afternoon, the contamination zone affecting local conditions in ways that didn't follow meteorological logic.

She noted it and kept climbing.

At the second rise, two and a half miles from camp, Owen's GPS began doing what it had done yesterday. Readings fluctuating, bearing shifting, the instrument arguing with itself in ways that instruments weren't supposed to. Owen switched to the paper map and compass, reading the terrain features against what the map showed, calling adjustments with the methodical patience of a man who had decided to trust math over technology.

"We're still on bearing," he said. "Half mile of this rocky section and then the terrain opens."

Emma was already feeling the pull.

It wasn't dramatic. Not a physical force, not something that moved her body without her permission. More like a compass needle responding to magnetic north, a directional quality in her awareness that said southwest, southwest, this way, getting stronger with each hundred yards of elevation gain. The circle was present in a way that other directions simply weren't, a weight in the southwest that had no physical explanation.

She didn't fight it. She noted it, the way she'd been noting everything, and kept moving.

The rocky section gave way at the three-mile mark to exactly what Owen had predicted: more open terrain, the trees spaced wider, the canopy higher, ground that was still rough with exposed root systems and loose stone but navigable without the constant hands-on climbing of the previous half mile. The sky was fully light now, clear and very blue, the kind of March sky that felt like a promise that the world knew how to be good at things.

Emma stopped at the high point of a ridge and looked southwest.

The clearing was visible from here. A natural amphitheater between two ridgelines, just as Robert Moore had described it in the journal that Emma had practically memorized over the past two weeks. Lower ground, sheltered, the kind of formation that occurred when two glacial movements had shaped a valley between them and left a bowl of relatively flat exposed bedrock in the center.

And in the center of that bowl, visible from a hundred yards even at this distance: the ash circle.

Ten feet across. Carved into exposed bedrock with the precision of people who had known exactly what they were doing and had taken the time to do it correctly. The ash compressed into the carvings over what must be centuries, dark against the pale granite, the symbols around the perimeter still legible to anyone who knew what they were looking at.

Emma stood on the ridge and looked at it for a long moment.

Rufus sat beside her. He was very still.

The pull was stronger here. Not uncomfortable. Not threatening. Just present, the way gravity is present, a fact of the landscape that the body understood without being told.

"There it is," Owen said quietly.

"There it is," Emma said.

She checked her satellite phone. One bar of signal on the ridge, barely enough.

She called James.

Four rings. He answered sounding like a man who had been awake all night, which he probably had.

"We're at the ridgeline above the site," Emma said. "I can see the circle from here. I'll perform the ceremony this afternoon when the solar position is right." She paused. "Walsh got out safely. Helicopter evacuation last night. He's on his way to a hospital in Kalispell."

A brief silence. "Good." James's voice carried something that wasn't just relief about Walsh. "Emma. The vote is tonight at seven. Werner filed three more motions this morning. Trying to disqualify Dr. Thomas on procedural grounds. Reeves is keeping the arrested operatives in county lockup and not letting Werner's lawyers near them until after the vote."

"The vote will go our way," Emma said. "I believe that."

"So do I. I just wanted you to know the timeline." A pause. "How are you doing? Really."

Emma looked at the ash circle a hundred yards below her, dark against pale rock, waiting for a hundred and eighteen years for someone who understood what it was.

"I'm standing on a ridge in Montana looking at a ceremonial site that my great-great-grandfather documented in 1907 but never visited," she said. "A site that belonged to the Morrison family until they were gone and there was no one left to protect it. I'm about to do what the last Morrison custodian never got the chance to do. I'm doing it with psilocybin mushrooms I'm going to harvest from the clearing in about an hour, using seventeen ceremony sequences I learned from a linguistics professor in Oxford, Ohio." She paused. "I'm terrified and I'm ready and those two things are not contradictory."

A brief silence on James's end. "Did you say mushrooms?"

"The ceremony requires them," Emma said. "It always has. The medicine is part of the preparation. Robert Moore took them. Mark took them. Every person who performed this ceremony took them. I'm not improvising, James. This is the protocol."

Another pause. Longer. "Okay," James said. "Okay." An awkward moment passes between them. "Be careful."

"I will." Emma looked at the circle one more time. "Win the vote, James."

"Seal the site, Emma."

She ended the call. Looked at Owen.

He was already looking at her with the expression of a man processing new information.

"The mushrooms," he said.

"They grow near the fallen pine at the clearing's edge," Emma said. "Moore documented it. Mark's journal confirmed it. Dr. Hanson and I discussed the protocol extensively. This isn't recreational, Owen. The medicine is how the ceremony works. It opens perception in specific ways that allow the closing sequence to function in both dimensions simultaneously."

Owen was quiet for a moment. "I know. I read the documentation." He paused. "I'm just calculating how long five to eight hours of psilocybin experience lasts."

"Long enough to perform the ceremony and seal the site," Emma said.

"And then some," Owen said.

"And then some," Emma agreed.

***

They made camp on the ridge above the clearing, Owen setting up while Emma sat with the circle visible below and ran the sequences until they were as natural as breathing.

The solar position would be right at approximately three-forty in the afternoon. Emma had four hours. She used them the way she'd been using every available hour for two weeks: preparation, review, stillness. The shadow dimension was active here, the contamination zone's effect on perception present and noted and set aside. She could feel her own shadow in it. She looked at it directly and didn't flinch and went back to the sequences.

At two-fifty Owen said: "Time to go find the fallen pine."

They descended into the clearing carefully, staying outside the circle's perimeter, moving along the edge of the amphitheater until they reached the tree line on the northwest side. The fallen pine was exactly where Mark's journal had placed it, a massive Ponderosa that had come down sometime in the past few decades, its root ball exposed, its trunk covered in the particular moss and lichen growth of something that had been horizontal for years.

And growing in the sheltered shadow beneath the trunk, exactly as documented: the mushrooms.

Emma crouched beside them. Psilocybin, the specific variety that Robert Moore had described, the variety the ancients had cultivated near these sites across seven locations on six continents because they understood what the medicine was for and had ensured it would be available to those who came prepared.

She harvested carefully, more than she thought she might need rather than less. The ancient instructions described the medicine in terms of what it was required to do: open perception to both dimensions simultaneously, hold that opening through seventeen ceremony sequences, allow the seeker to perceive the shadow with full clarity. There was no measured dose. There was enough and not enough, and Dr. Hanson had been unambiguous when they'd discussed it in Oxford: for a closing ceremony of this magnitude, in a site this contaminated, erring toward more was the only responsible choice. The ceremony failing because the medicine was insufficient was not an outcome Emma was willing to accept.

Owen watched without speaking.

Emma stood. Looked at the mushrooms in her hand. Looked at the ash circle twenty feet away.

"Onset is thirty to forty-five minutes," she said. "I place the cardinal materials first. By the time I begin the sequences the medicine will be working."

"How will I know if something is wrong?" Owen asked.

"Rufus will tell you," Emma said. "Watch him. He'll know before either of us."

She looked at Owen for a long moment. At the man who had driven to Moores Hill with Baker's coordinates on a Thursday morning that felt like a year ago. Who had been in every investigation, every discovery, every moment that had led to this clearing.

"Thank you for coming," she said.

"I wasn't letting you do this alone," Owen said. Simply. As fact.

Emma nodded. Then she took the mushrooms.

***

She placed the cardinal materials while the medicine was still quiet in her system, working methodically around the circle's perimeter. North: meteorite iron filings settled into the carved channel. East: ancient salt catching the afternoon light. South: pure silver pieces placed at the anchor point. West: ash from the circle itself, completion, the cycle closing.

Four positions. Four elements. Everything as documented.

By the time she stood at the circle's edge to begin the sequences, the medicine had begun its work.

Not dramatically. Not in any way that announced itself as different from the contamination zone's existing perceptual effects. More like a gentle lifting of the world's foreground, a quality of attention that had expanded slightly beyond its usual range, colors becoming more precise rather than more vivid, the granite under her boots more granite than granite had been a moment ago.

Emma was aware of it and noted it and began the first sequence.

She looked up at Owen and Rufus on the slope above the clearing. Owen raised a hand. Rufus sat absolutely still, watching her with those dark attentive eyes.

"Stay with Owen," Emma said to Rufus. "Outside the circle. Whatever you hear or see from me inside, stay outside."

Rufus looked at her for a long moment. Then he moved to Owen's side with the reluctant acceptance she'd come to recognize.

Emma turned back to the circle. Closed her eyes. Found the first sequence.

And began to speak.

The medicine and the ceremony met each other the way two rivers meet, not collision but convergence, each one making the other more fully itself. The ancient syllables moved through the clearing and the expanded perception the medicine had opened received them differently than normal consciousness would have, the words landing in multiple dimensions simultaneously, the way they had been designed to land, the way they could only land with the medicine present.

Second sequence. The ash in the northern carving shifted.

Third sequence. The temperature dropped another five degrees. Emma felt it as interesting rather than alarming, the cold having a texture now, a particular quality she could examine.

Fourth sequence. And here was where the medicine fully arrived.

The dimensional space opened with a clarity that took her breath away. Not the contamination zone's misaligned wrongness, not the subtle sense of two realities running out of phase. This was what the ceremony was designed to produce: both dimensions simultaneously, clearly perceived, correctly aligned, the physical world and the shadow world in right relationship to each other for the first time Emma had ever experienced it.

She could see the clearing. The granite. The ash circle glowing faintly at the cardinal points. The afternoon sky above the ridgeline, impossibly blue, each cloud a precise and considered thing.

She could also see through all of it, alongside all of it, into the dimension that existed parallel to the physical. The space where consciousness operated without body. Where the shadow lived.

Fifth sequence. Emma felt the contamination directly, thirty years of it, Mark's darkness and terror and ten-year losing war, the seven dead people's broken consciousness, all of it present in the bedrock beneath her feet.

Sixth sequence. She kept speaking. The medicine kept the two dimensions open and clear.

And then at the seventh sequence the shadow came.

Her shadow. Not Mark's. Not the contamination's accumulated weight. Hers.

And Emma looked at it with eyes that the medicine had opened and a mind that two weeks of preparation had made ready and the full attention of someone who had read Mark's August 1993 journal entry and understood exactly what this moment was and what it required.

She looked at her shadow directly.

All of it. Her capacity for cruelty. For selfishness. For predation. Every dark impulse she had ever suppressed or set aside or chosen not to act on. Present and visible and real and completely hers.

The medicine didn't make it worse. It made it clearer. Stripped away the noise and showed her the signal: this is here, this is human, this is what you contain, this is what every person who has ever stood near an ash circle has seen because this is what it means to be fully alive.

Emma looked at it and she said yes.

Not to the darkness. To the truth of it. To the fact of her own complete humanity, light and shadow both, the full range, acknowledged without condition.

The shadow, fully seen, began to integrate.

And Emma kept speaking. The eighth sequence. Steady and precise and certain. Both worlds open. The medicine holding the door. The ceremony doing the work.

She was in the circle.

She was in both worlds simultaneously.

And she was choosing.

CHAPTER 16: THE MORRISON FILE

Thursday morning. The vote was tonight at seven.

The morning came in gray and cold, the kind of March morning that couldn't commit to the season it wanted to be.

James had slept three hours in the Carnegie Hall security office and woken to eight messages: Margaret confirming Dorothy Webb would be at the hearing and had been preparing remarks since Tuesday, Ashford sending the finalized petition invalidation brief, Reeves with an update on the two arrested operatives who were still not talking but whose fingerprints had returned no matches in any domestic database, Owen sending photographs of the laptop emails from Montana, and four messages from council members that ranged from supportive to cautiously noncommittal.

The two arrested operatives with no domestic fingerprint matches told James something useful. These were not local contractors or regional hired help. They were the kind of people whose identities existed only in the places their employers wanted them to exist. The organization Werner represented had international reach. Thirty years of operation across four continents didn't happen any other way.

He wrote this down in the case notes he'd been keeping since day one and added it to the council briefing packet he was building for the seven o'clock hearing.

Dr. Thomas arrived at Carnegie Hall at nine to complete her assessment documentation. She moved through the building with the same efficient precision she'd brought on Wednesday, adding measurements and photographs to the preliminary findings, building the kind of thorough report that held up under cross-examination. She asked James two questions about the attacks he hadn't answered in their initial conversation and he answered them. She didn't ask about the false wall or what lay beneath it and he was grateful.

"I'll be ready for tonight," she said when she finished. "I've done this before. I know how Werner's people cross-examine forensic assessments. I know the angles they'll try."

"What are the angles?" James asked.

"Selection bias: I only looked at what the historical society's side wanted me to see. Chain of custody: the damage wasn't properly documented before I arrived so I'm building a narrative on contaminated evidence. Financial interest: I was hired by the historical society, therefore my findings serve their interests." She looked at him calmly. "My response to all three is the same. I followed standard forensic assessment protocol. The evidence speaks for itself. And if they want to argue that damage inflicted by pipe cutters is consistent with natural pipe failure, they're welcome to make that argument in front of a room full of Moores Hill residents who know what happened to Officers Daniels and Kowalski."

James looked at her. "You heard about that."

"Everyone in three counties heard about that," Dr. Thomas said.

***

The town council chambers held two hundred people when pressed and was pressed hard by seven o'clock Thursday evening. James had been there since five, helping Margaret arrange the historical society's presentation materials, reviewing the footage one final time, running through the sequence of arguments with Ashford and Dr. Thomas the way you run through a plan one last time before executing it, not because you've forgotten the plan but because the act of saying it aloud makes it real in a way that thinking it doesn't.

Dorothy Webb arrived at five-thirty, eighty-one years old and moving with the particular unhurried purpose of someone who has decided exactly what they intend to do and is not interested in being rushed toward or away from it. She'd dressed carefully: good clothes, the kind worn for occasions that mattered. She sat in the front row of the gallery and arranged her notes and looked at the council dais with the expression of someone who had been coming to Moores Hill civic meetings for sixty years and understood that what happened in rooms like this one was what actually shaped a community's life.

James sat beside her for a few minutes before the hearing started.

"What are you going to say?" he asked.

"The truth," Dorothy said. "Which is that Carnegie Hall isn't a building. It's a promise this community made to itself about what it valued. Buildings are structures. Carnegie Hall is an argument. It argues that a town of six hundred people can build something that lasts. That what we make together outlasts the people who made it." She looked at him. "I'm going to tell them about my grandmother's grandmother. I'm going to make them understand that what they vote on tonight isn't about structural reports. It's about whether Moores Hill keeps its promises."

James left her to her notes and took his position at the historical society's table.

Werner arrived at six-fifty with Torres and two other lawyers James hadn't seen before. They took their seats with the particular coordinated efficiency of a team that had done this many times. Werner looked at James across the chamber and nodded once, the professional acknowledgment of an opponent he respected and intended to defeat.

James nodded back.

Mayor Ashcraft called the hearing to order at seven-oh-four.

Torres went first. His presentation was identical in structure to Tuesday's but refined, the procedural vulnerabilities he'd exposed in the Tuesday hearing addressed, the weaknesses Werner had identified now shored up with additional documentation. He had responded to the Whitfield problem by bringing a second engineer's assessment, a man named Dr. Alan Briggs whose credentials were verifiably current, who had conducted his own inspection of the building in the forty-eight hours since the Tuesday hearing and whose findings aligned with Torres's original report.

James watched the council members' faces while Briggs presented. This was Werner's adaptation. Ashford's petition invalidation had neutralized Torres's report, so Werner had obtained a new one. Clean credentials. Recent inspection. The same findings dressed in fresh paperwork.

Werner addressed the council before James could respond. "Your honor, the historical society spent forty-eight hours attacking the procedural validity of our original assessment rather than its substance. That substance has now been independently confirmed by a credentialed engineer. The council has two structural assessments from qualified engineers finding the building unsafe and one assessment from an engineer hired specifically by the party that opposes demolition. The preponderance of evidence supports condemnation."

It was a good move. James had anticipated something like it. He stood without being called on, which drew a look from Mayor Ashcraft, and she nodded permission.

"Dr. Briggs conducted his inspection of Carnegie Hall Wednesday," James said. "The same day that three individuals breached the building's east wall with a hydraulic cutting tool, were confronted by police, and were detained. Two of them are currently in Dearborn County custody." He pulled up the footage on his laptop and connected it to the projector. "This is the east wall breach. Dr. Briggs inspected a building in which a hole had been cut through the original brick by people who have been attacking this building for twelve days. His assessment of wall integrity reflects damage they created."

He played the breach footage. The hydraulic cutter. The opening appearing in original 1907 brick. The confrontation with Martinez.

The chamber was very quiet.

"Furthermore," James said, "in the course of Wednesday night's incident, evidence was recovered suggesting that the organization behind the Safety Coalition is targeting Carnegie Hall not for safety reasons but for access to what lies beneath it. This organization is under active investigation by the Dearborn County DA's office for identity fraud, criminal trespass, assault on police officers, and criminal mischief. This council is being asked to vote on a condemnation petition filed by an organization whose principals are currently subjects of a criminal investigation."

Werner was on his feet. "The criminal allegations against unidentified individuals have no bearing on the structural merits of this petition. Carnegie Hall either meets safety standards or it doesn't. The question of who filed the petition doesn't change the physical reality of the building."

"The physical reality of the building," Dr. Thomas said from her seat, rising without being called, "was manufactured. I've documented it in forty-seven pages that were filed with the council clerk at nine o'clock this morning and that I'm prepared to walk this council through in detail. This building was deliberately damaged to create the appearance of structural failure. Both of the reports you have heard tonight assessed damage that was created by the same organization that filed this petition. That is not independent assessment. That is circular evidence."

Werner filed a procedural objection. Mayor Ashcraft overruled it.

Ashford presented the petition invalidation argument for the third time, this time with an addendum addressing Briggs's report specifically. The addendum was precise and thorough and took eleven minutes to deliver. Werner's objections got shorter as the hearing progressed, the particular sign of a lawyer who is running out of angles.

The public comment period was thirty-five minutes. Fourteen residents spoke. Eleven in favor of preservation. Three in favor of condemnation, two of whom James was fairly certain had been approached by the Safety Coalition, the third of whom was a retired contractor who had genuine concerns about the building's age and expressed them honestly and without apparent coordination.

Dorothy Webb spoke last.

She stood at the public microphone with her notes in her hand and looked at the council for a moment before speaking.

"My grandmother's grandmother graduated from Moores Hill College in 1912," she said. "Her name was Eleanor Ashford. She was the first woman in her family to attend college. She was the first woman in this county to earn a degree in mathematics. She used to say that Moores Hill College and Carnegie Hall gave her a life she couldn't have had anywhere else. She talked about that building her whole life. When the college closed she grieved it like a death." Dorothy paused. "Eleanor Ashford has been dead for sixty years. But I still hear her talking about Carnegie Hall. And I think that's what a landmark is. It's not a structure. It's a voice. It's the voice of people who lived here before us, who made something here, who left it for us to take care of." She looked at the council members one by one. "I'm eighty-one years old. I've been coming to civic meetings in this town for sixty years. I've seen this community make hard choices. Good choices and bad ones. Tonight I'm asking you to make a good one. Don't let Carnegie Hall go. Don't let Eleanor Ashford's voice go silent because someone from Cincinnati filed some paperwork."

She sat down.

The gallery was absolutely quiet for three full seconds.

Then Tom Hargrove started clapping. Not enthusiastically, not performatively. Just the solid steady applause of a man who had heard something that needed to be acknowledged. Three other people joined him. Then more.

Werner did not applaud. He was writing notes.

Mayor Ashcraft called for council deliberation at eight-forty-seven.

The deliberation lasted forty minutes. James sat at the historical society table and watched and listened and catalogued every exchange. Mayor Ashcraft ran it with the controlled precision of someone who understood that how a vote was conducted mattered as much as what the vote was. Each council member spoke. Hargrove and Simmons and Thornton were clear: the petition was built on fraud, the damage was manufactured, the building was sound, condemnation was not warranted. Linda Hayes was more cautious, acknowledging the fraud evidence but expressing concern about the two legitimate structural assessments. The remaining two members were the variables James had been unable to fully read through the week.

Robert Yost, who taught history at the county high school and had never spoken to James directly about Carnegie Hall, asked a single question: "If we vote against condemnation tonight and something happens to that building, who is responsible?"

Mayor Ashcraft said: "The council's responsibility is to make decisions based on evidence. The evidence presented tonight establishes that the structural concerns were manufactured. If the council votes based on fraudulent evidence and the building comes down as a result, that responsibility lies elsewhere."

Yost nodded once and said nothing more.

The vote was called at nine-forty-seven.

Seven council members. Four votes needed to condemn.

Mayor Ashcraft voted against condemnation.

Tom Hargrove voted against.

Carol Simmons voted against.

Robert Thornton voted against.

Linda Hayes voted for condemnation.

The remaining two members: one against, one abstention.

Four against. One for. One abstention. One for condemnation.

Motion failed. Carnegie Hall was not condemned.

The gallery reacted with the particular kind of relief that isn't celebratory so much as exhaled, the sound a community makes when something they were afraid of losing turns out to be still there.

Margaret Hendricks had her hands over her mouth. Dorothy Webb sat very straight in her front-row seat and looked at the council dais with the expression of someone who has waited for something for a long time and is allowing themselves to feel it.

James let himself feel it for approximately ten seconds. Then Werner stood.

"The Safety Coalition will be filing an emergency appeal with the county," Werner said. His voice was professionally level, carrying none of the frustration the evening had to have cost him. "Additionally, we will be seeking an emergency injunction based on imminent public safety risk. A local political outcome does not override public safety law. We intend to pursue every available avenue to ensure this community is protected."

Mayor Ashcraft thanked him for his participation and adjourned the hearing.

***

James was the last to leave the historical society table. He was packing his laptop when Werner appeared beside him, not in the corridor this time, right there in the chamber as the last residents filed out.

James kept packing.

"Congratulations," Werner said. "You ran a good campaign."

"It wasn't a campaign," James said. "It was the truth."

"The truth." Werner considered this. "You're going to keep believing that. I respect it." He paused. "Mr. McClanahan. The appeal will be filed tomorrow. The injunction petition by end of week. We have resources you haven't seen yet. Tonight's vote is a setback. It's not an ending."

"I know," James said. He zipped his bag. "You told me that already."

"I did." Werner was quiet for a moment. "Your colleague in Montana. Is she performing the ceremony tonight?"

James looked at him directly. "I don't know what you're talking about."

Werner almost smiled. Not the professional smile. Something smaller and less calculated, the expression of a man who has accepted something he hadn't expected to accept. "You're going to find out what convergence means," he said quietly. "When she seals the Montana site. If she seals it. You're going to feel it. And then you're going to understand why we've been doing this for thirty years." He picked up his briefcase. "We're not your enemies. I know that's difficult to believe given the past two weeks. But we're trying to prevent something that none of you are prepared for."

James said nothing.

Werner looked at him for a moment longer. Then he walked out of the council chambers and James heard his footsteps recede down the corridor and the main door open and close.

James stood alone in the empty chamber for thirty seconds.

Then he pulled out his phone and called Owen.

The satellite connection was thin but held. Owen answered on the second ring, his voice carrying the particular quiet of someone maintaining a vigil.

"How did it go?" Owen asked.

"We held it. Four to one against condemnation. Werner is filing appeals but the building is safe tonight." James paused. "How is Emma?"

"She's in the circle," Owen said. "Has been for about two hours. I can see her from the ridge." A brief silence. "James. Whatever she's doing down there, it's working. The temperature in the clearing lifted about forty minutes ago. The wrong cold. It just lifted."

James sat very still in the empty council chamber.

"Tell her when she comes out," James said. "Don't interrupt her."

"I know," Owen said. "I'm not going anywhere."

James ended the call and sat in the basement of Carnegie Hall with the laptop bag on the table beside him and the chairs around him still holding the slight warmth of the hundred and fifty people who had sat in them an hour ago.

Outside Carnegie Hall, eight police officers stood watch over a building that a town had just voted to keep.

In a Montana wilderness clearing, Owen Mitchell sat at the edge of a ridge with a German Shepherd pressed against his leg and watched a woman perform a ceremony older than the country they were standing in.

James stayed where he was.

Whatever convergence meant, it was happening now.

And Carnegie Hall was still standing.

CHAPTER 17: THEY KNOW

The shadow did not look the way Emma had expected.

She'd imagined something monstrous. Something clearly other, clearly wrong, the kind of darkness that announced itself so you knew what you were dealing with. What she saw instead was herself. Completely and without distortion, herself. Not a twisted version. Not an exaggerated version. Just Emma Caldwell, standing in an ash circle in Montana wilderness, with every capacity she had ever possessed fully visible, the ones she used and the ones she didn't, the ones she was proud of and the ones she had never once acted on and had spent years pretending didn't exist.

The medicine made it clear in a way that nothing else could have. Stripped away the comfortable distance between Emma and the truth of herself, removed the fog of everyday consciousness that allowed human beings to function without looking directly at what they were capable of, and showed her the signal underneath all the noise.

She looked at it. All of it. The capacity for cruelty. For selfishness. For predation. Every dark impulse she had ever suppressed or set aside or chosen not to act on. Present and visible and real and completely hers.

It was not separate from her. That was the thing. The shadow was not an addition to who she was. It was a dimension of who she was. The darkness and the light using the same infrastructure, the same intelligence, the same capacity for love and care and loyalty that had driven her across the country to seal a site and pull a stranger out of a drainage. The same Emma, all the way through.

This is here. This is mine.

She held the shadow's gaze and the shadow held hers and neither of them flinched.

And then Emma did the thing that Mark Caldwell had not been able to do in August 1993 in this same circle with this same ceremony showing him the same truth about himself.

She said yes.

Not to the darkness. Not to the capacity for cruelty or predation or any of the things the shadow had shown her. She said yes to the fact of it. Yes, this is real. Yes, this is mine. Yes, I contain this. Yes, I have always contained this. Yes, every human being who has ever stood near an ash circle has seen exactly this same truth about themselves because this is what it means to be human, to have the full range, to be capable of everything the species is capable of, good and terrible and everything between.

She said yes to the truth of herself without condition.

The shadow, fully seen, fully acknowledged, fully claimed as hers, began to fold back in. Not disappear. Integration, not elimination. The shadow becoming part of the whole rather than a severed thing that operated in the dark. Hers. Fully and consciously hers.

The contamination around her reacted.

Ninth sequence. The contamination recognized the language. Something in the accumulated darkness of thirty years shifted in response to the words, the way a lock shifts when the right key finds the right tumbler. Not resistance. Something closer to the exhausted relief of something that has been wound too tight for too long and is finally being allowed to release.

Tenth sequence. The ash in the southern carving began to move. Organized movement, the ash circling within the channel of the carving in a slow deliberate spiral. The site was not just responding to the language. The site was responding to her. To the custodian blood. To the medicine that had opened her perception wide enough to work in both dimensions simultaneously the way the ceremony required.

Eleventh sequence.

Emma felt the contamination beginning to drain. The sensation of something that had been filling the circle for thirty years moving toward release, the way a long-held breath releases when permission is finally given. Mark's darkness dispersing. The seven dead people's terror and broken consciousness releasing from the bedrock.

She could feel each of them as they went.

Marcus Chandler, the first. She felt the shape of what he'd seen and how it had broken him, a version of the same shadow she'd just faced, the same human truth, unprepared and alone and running. She felt him release.

The six who came after, each one shown what Marcus had been shown, none of them prepared, all of them broken in different ways. She felt each one release in turn.

Not absolution. The ceremony wasn't undoing what had happened to them. It was releasing what had been trapped here by what happened to them.

Twelfth sequence.

Owen's presence at the boundary. She could feel him without seeing him, the awareness of someone she trusted anchoring the edge of the space. He wasn't coming in. He'd promised.

Rufus. His presence was different from Owen's, denser, more immediate. Whatever Rufus was, he was fully present at the edge of this circle in a way that felt like witness. The guardian who had brought something important to the place it needed to be and was now watching the thing it was always moving toward.

Thirteenth sequence.

The ash in all four cardinal carvings was moving now, the same slow spiral in each channel. The temperature in the clearing had dropped so far that her exhaled breath was a visible cloud. Emma noted this as interesting. The medicine was doing something extraordinary to her relationship with interesting. Everything was interesting. The cold was interesting. The ash spiral was interesting. The fact that she was standing in both dimensions simultaneously was the most interesting thing that had ever happened to her and she was handling it with the focused competence of a woman who had prepared carefully and taken perhaps slightly more mushrooms than was strictly necessary for the task at hand.

She kept speaking. The sequences held.

Fourteenth sequence.

The dimensional space began to clarify, the misalignment of the contamination zone resolving into something that was both dimensions simultaneously, clearly and without distortion. The physical and the dimensional in proper relation to each other.

This was what the ceremony was designed to restore.

Fifteenth sequence.

And then Emma felt something she hadn't been prepared for.

The other six sites.

Not visually. Not as a hallucination. More like the sense of connection extended across the whole network. Six other points of awareness in the dimensional space, six other ash circles in six other places on the planet, each one registering what was happening in Montana.

Three of them were active. Functioning. Peru. Egypt. England. Their custodian families had maintained the knowledge through everything. Emma felt their attention, not as conscious thought, not as communication, but as presence. Acknowledgment.

One was Moores Hill. Sealed. Protected. Waiting.

Two were silence. Easter Island. Göbekli Tepe. The Safety Coalition had reached them first. Emma felt their absence as a specific kind of void in the network, not pain exactly, just the undeniable fact of two gaps that could not be filled.

Montana was closing now. Five of seven. The network incomplete but breathing again.

This was convergence. Not an event. A state. The seven-site network functioning as a whole. The Safety Coalition had destroyed two sites to prevent it. Had been trying to destroy Carnegie Hall to prevent it.

Emma didn't know yet what a fully restored network would do.

But she was going to complete the ceremony regardless.

Because seven people were dead in this clearing. Because Timothy Walsh had spent two months in a creek drainage. Because Mark Caldwell had come here in 1993 in good faith and been destroyed by what he found because no one was maintaining the knowledge anymore.

Because she was the custodian and the ceremony was almost done.

Sixteenth sequence.

The ash circle pulsed. The dark ash in the carved channels brightened for a moment, something very old and very patient finally recognizing that the waiting was almost over. Emma felt it through the soles of her boots and through the cold air on her face and through the dimensional space she was still perceiving, both worlds present and clear and correctly aligned.

She thought about her mother, Linda Caldwell, who had spent twenty years protecting a building she knew mattered without knowing why. Who had died for it.

She thought about Robert Moore, who had stood at the Moores Hill site in 1907 and been shown the same truth Emma had been shown tonight, and who had not been able to say yes to it.

She thought about Mark Caldwell, the good man who had tried.

She was the fifth. And she understood it.

The seventeenth sequence.

Emma spoke the final words of the closing ceremony with the precision and care and full attention of every preparation she had made. Each syllable exact. Each transition between phrases clean. The timing exactly as Robert Moore had documented.

The last word left her mouth and landed in the Montana air.

And the ash circle completed itself.

Emma felt it close.

The way a long-held breath fully releases when everything in the body that was holding it lets go simultaneously. The contamination that had been accumulating since 1993, thirty years of it, released from the bedrock in a single long exhalation and dispersed into the surrounding wilderness and was gone.

The cold in the clearing lifted.

The contamination cold. The wrong cold. Gone.

Emma stood in the ash circle in the natural temperature of a Montana evening at elevation and breathed.

The two-dimensional perception remained for a moment longer. She could still feel the network, the two functioning custodian sites on the other side of the world sending something that felt like recognition through the dimensional space. Three out of seven. More complete than an hour ago.

Then the dimensional perception eased. The world returned to its single register.

Emma was standing in a circle carved into Montana bedrock with the ash in the channels still and dark and undisturbed.

She collected the ceremonial materials from the cardinal points, moving clockwise, securing each element carefully. Shouldered her pack. Stood at the circle's edge one final moment.

"Thank you," she said. To the circle. To the ancients. To Robert Moore who hadn't been able to do this and had known it. To Linda Caldwell. To Mark.

She turned away and started up the slope.

And that was when the mushrooms, which had been admirably cooperative during the ceremony and had apparently decided they had been patient long enough, arrived in full.

***

Owen saw her coming up the slope and stood up.

Emma was moving carefully. Not unsteadily. Carefully. The way a person moves when each footstep is a complete and fascinating event in itself. She reached the top of the ridge and stopped and looked at Owen and then looked past him at the sky, which had shifted into the deep blue of early evening and was doing something that required her full attention for a moment.

Owen waited.

Emma looked back at him.

"It worked," she said.

"I know," Owen said. "I watched. Are you okay?"

She considered this. Not the way a person considers a simple question but the way a person considers something that deserves genuine examination. After a moment she nodded slowly. "Yes," she said. Then she sat down on the granite, not urgently, just sat down, and looked at the clearing below.

Owen sat down beside her. Rufus came and pressed against her leg and she put her hand on his back without looking at him, the automatic gesture of someone confirming that a thing is real.

They sat.

The sky deepened. The first star appeared on the eastern horizon. Emma saw it and went very still, her attention narrowing to that single point of light with the complete focus of someone who has never properly considered a star before and is now doing so for the first time.

Owen watched her. He'd been a journalist for fifteen years. He knew how to wait.

Three minutes passed.

"Owen," Emma said, without looking away from the star.

"Yes."

A long pause. Whatever she'd been about to say had gone somewhere else. She was quiet for another full minute.

"Never mind," she said.

Owen pressed his lips together.

Rufus's tail wagged once.

Emma looked at the clearing below. At the ash circle, dark and still, the cardinal materials placed and the contamination gone and the wrongness lifted and the ceremony complete. She looked at it for a long time with an expression Owen couldn't read, something between recognition and wonder, the expression of a person seeing something familiar from an entirely new angle.

Then she looked at her hands.

Owen watched her look at her hands. This took a while.

"Owen," she said.

"Yes."

She held up her hands slightly, not showing them to him, just acknowledging their existence. "These," she said, and then stopped.

"Yes," Owen said carefully.

"Nothing," Emma said. "Sorry." She put her hands back in her lap and looked at the star again.

Owen looked at Rufus. Rufus looked back at Owen with an expression that Owen could only describe as deeply patient. His tail moved in a slow comfortable wag. He was pressed against Emma's leg and she was absently running her hand through his fur and had been for some time without appearing to notice she was doing it.

Owen got out his notebook. He had a feeling he was going to want to write some of this down.

The stars came out one by one. Emma tracked each new one the moment it appeared, her attention moving across the sky with the unhurried thoroughness of someone taking inventory. She didn't comment on them. She just looked.

After a while she said: "James."

Owen looked up from his notebook. "What about James?"

Emma appeared to consider whether she had anything further to add. She did not. "Nothing," she said. "Just." A pause. "James."

"The vote held," Owen said. "Carnegie Hall is safe. I called him while you were in the circle."

Emma turned to look at him. This information was arriving from a very long distance and taking its time getting there. Then something settled in her face. "Good," she said. "Good." She looked back at the sky. "That's good."

"It is," Owen said.

Another long silence. Owen wrote in his notebook. Emma watched the stars accumulate. Rufus dozed against her leg.

Then Emma said, very quietly and with complete sincerity: "Owen, the meteorite iron is from outer space."

Owen stopped writing.

"The iron filings," Emma continued, with the careful precision of someone working out something important. "They're from a meteorite. Which came from space. I put them in the circle." A pause. "I put space in the circle."

Owen looked at her. She was not joking. She was not being absurd. She had arrived at this observation through what was clearly a significant interior journey and was sharing the conclusion with him the way a scientist shares a result.

"You did," Owen said.

Emma nodded slowly. "Robert Moore did too," she said. "At the Moores Hill circle. In 1907." She was quiet for a moment. "He never understood that."

Owen wasn't entirely sure what to do with that but he wrote it down.

Rufus opened one eye, looked at Emma, closed it again.

Owen built a fire because the temperature was dropping and Emma hadn't moved in forty minutes and he wasn't sure she was going to. The fire caught and Emma watched it with the same complete attention she'd given the stars, her face lit warm gold in the flickering light, her expression entirely still.

At some point she ate without Owen entirely noticing when she'd started. She accepted water when he handed it to her. She gave no indication that any of these things were unusual.

The fire burned down and Owen built it back up.

Emma said: "I could feel them go."

Owen looked up. "The contamination?"

"The people," Emma said. "The ones who died here." She was looking at the fire, not at him. "One at a time. I felt each one." A long pause. "Marcus Chandler went first."

Owen was very still.

"I don't know if that's something I'm supposed to say," Emma said. "It might just be the mushrooms."

"Tell me anyway," Owen said quietly.

She did. Slowly, with long pauses between sentences, she described what she'd experienced from the eleventh sequence onward, the contamination releasing, the people releasing with it, the network felt for the first time. She spoke the way someone speaks when they're accessing something that is still very present and very delicate, choosing each word carefully, taking her time.

Owen wrote all of it down.

When she finished she was quiet again for a long time. The fire had burned low. The stars were enormous above the Montana ridgeline, more stars than either of them had ever seen, the Milky Way visible as a smear of pale light across the dark.

Emma looked up at it.

"Owen," she said.

"Yes."

"I think I understand convergence."

Owen's pen stopped. "What is it?"

A long pause. Something in her expression suggested the answer was fully formed somewhere inside her and the challenge was finding the surface for it.

"The network," she said slowly. "All seven. When they function together. It's not an event. It's a state." She was quiet. "When all seven are properly maintained. The medicine works correctly everywhere. The shadow integration. The healing." She paused again. "That's what they're afraid of."

"The Safety Coalition," Owen said.

"A world where people can face their shadows properly," Emma said. "And integrate them. Instead of running." She looked at the fire. "Mark ran. That's what happened. He saw it and he ran for ten years and he lost." A long pause. "They want people to keep running."

Owen looked at her. "You think that's it? That's what convergence prevents?"

Emma was quiet for a long time.

"I don't know," she said finally. "I think that's part of it. I think there's more I couldn't see." She looked at the stars. "I'll know more when the mushrooms wear off."

Owen wrote that down too.

Later, when the fire had burned to coals and Rufus was deeply asleep and Emma's eyes were half-closed, she said one more thing.

"Owen."

"Yes."

"Don't put the outer space thing in the article."

Owen stopped writing. "Why not? It's genuinely interesting."

"It is," Emma said. "But I said it like that. And James will know."

Owen looked at her. Emma's eyes were fully closed now, her breathing slowing toward sleep.

"Know what?" Owen said.

But Emma was already gone, tilted sideways against Rufus, asleep between one breath and the next, leaving Owen alone by the coals with his notebook and the Montana sky and the sealed ash circle below and absolutely no intention of leaving that observation out of the article.

***

She woke Friday morning with the particular clarity that follows a significant psilocybin experience. Not the groggy uncertain morning of too much alcohol. Something cleaner than that. The world rearranged and the rearrangement an improvement.

Owen had coffee ready.

"How do you feel?" he asked.

"Clear," Emma said. She meant it in more than one way.

She accepted the coffee. Looked at the clearing below. The ash circle dark and still in the morning light. Just granite and ancient carvings and the particular silence of something that had been waiting a very long time and had finally been given what it needed.

"It worked," she said.

"It did," Owen said. "Emma. What you did down there."

"I know," Emma said quietly. She drank her coffee. After a moment: "How much of last night do I need to be embarrassed about."

Owen considered this. "The outer space observation was genuinely insightful," he said. "The convergence theory you worked out by the fire was remarkable. The thing about Mark running." He paused. "All of that goes in the book."

"That's not what I asked," Emma said.

"You fell asleep mid-sentence," Owen said.

"That was the mushrooms," Emma said.

"Obviously," Owen said.

"And whatever I said before that."

"Also the mushrooms," Owen agreed.

Emma looked at him over her coffee with the expression of someone who suspects she is not getting the full picture but has decided to accept the summary. "Good," she said.

Rufus walked over and sat in front of her and looked at her steadily.

Emma looked back at him. "We still have an understanding," she told him.

His tail wagged once. Settled.

They broke camp efficiently, loaded their packs, and started the long hike out. Fifteen miles back to the Expedition. A long drive to Kalispell. A flight home to Indiana.

Moores Hill. Carnegie Hall. Werner's appeals. The work that was still waiting.

Emma walked the first mile in silence, the ceremony and the medicine and the long night settling into her body as memory rather than experience. At the top of the first rise she stopped and looked back at the clearing one final time.

The ash circle was visible from here, small and dark against the pale granite, sealed and silent and exactly as it should be.

She turned away and kept walking.

Rufus walked beside her, close and steady, the guardian who had brought her here and was now walking her home.

She had a long hike ahead of her.

She didn't mind at all.

CONVERGENCE & RESOLUTION

CHAPTER 18: THE CUSTODIAN

They left the trailhead camp at first light Friday morning.

Emma shouldered her pack and looked back at the clearing one final time from the ridge before the terrain dropped away and blocked the view.

The ash circle was visible from here, small and dark against the pale granite, sealed and silent and exactly as it should be. The cardinal materials still in place. The ash in the channels undisturbed. Whatever the ancients had built here, whatever the Morrison family had protected for generations before colonization broke the knowledge lineage, whatever Mark had broken open in 1993 and whatever Emma had closed the night before, it was finished now. Done. The site was not a wound anymore. It was simply old ground with old carvings, waiting to be properly understood by people who knew what they were looking at.

Emma turned away and started down the slope.

Rufus fell into step beside her. Owen followed three paces back with his pack and his notebook and the particular quiet of a man who understood that the first miles of this hike needed to belong to Emma.

The wilderness had changed overnight.

Not visibly. The trees were the same trees, the granite the same granite, the creek drainage they crossed in the first hour still running cold and clear with snowmelt. But the quality of the air was different. The contamination zone's persistent wrongness, the sense of two realities slightly out of phase, the auditory effects and the temperature drops that had no meteorological explanation, all of it was gone. The wilderness was simply wilderness again. Cold and demanding and indifferent in the way that honest wilderness is indifferent, not hostile, not wrong, just entirely itself without any overlay of human darkness deposited into its bedrock.

Emma walked and let the miles do what miles do.

She'd been expecting something more dramatic. Some sense of completion that announced itself. What she felt instead was something quieter and more lasting. The absence of a weight she'd been carrying so long she'd stopped noticing it as a weight. It had just been the way things felt. And now it wasn't there and the world felt different in the way a room feels different when you remove a piece of furniture that was always in the way. You don't notice the furniture specifically. You just notice that there's more room to move.

She thought about Mark.

Not the trial version of Mark. Not the monster the evidence had built across six weeks in a Dearborn County courtroom. The man in the 1991 journal. The one who'd helped Linda move the couch and missed his brother and taught Emma to drive in the grain elevator parking lot and made terrible jokes at Christmas. The man who'd gone to Montana in August 1993 because he thought he was doing the right thing for his family.

She'd faced the same shadow Mark had faced. Seen the same truth about herself. The same capacity for darkness that lived in everyone who had ever stood near an ash circle and looked honestly at what they were made of.

The difference was she'd known what she was seeing.

Mark had seen his darkness and thought: this is who I really am. This is my true nature finally revealed. And he'd spent ten years fighting that interpretation before he lost the fight and became it.

Emma had seen her darkness and thought: this is what I'm capable of. This is potential, not destiny. This is the full range of what it means to be human. And she'd said yes to the truth of it without making the mistake of identifying with it.

That distinction was everything. That was the entire purpose of the medicine and the ceremony and the preparation. Not to show people they were monsters. To show them they contained the full range and then give them the framework to choose consciously which parts they acted from.

The ancients had understood this. Had built the medicine and the ceremony and the sites into a system designed to produce exactly this outcome. Properly used, properly prepared, properly guided, the experience produced integration. Improperly used, it produced what it had produced in Marcus Chandler and seven others and Mark Caldwell. Not because the sites were evil. Because the knowledge had been lost.

Emma had found the knowledge. Had used it correctly. Had come back intact.

She thought about what that meant for the network. For the two custodian families who had felt Montana seal and had sent their acknowledgment through the dimensional space. People she'd never met, in places she'd never been, maintaining knowledge she'd only recently recovered, had felt what she did last night and had recognized it. Three out of seven. The network incomplete but functioning.

She needed to find them.

Not today. Today was for walking fifteen miles through Montana wilderness and getting to the Expedition and driving to Kalispell and getting on a plane home. But soon. When she was rested and clear and ready to have the most important conversation of her custodian life with people who actually understood what that meant.

At the three-mile mark, where the terrain opened into the wider drainage they'd followed on the hike in, Emma pulled out her satellite phone.

She called Dr. Hanson.

The linguistics professor answered on the third ring, her voice carrying the alert quality of someone who had been waiting for this call.

"Emma."

"It worked," Emma said. "The ceremony is complete. The Montana site is sealed. The contamination is gone."

A silence on the other end that Emma recognized as Dr. Hanson processing something significant.

"You're certain," Dr. Hanson said. It wasn't a question exactly. More like a person who needs to hear something twice before they can fully receive it.

"I'm standing four miles from the site on a clear morning in March and the wilderness is exactly what it should be," Emma said. "The temperature dropped five degrees when I entered the contamination zone on Wednesday. It hasn't dropped since the ceremony completed last night. The perceptual effects are gone. The site registers differently. I can't explain that last part in any way that would satisfy a peer review committee but I know what contaminated feels like and this isn't it."

"The seventeen sequences," Dr. Hanson said. "The pronunciation held?"

"Every syllable. Your work made it possible. I want you to know that."

Another silence. "Emma. Do you understand what you've done? There's no documented case of a successful closing ceremony in any academic literature. The sites have been considered sealed by destruction or by natural deterioration for as long as anyone has been studying them. What you did last night is the first verified ceremonial sealing in the modern record."

"I need it documented," Emma said. "Whatever you can put on paper through academic channels. I'm sending you photographs, GPS coordinates, timeline. Not because I need validation. Because the Anti-Custodians have been arguing for thirty years that the sites can only be managed through destruction. I need there to be a record that says otherwise. A record that exists outside my personal documentation and outside anything the Safety Coalition can discredit."

"I can do that," Dr. Hanson said. "It'll take time. Peer review, institutional sign-off. But yes. I can document this."

"One more thing," Emma said. "The medicine. For the record, I used psilocybin mushrooms harvested from the site according to the protocols Robert Moore documented. The ceremonial dose. Not recreational. Not exploratory. The specific preparation described in the original documentation."

A pause. "I'll note that you followed the documented ceremonial protocol," Dr. Hanson said carefully.

"That's exactly right," Emma said. "I followed the documented ceremonial protocol."

She ended the call. Owen had come up beside her without her noticing, his pack adjusted, his notebook in hand.

"The academic record," he said.

"The Anti-Custodians have lawyers and shell companies and thirty years of institutional infrastructure," Emma said. "We need a paper trail that doesn't belong to us. Documentation that exists in the world independent of anything we control."

Owen wrote something in his notebook. "I'm putting that in the book."

"I assumed," Emma said.

They kept walking.

***

The terrain was different on the way out than it had been on the way in. Technically it was identical, the same rock faces and drainage crossings and elevation changes. But Emma was moving through it differently. On the hike in she'd been building toward something, focused forward, the ceremony ahead of her and the contamination zone pressing in around her and the weight of everything the site had accumulated over thirty years making the air heavy with wrongness.

Now the wrongness was gone and the air was just air and Emma was carrying something different than she'd carried in. Not lighter exactly. More settled. The way you carry something that has found its proper place rather than something you've been struggling to balance.

Rufus ranged ahead and returned, ranged and returned, the pattern she'd come to rely on. But his ranging had changed too. On the hike in he'd been taut with something, alert in the specific way of an animal tracking a threat. Now he moved through the wilderness with the easy attentiveness of a dog who is simply present in good country. Whatever he'd been holding against, it was gone.

At the eight-mile mark, where they stopped to eat and rest and check their bearing against Owen's topographic map, Emma photographed the creek drainage and the terrain and noted the GPS coordinates in her documentation file. Building the record. Creating the evidence that sealing was possible and that the Montana site was now stable.

She found herself thinking about Walsh.

Wherever he was, in a hospital in Kalispell probably, beginning the long work of processing what the site had shown him. Two months in that drainage with his shadow running loose and no framework for integration and no medicine calibrated for the closing ceremony and no one to tell him what he was experiencing was human rather than monstrous. He'd survived it through sheer survival instinct, the discipline of a man who knew wilderness and had used that knowledge to stay alive while everything else fell apart.

She hoped someone was with him. She hoped someone was telling him that what he'd seen in the circle was the truth about himself and not his identity. That there was a difference between capacity and destiny. That Mark Caldwell had made one choice and Emma Caldwell had made another and Walsh could make his own choice when he was ready.

She made a note to follow up with the Kalispell hospital when she got back to cellular range.

Owen was watching her from across the creek.

"Walsh," he said. Reading her the way he always read her, the occupational habit of a journalist who had been paying close attention to Emma Caldwell for three years.

"I want to make sure someone explains what happened to him," Emma said. "Not the contamination. The shadow. What he saw. He needs a framework for it."

"Dr. Hanson," Owen said.

"Yes." Emma put away her phone. "I'll ask her."

They ate. Rufus accepted trail mix from Emma's hand with the dignified gratitude of a dog who has earned his keep. The Montana afternoon moved through its light changes above the tree canopy, clear and cold and entirely ordinary.

Emma thought about ordinary.

She'd been chasing ordinary since her mother died. Some version of the life she'd had before the journals and the cipher and the trial, before the trafficking network and Baker's death, before the custodian revelation and Montana and the ceremony. Some version of being Emma Caldwell the data security analyst from Nashville who had a normal job and a normal apartment and called her mother on weekends.

That version was gone. Had been gone for a year. She understood now that it wasn't coming back and that this was alright. The life she had instead was harder and stranger and more dangerous and it was also the life that actually fit who she was. The life where the skills she'd spent her career building, pattern recognition, investigative methodology, the ability to hold large amounts of complex information and find the thread that connected them, turned out to be exactly the skills that the custodian work required.

She hadn't been preparing for a career in data security.

She'd been preparing for this.

The thought didn't arrive with any drama. Just settled in beside her on a rock in a Montana creek drainage while Rufus finished his trail mix and Owen wrote in his notebook. Settled in and stayed.

"Owen," Emma said.

He looked up.

"I'm glad you came."

Owen looked at her for a moment. "I know," he said. "I was always going to."

Emma nodded. She shouldered her pack and stood up.

"Eight miles," she said.

"Seven and a half," Owen said, checking the map.

"Seven and a half," Emma agreed.

They kept walking.

***

They reached the Expedition at the trailhead just after dawn Saturday morning, having camped one final night in the drainage below the ridge. Emma loaded her pack into the cargo area and stood for a moment in the cold morning air looking back at the wilderness. Somewhere in there, fifteen miles northeast, the ash circle sat sealed in its granite bowl. The cold was the cold of early morning in the mountains. Natural. Clean. Exactly what cold was supposed to be.

Rufus jumped into the back seat and settled immediately. He was done with Montana. His business here was complete.

Owen drove. Emma sat in the passenger seat and watched the wilderness give way to the Flathead Valley and then to Whitefish and then to the highway south toward Kalispell. The mountains receded in the side mirror. The landscape flattened. The world became road and farmland and the ordinary human geography of a place that people lived in and drove through and didn't think about too carefully.

She called the Flathead Valley Medical Center from the highway and asked about Timothy Walsh. A nurse told her he'd been admitted Thursday night, that he was stable and receiving psychiatric evaluation, and that the family had been notified. Emma identified herself as someone who had located him in the wilderness, gave her number, and asked that the attending physician call her when able.

Twenty minutes later her phone rang.

The doctor was careful and professional and had clearly been briefed that Walsh's situation was unusual. Emma told him what she'd told the paramedics. Psilocybin psychosis. Prolonged exposure without adequate preparation. The psychological fracture that resulted. She told him that Walsh had been remarkably functional given what he'd experienced, that his survival discipline had kept him alive when most people would have died, and that when he was ready to process what he'd seen she knew someone who could help him understand it.

She texted Dr. Hanson's number to the hospital.

Then she put her phone in her lap and watched Kalispell appear ahead through the windshield, the mountains behind them now, the valley opening up, the ordinary world reasserting itself in all its unremarkable necessary detail.

She was going home.

The flight from Kalispell to Indianapolis with a connection in Denver took six hours. Emma slept through most of it, genuinely and completely, the sleep of someone whose body has finally been given permission to rest. Rufus was a warm weight at her feet. Owen was across the aisle writing in his notebook with the focused attention of a journalist who has been carrying a story for days and is finally somewhere quiet enough to get it down.

Emma slept and dreamed of Carnegie Hall's bell tower visible through a kitchen window and the particular quality of Indiana light in late March and Sarah McClanahan's voice telling someone they needed to eat.

She woke over the flat middle of the country somewhere between Denver and Indianapolis and looked out the window at the darkness below and thought about the two custodian families out there somewhere, in places she didn't yet know, maintaining knowledge she'd almost lost, waiting for someone to make contact.

She was going to write them letters.

Actual letters, on paper, sent through the mail. It felt right. The digital world was fast and efficient and completely wrong for what needed to be communicated. You didn't introduce yourself as a fellow custodian of an ancient shamanic network via email. You wrote a letter. You took your time. You let the words carry the weight they needed to carry.

She would write them when she got home.

After she slept for approximately sixteen hours.

The plane descended into Indianapolis through a clear Saturday night and Emma watched the grid of lights below resolve into recognizable geography. The highway she'd driven to the airport five days ago. The suburbs. The city.

Somewhere south of all of it, too small and too dark to see from altitude, Moores Hill waited.

597 people. One historic building. A sealed chamber beneath Main Street.

And an ash circle in Indiana bedrock that had been waiting since before the town existed for a custodian who understood what it needed.

Emma understood what it needed.

She was almost home.

CHAPTER 19: SACRED MEDICINE

James was still at Carnegie Hall when Emma called Thursday night to tell him the site was sealed.

He'd been in the basement security office for the better part of eighteen hours by then, running on coffee and the particular focused energy that sustained him through things that mattered. The two arrested operatives were in Dearborn County lockup. Their lawyers had arrived by midnight and had begun the process of making noise about unlawful detention and excessive force and a half dozen other complaints that James recognized as the standard opening moves of people who understood the legal system as a tool rather than a constraint. Reeves had eight officers on rotating shifts at Carnegie Hall and had personally walked the building three times since the arrests.

The building was holding.

And then Emma's voice on the phone, thin and certain from a Montana wilderness, telling him it was done.

James sat in the basement for a long moment after the call ended. Around him Carnegie Hall held its century-old silence, the particular acoustic character of a building that had been standing since 1907 and had absorbed more history than any structure its size had any right to contain.

Twenty feet below his feet, an ash circle sat sealed in its bedrock. Had sat sealed since Robert Moore put it there in 1907 out of fear and guilt. Would sit sealed now with something better than fear beneath it.

James thought about Emma standing in that circle in Montana wilderness, speaking ancient words she'd learned from a linguistics professor in Oxford, Ohio, facing whatever the medicine showed her and choosing. Making the choice Mark Caldwell had not been able to make.

He thought about the town outside these walls. 597 people who had spent three years asking themselves how they could have trusted Mark Caldwell so completely. How they could have eaten at his table and bought cars from his dealership and watched him sit in the church pew and never seen it. The question that had been eating at Moores Hill since the verdict, the question that had no good answer in any version of the story where Mark was simply a monster the town had failed to recognize.

But in the version where Mark was a good man who found something he wasn't prepared for and lost a ten-year private war against what it showed him, the town had done nothing wrong. The town had known him correctly. The monster wasn't the man they'd trusted. The monster was what the man became after Montana.

Emma had faced the same thing Montana had given Mark and come back herself. That mattered in ways James was still working out. It mattered for the town and it mattered for the series of events that had brought them all to this week and it mattered for whatever came next.

He made fresh coffee. Settled in for the rest of the night.

***

Friday morning arrived gray and cold with three inches of new snow on Main Street that nobody had predicted.

James stood at Carnegie Hall's front entrance and watched Moores Hill wake up to the snow with the resigned practicality of a small town that had been dealing with Indiana weather for a hundred and fifty years. Trucks with plows attached working the main roads. Sarah McClanahan's diner lights on earlier than usual, warm yellow rectangles against the white street. The particular quality of a small town morning after something significant has happened, the awareness moving through the community before most people had consciously processed what they were aware of.

Carnegie Hall had survived. The vote had held. Two people had been arrested trying to break through its walls. The full story was still assembling itself in the community's understanding but the essential fact was present: the building was still there and the people who'd tried to take it down had failed.

Reeves arrived at eight with a fresh unit rotation and a folder of paperwork that James recognized as the formal documentation of the previous night's events. He went through it with James over coffee in the historical society kitchen, the same kitchen where Margaret kept supplies for exactly this kind of occasion.

"The DA is reviewing the arrest footage," Reeves said. "Breaking and entering. Criminal trespass. Destruction of property. Assault on a police officer from Thursday's trunk incident." He looked at James over his coffee. "That last one is the one they're going to feel. My officers were unlawfully restrained and locked in the trunks of their own vehicles. That doesn't go away with good lawyers."

"What about Werner?" James asked.

Reeves's expression shifted slightly. "Werner filed three appeals by nine AM. County level. The first one challenges the vote on procedural grounds. The second challenges the admissibility of your security footage. The third is an emergency injunction request based on public safety grounds." A pause. "His clients are in lockup but Werner himself is operating like nothing happened. Like Thursday night was a setback, not a defeat."

James had known Werner would come at it from every available angle. It was what a professional did when the direct approach failed. What interested James more was what Werner would do when he ran out of angles.

He spent the morning at his laptop, sending documentation to the council members who'd voted against condemnation. Building the record. Making sure every piece of evidence from every camera on every night of the twelve-day campaign was organized and accessible. If Werner was filing appeals, James was building the case that would defeat them.

Margaret arrived at ten and walked the building with the expression of someone confirming that something they'd feared losing was still there. She ran her hand along the hallway wall the way people touch things that have been threatened. Dorothy Webb came in mid-morning with a plate of something she'd baked and the particular satisfied energy of a woman who had spoken her piece in front of a town council and had been heard.

"My grandmother's grandmother would be pleased," Dorothy said.

"She would," James said.

"Are they really going to keep fighting?" Dorothy asked.

"Werner will file appeals," James said. "It'll take months to work through the system. But the evidence is public now. The arrests are recorded. Their credibility is badly damaged." He paused. "They're not done. But they're not going to win this."

Dorothy nodded. She looked at the hallway, at the photographs of Moores Hill's history that lined the walls, at the particular way afternoon light came through the windows and fell across the wooden floors that had been there since 1907.

"Then we'll keep watching," she said. "That's what this town does. We keep watch over what matters."

James thought that was exactly right.

***

Werner found him Saturday afternoon.

Not at Carnegie Hall. James was at Sarah's diner, eating a late lunch he'd been putting off since morning, sitting in a corner booth with his laptop and a plate of whatever Sarah had put in front of him because she'd decided he wasn't eating enough and had taken matters into her own hands.

Werner came through the door at two-seventeen, alone, without the briefcase and without the other lawyers and without the professional armor of the hearing room. He was wearing a jacket and slacks instead of his courtroom suit. He looked like a man who had decided to have a conversation rather than a confrontation.

He looked at James across the diner. James looked back.

Werner walked over.

"May I?" He indicated the seat across from James.

James closed his laptop. "Sit down."

Werner sat. Sarah appeared from behind the counter with the automatic hospitality of a woman who had been running a diner in a small town for twenty years and fed everyone who came through the door regardless of her opinion of them. She put coffee in front of Werner without being asked and went back to the counter without comment.

Werner looked at the coffee. Then at James.

"I'm not here about the appeals," he said.

"Then why are you here?"

"Because I want you to understand something before I leave." He said it simply, without the professional gloss of the courtroom. "We're not going to stop. The appeals will run their course and we'll lose most of them and Carnegie Hall will stand. I know that. Our legal position is damaged. Our operational capacity in this region is effectively finished. Two of our people are facing serious charges." A pause. "But the organization will continue. In other places. With other sites."

"I know," James said.

"Then I want you to understand why." Werner wrapped his hands around the coffee cup. "I've been doing this work for eleven years. Before me, others did it for twenty years. Before them, Aldridge did it for thirty years starting in 1990. In that time we have documented thirty-one incidents at seven sites where individuals accessed ceremonial spaces without preparation. Twenty-two deaths. Nine psychological breaks of varying severity." He looked at James directly. "We are not the villains of this story, Mr. McClanahan. We are people who looked at what these sites do to unprepared human beings and decided that destruction was more merciful than preservation."

"You were wrong," James said.

"Were we?" Werner's voice was not combative. He genuinely appeared to be asking. "Your colleague sealed Montana. One site. With days of preparation instead of the months the ceremony requires, a linguistics professor she found by cold calling academic databases, medicine harvested from the site itself, and the specific bloodline connection that the ceremony requires." He paused. "She succeeded because of who she is and what she carries in her blood and because she was willing to walk into a site that had killed nine people with inadequate preparation and say yes to what it showed her. How many people on this planet can do that? How many will ever be able to do that? The knowledge was nearly gone. It nearly died with Robert Moore in 1907. It nearly died again when your colleague's mother died. If Emma Caldwell had died in Montana, or had made a different choice in that circle, the knowledge would be effectively gone again." He looked at the table. "We don't destroy sites because we want to. We destroy them because we've watched them kill people for thirty years and we don't believe the knowledge can be reliably maintained."

"Emma maintained it," James said.

"Emma is exceptional," Werner said. "And exceptional people are not a preservation strategy." He was quiet for a moment. "Mark Caldwell was not exceptional. He was a decent man who made one catastrophic mistake and spent the rest of his life becoming its consequences. He's not unusual. He's the rule. Exceptional people like your colleague are the exception."

James thought about that. About Emma standing in the Montana clearing with the medicine and seventeen ceremony sequences and the full weight of custodian preparation. About how close it had all come to not happening. If Linda Caldwell hadn't hidden the journals. If Emma hadn't decoded the cipher. If Dr. Hanson hadn't been able to translate the sequences. Any one of those links failing and the knowledge died.

Werner was not wrong about the fragility of it.

He was wrong about what that meant.

"The answer to fragile knowledge isn't destruction," James said. "It's transmission. It's finding the custodian families. It's rebuilding the network. It's making sure the knowledge doesn't depend on one exceptional person in one exceptional family."

"That's the theory," Werner said. "The practice is thirty-one incidents and twenty-two deaths."

"The practice before Emma," James said. "The practice when the knowledge was nearly gone and sites were activating without anyone knowing how to close them. That's not the practice going forward."

Werner looked at him for a long moment. Something in his expression shifted, not concession exactly, but the particular quality of a man who is genuinely considering a position he'd dismissed.

"Maybe," he said. "We'll see." He stood up. "Tell your colleague she made the right choice in that circle. Whatever she saw. Whatever it showed her. She made the right choice." He paused. "Mark Caldwell made the wrong choice. That's why we exist. To prevent more Marks. But if the custodian network can actually be rebuilt. If the knowledge can actually be maintained reliably." He didn't finish the sentence. Just picked up his coffee cup, drank the last of it, and set it back down.

"If that becomes true," he said finally, "then we were wrong. I'll accept that when I see it."

He put money on the table for the coffee. More than it cost. Then he walked out of Sarah's diner and James watched him go through the window, down the Main Street sidewalk, past the Carnegie Hall bell tower visible above the roofline, and out of sight.

James sat with his cold lunch and his open laptop and the particular quiet of a Saturday afternoon in Moores Hill after something large had finished happening.

His phone buzzed. A text from Reeves: Werner checked out of his Cincinnati hotel this morning. Rental car returned at Columbus airport. No forwarding information. Just gone.

James put his phone down.

He thought about what Werner had said. About thirty-one incidents and twenty-two deaths. About the fragility of the knowledge and the rarity of people like Emma and the genuine difficulty of Werner's position, a man who had spent eleven years trying to prevent harm and had ended up causing a different kind of harm instead.

Not a villain. A man who had looked at a real problem and chosen the wrong solution with genuine conviction.

James didn't forgive him for what the organization had done. For the four sites destroyed and the families of custodians who would never recover their lost knowledge and the coordinated criminal campaign against Carnegie Hall and the officers Daniels and Kowalski locked in their own trunks on Main Street.

But he understood him now in a way he hadn't before.

And understanding was not the same as forgiving and it was not the same as forgetting and it was not the same as stopping.

James reopened his laptop. He had appeals to prepare for. Evidence to organize. A case to build that would survive Werner's lawyers for as long as they kept filing.

Carnegie Hall needed to be defended not just for the next few months but for the years and decades ahead. The Safety Coalition might be damaged but Werner had been right about one thing. They were not finished.

Neither was James.

Sarah appeared at his elbow and took his cold plate away and brought him something hot without asking what he wanted, which was how Sarah operated and had always operated and James had stopped fighting it years ago.

"You look like someone who needs feeding," she said.

"I'm fine," James said.

"You look like someone who's been awake for thirty-six hours and is running on coffee and stubbornness," Sarah said. "Same thing you look like after every investigation. Eat."

James ate.

Outside, Carnegie Hall stood on Main Street in the March snow, red brick and white trim and bell tower rising above the roofline exactly as it had risen above the roofline since 1907. Protected. Sealed. Safe.

For now.

James intended to make for now into a very long time.

He ate Sarah McClanahan's food and worked on his laptop and waited for Emma to come home.

CHAPTER 20: WHAT WAS BROKEN

Emma came home to lights on.

She turned onto Oak Street at nine-fifteen Saturday evening, Rufus in the passenger seat, Owen's rental following her through town. The farmhouse windows were lit from inside, warm yellow against the cold March dark, and there was a car she recognized as James's parked at the curb and another she recognized as Sarah McClanahan's pickup in the driveway.

Emma sat in the parked car for a moment with the engine running, looking at the lit windows, and felt something release in her chest that she hadn't fully known was still held.

Home.

She got out. Rufus jumped out and went directly to the front porch as if he'd always known this was where he was supposed to be, which Emma had come to believe he probably had. Owen parked behind her and climbed out with his pack and his notebook and said nothing, just fell into step behind her, which was the right thing.

James opened the front door before she reached it.

He looked at her the way he'd been looking at her since her mother died, with the careful attention of someone who was always checking whether she was okay and never quite saying so directly. He looked at Montana in her face and whatever he saw there settled something in his own expression.

"Hey," he said.

"Hey," Emma said.

She walked past him into the house and into the smell of Sarah McClanahan's cooking, which was one of the reliable constants of the universe and which Emma had apparently needed without knowing she needed it. Sarah was at the stove in Emma's kitchen with the complete authority of a woman who understood that the way to help someone who has been through something significant is to feed them while they process it.

"Sit down," Sarah said, without turning around. "Both of you. Owen too."

They sat.

The kitchen table had been cleared of everything except the things that belonged there, a far cry from the journals and laptops and evidence folders it had been supporting for the past two weeks. There was food in various stages of completion on the counter. There were four mismatched coffee mugs that Sarah had apparently found in Emma's cabinets and deployed without asking. There was the particular quality of warmth that a kitchen takes on when someone who knows what they're doing has been cooking in it for a few hours.

Rufus went under the table and settled at Emma's feet with the certainty of a dog who has decided where he belongs.

James sat across from Emma. Owen beside her. Sarah moving between counter and stove with the unhurried efficiency of someone who has done this many times and understands that the food and the presence are doing their work without needing to be supplemented by conversation.

Emma looked at the kitchen window.

Carnegie Hall's bell tower was visible above the neighbor's roofline, lit against the dark sky, exactly where it had always been. The same view she'd had from this window for the two weeks before Montana. The same view her mother had had from this window for thirty-five years of protecting a building she'd known mattered without knowing why.

Emma knew why now.

"Werner is gone," James said. It wasn't a question. He'd seen her face.

"Good," Emma said.

"He came to see me. Yesterday. At the diner."

Emma looked at him. "What did he say?"

James told her. All of it. The thirty-one incidents and twenty-two deaths and Werner's genuine belief that destruction was more merciful than preservation. The acknowledgment that if the network could actually be rebuilt he'd been wrong. The way he'd walked out and disappeared.

Emma listened without interrupting. When James finished she was quiet for a moment.

"He's not wrong about the fragility," she said. "The knowledge was almost gone. If my mother had hidden those journals somewhere else. If Charlotte's Web hadn't been on my childhood bookshelf. If Dr. Hanson hadn't been able to translate the sequences." She paused. "A lot of things had to go right."

"They did go right," James said.

"This time," Emma said. "Werner's point is that relying on exceptional circumstances isn't a strategy." She looked at the window again. "He's right about that. Which means my job isn't just to be the custodian. It's to make sure the knowledge doesn't rest on one person ever again."

Sarah set plates in front of all three of them without ceremony and sat down at the fourth chair, which Emma understood as Sarah's particular way of saying she was part of this conversation whether anyone had asked her or not.

"The two families," Owen said. "The ones you felt in the circle."

"I'm going to write them letters," Emma said. "This week. Introduce myself. Tell them what happened in Montana. Ask them what they know that I don't." She looked at her plate. The food was excellent and she was hungrier than she'd realized. "There's a lot I don't know. I sealed one site with seventeen ceremony sequences that I learned in a professor's office. The families who have maintained their knowledge for generations know things I haven't even thought to ask about yet."

"They felt the Montana sealing," Owen said. "They acknowledged it. They know you exist."

"They know someone exists," Emma said. "They don't know it's me. They don't know the American lineage almost died entirely. They don't know any of it." She ate for a moment. "The letters need to be careful. I don't know who else might be watching those families. The Safety Coalition has been monitoring the sites for thirty years. They know who the active custodians are."

James was already nodding. "We approach it like an investigation. Careful. Methodical. No direct digital contact initially."

"Letters," Emma said. "On paper. The slow way."

Sarah had been listening to this with the expression she used when she was absorbing information she didn't fully understand but was filing carefully for later. She looked at Emma.

"Are you okay?" she said. Not the polite version of the question. The Sarah McClanahan version, which meant... tell me the truth.

Emma looked at her.

Sarah McClanahan had known Emma since Emma was a child. Had been one of Linda Caldwell's closest friends. Had sat across this same table from Emma the week Linda died and brought food and told her she needed to eat and hadn't asked any questions Emma wasn't ready to answer. Had lost her own cousin Sarah Bennett to Mark Caldwell twenty years before Emma knew what Mark was.

"I'm okay," Emma said. "Really."

Sarah studied her face the way only someone who had been watching you for thirty-two years could study a face. Then she nodded. "Good," she said. "Because you look like yourself again. You didn't look like yourself when you left."

Emma thought about that. About what looking like yourself meant after you'd stood in an ash circle in Montana and faced the full range of what you were capable of and said yes to all of it and come back.

Maybe that was it exactly. She looked like herself again because she finally was herself. Completely. The shadow integrated rather than severed. The full range acknowledged rather than partitioned. Not a better version or a worse version. Just the complete one.

"I'll take that," Emma said.

They ate. The four of them around the kitchen table in the house where Emma had grown up and where her mother had hidden sixteen journals in the attic and where the investigation into Mark Caldwell had begun and where Emma had decoded the Charlotte's Web cipher at two in the morning and where Clue-Minati Investigations had first taken shape over coffee and evidence boards. The house that was hers now.

Owen talked about the book he was going to write. Not the timeline or the structure, just the fact of it, the way he talked about things when they were real enough to name but not yet ready to be examined too closely. James talked about the appeals Werner had filed and the legal strategy he was building to defeat them. Sarah talked about nothing in particular, which was how Sarah maintained a conversation she wanted to be part of without forcing the subject, a skill Emma had watched her deploy her entire life.

Rufus slept under the table.

It was, Emma thought, exactly what coming home was supposed to feel like.

***

They stayed until nearly midnight. Sarah cleaned up with the thoroughness of someone who considers leaving a kitchen in any state other than perfect a personal failure. James went through the Carnegie Hall documentation with Emma for an hour, making sure she was current on everything that had happened while she was in Montana. Owen sat at the table with his notebook until Sarah told him he was keeping people up and he closed it.

When they were gone Emma sat alone at the kitchen table with the house quiet around her.

Rufus had moved from under the table to beside her chair, pressed against her leg, his breathing slow and even. Not asleep. Just present.

Emma opened Robert Moore's journal to the last entry. The one dated 1907, the year he'd built Carnegie Hall over the sealed site, the final piece of his documented reckoning with what he'd found and what he'd done with it.

She'd read this entry dozens of times. It had different weight now.

Robert Moore had stood in the Indiana bedrock beneath this very building and seen exactly what Emma had seen in Montana. The same shadow. The same human truth. And he hadn't been able to say yes to it. Had sealed the site out of the fear that acknowledgment produced in him, the fear that the shadow he'd seen was who he really was rather than what he was capable of.

He'd spent the rest of his life in that mistake. Had built a building over the site as if concrete and stone could hold down what he'd seen. Had written journals documenting everything and then locked the knowledge away and let the transmission die.

Emma felt for him in a way she hadn't before Montana. She understood now what it cost to stand in that circle unprepared and alone, without medicine calibrated to the ceremony, without any framework for what the experience was designed to do. Robert Moore hadn't had any of those things. He'd stood in bedrock in Indiana in 1907 and looked at the full truth of himself with no preparation and no guidance and had done the only thing available to him, which was to run from it as elegantly as he could.

He'd run for the rest of his life.

She placed the journal carefully on the table. Then she got her pen and her own notebook and she wrote.

Not the ceremony sequences. Not documentation. A letter. The first of what she understood would be many.

To whoever is currently maintaining the knowledge at your site. My name is Emma Caldwell. I am the custodian of the Carnegie Hall site in Moores Hill, Indiana. Three weeks ago I performed a successful closing ceremony at the Montana site, which had been contaminated since 1993. I felt your acknowledgment through the network when the ceremony completed.

I am writing because I believe we need to know each other.

She wrote for an hour. Carefully, taking her time, letting the words carry what they needed to carry. When she finished she read it through twice and made two small corrections and folded it and set it aside.

Tomorrow she would find addresses. Figure out how to reach people whose locations she knew only as dimensional presences in an ash circle in Montana. Build the bridge between the custodian she was now and the network she was part of.

Tonight she went upstairs and opened her bedroom window an inch the way she always did regardless of temperature and lay down on her childhood bed in the room with the posters on the walls and Charlotte's Web on the shelf and the quilt her grandmother had made, and she slept.

Below the window, Carnegie Hall's bell tower was visible against the night sky.

Below the tower, twenty feet into the bedrock of Main Street, an ash circle waited.

Protected. Sealed. Exactly as it should be.

Rufus lay across the bedroom doorway in the way he'd apparently decided was his permanent position, guardian of thresholds, and Emma fell asleep to the sound of the town settling into its Saturday night silence.

She was home.

She was the custodian.

Both of those things were true at the same time and would be true for the rest of her life.

That was enough.

CHAPTER 21: KEEP IT SEALED

The week after Montana had a different quality than any week Emma could remember.

Not quieter exactly. The Werner appeals were moving through the county system and James was filing counter-documentation daily and Reeves was coordinating with the DA's office on the criminal charges against the two arrested operatives and the ordinary machinery of legal consequence was grinding forward with the particular slowness of legal machinery everywhere. Clue-Minati had three pending inquiries that had accumulated while Emma was in Montana, two of which were straightforward enough to address remotely and one of which was going to require actual investigation. Owen was in Indianapolis working on the book proposal, calling Emma every other day with questions about sequence and tone. Dr. Hanson sent a preliminary framework document for the academic paper on Monday, fourteen pages of careful scholarly language that Emma read twice and found both accurate and completely insufficient for what had actually happened.

Life had not stopped happening while Emma was in Montana. It had just been waiting.

But the quality of the week was different. The weight that had been present since her mother died, the accumulated pressure of investigation and threat and the knowledge of what lay beneath Carnegie Hall and what was happening in Montana, that weight was gone. Not replaced by lightness. Replaced by something more useful than lightness. Clarity. The particular state of a person who has finished something significant and is now simply present in their life without the interference of the thing they were building toward.

Emma worked. She returned phone calls. She ate regular meals for the first time in two weeks. She slept eight hours a night in her childhood bedroom with Rufus across the doorway and woke without the ceremony sequences running automatically through her mind, which was how she knew the urgency had genuinely passed.

On Wednesday she drove to Carnegie Hall.

Margaret was in her office when Emma arrived, reviewing tour schedules with the focused energy of a woman who had been managing a crisis for two weeks and was now redirecting that energy into the work she'd been doing for twenty years. She looked up when Emma appeared in the doorway and her expression did something complicated that resolved into relief.

"You look good," Margaret said.

"I feel good," Emma said.

"The board wants to thank you. Formally. We were going to wait until you'd rested but Dorothy Webb has been calling me every day asking when she can see you."

"Tell Dorothy I'll come to the next board meeting," Emma said. "Tell her I'll bring something from the diner."

Margaret smiled. "She'll appreciate that." She paused. "Emma. What you did. James told us the building is safe now. Really safe. Not just from the Safety Coalition but from whatever was under it."

"The site was contaminated," Emma said carefully. "That contamination is gone now. The site is sealed correctly. Carnegie Hall is built over something very old and very significant and it needs to stay standing." She met Margaret's eyes directly. "That's what my family has been protecting for a hundred and eighteen years. I understand that now. And I intend to keep doing it."

Margaret looked at her for a long moment. "Your mother would be proud," she said.

Emma heard that differently than she had before Montana. Before, the statement had carried the ache of something lost. Now it carried something more complete. Her mother had spent twenty years protecting this building while documenting a killer, had died for both of those missions, had passed the knowledge forward through sixteen journals hidden in an attic under a loose floorboard. Linda Caldwell had been a custodian without knowing the word for what she was.

"Yes," Emma said. "She would."

She went downstairs.

James was in the basement security office, where Emma had come to understand he spent more time than he spent anywhere else these days, running on the particular fuel of someone who has found the work that actually fits who they are. He looked up when Emma appeared and something in his expression settled.

"I need to go into the chamber," Emma said.

"I know," James said.

He disabled the security at the false wall release mechanism and they went through together, down the tunnel, into the carved stone passage that twenty feet below Main Street opened into the chamber Robert Moore had sealed in 1907. James carried a flashlight. Emma carried Robert Moore's journal and a pen.

The chamber was exactly as they'd left it. The carvings. The symbols around the perimeter. The ash circle carved into the bedrock, the same ancient language as Montana, the same precision, the same intention, waiting.

Emma stood at the chamber's edge and looked at the circle.

She'd been here before. Had stood in this chamber and felt the pull and understood that what lay beneath Carnegie Hall was the same thing that lay beneath the Montana wilderness. But she hadn't been ready then. Had needed Montana first. Had needed to face the shadow and say yes to it and perform the closing ceremony and come back intact before she could stand here with the full understanding of what this site was and what it required.

She was ready now.

She didn't perform a ceremony. The Carnegie Hall site was sealed, had been sealed since 1907, was not contaminated and did not need closing. What it needed was acknowledged. Witnessed. Confirmed by the custodian who had taken responsibility for it.

Emma walked the perimeter of the chamber slowly, the way she'd walked the Montana circle before the ceremony. Noting the carvings. Reading the symbols that Dr. Hanson had translated, the proto-Indo-European ceremonial language that had been carved here by people who understood that this ground was sacred and that sacred ground required marking and protecting and maintaining.

She stopped at the northern anchor point.

Crouched down.

The bedrock was cold under her fingertips. Ancient and patient and completely indifferent in the way that stone is indifferent, holding its carvings for centuries and millennia without any need for recognition.

On the northern wall of the chamber, in the original stonework, she could see Robert Moore's inscription. Small. Careful. The handwriting of a man who had been a geologist and a builder and a custodian who had not known he was a custodian until he found this chamber.

R.M. 1907.

That was all. Just his initials and the year. The minimal acknowledgment of someone who had sealed something here and couldn't fully explain why but had understood that the act needed to be marked.

Emma looked at it for a long time.

Then she opened her pen and found the clear stone surface beside Robert Moore's inscription and added her own.

E.C. 2026.

Not claiming ownership. Acknowledging continuity. The line that ran from Robert Moore through Margaret Moore Hendricks through Sarah Hendricks Ashcraft through Linda Caldwell to Emma, each generation protecting what they could understand of what they'd been given, arriving at this moment where someone finally understood all of it.

She capped her pen and stood up.

James was watching from the chamber entrance. He'd stayed back, giving her the space. He looked at the inscription and then at Emma and nodded once.

They went back up through the tunnel, through the false wall, into the basement of Carnegie Hall, into the building's ordinary life above.

***

The Ashcraft families were on her mind.

She'd been thinking about them since the ceremony, since the moment in the fifteenth sequence when she'd understood that the Ashcraft name in Moores Hill wasn't coincidence. The stonemason lineage. Ash-Craft. The families who had carved and maintained the ash circle markers for generations before colonization broke the knowledge transmission. Who had kept the name and lost the mission.

Mayor Patricia Ashcraft had voted against the condemnation. Had said in my town with a particular quality that Emma now heard differently.

She didn't approach this directly. She was careful, the way she was careful about everything that touched the sites. But she began, in the week after Montana, to research the Ashcraft families in Moores Hill. Not through official channels. Through conversation. Through the historical society's records that Margaret was happy to share. Through the kind of slow patient genealogical work that Owen had taught her by example across two investigations.

What she found was consistent with what she'd understood from the ceremony. The Ashcraft families in Moores Hill went back to the earliest settlement records. They'd been here before the town was named, before the postal service made its famous error, before Carnegie money built the Hall on Main Street. They'd been here when the ash circle was still in use, when the knowledge was still alive in the community, when the ground beneath what would become Carnegie Hall was understood to be significant ground.

The knowledge had broken. The name had survived. The families were still here.

Emma wrote that down in her custodian notebook and set it aside. This was a thread for later. For when the immediate work was done and the letters to the international families had been answered and the network was beginning to take shape. The Ashcraft thread was going to matter. She was certain of it.

She was glad she knew it was there.

On Friday she received the first response to one of her letters.

She hadn't been able to write to them directly. She didn't have addresses. She had dimensional coordinates from the ceremony and Robert Moore's documentation of the seven sites and the investigative instincts of someone who had spent two years learning how to find things that didn't want to be found. She'd done what a data security analyst does when direct contact isn't possible. She'd left a signal in a place where the right people would find it. A post on an academic forum dedicated to indigenous ceremonial practices, worded with enough specificity that anyone maintaining active knowledge of the sites would recognize it immediately and anyone else would dismiss it as scholarly speculation. She'd identified herself only as the American custodian and described the Montana sealing in terms precise enough to be verifiable.

They had found her.

The response came by email, which surprised her, from an address she didn't recognize, a single line.

We felt Montana. We have been waiting for this contact. When can we speak?

Emma read it three times. Then she called James.

"One of the families responded," she said.

A brief silence. "Which one?"

"I don't know yet. The email doesn't identify location. But the language is right. They felt the Montana sealing. They've been waiting." She paused. "James. They've been waiting. While we were trying to figure out what the sites were, while the Safety Coalition was destroying them, while the knowledge was dying in the American lineage, these families were just. Waiting. Maintaining their sites. Hoping someone would make contact."

"How long?" James said.

Emma thought about the dimensional network. About the two presences she'd felt during the ceremony, the quality of attention they'd given to what was happening in Montana. The particular patience of it. Not urgent. Not desperate. Just present and attending and waiting.

"A long time," she said.

She replied to the email that afternoon with the careful deliberateness she'd brought to the original letters. Identifying herself. Naming the site she was responsible for. Describing the Montana ceremony briefly, the contamination that had been there and was gone, the sealing that had worked. Asking who they were and where and what they knew.

The reply came within the hour.

Our name is not important yet. What is important is that you sealed a contaminated site alone, with partial knowledge, using medicine and a ceremony you learned from documents rather than transmission. That you succeeded is remarkable. That you came back intact is more remarkable. We would like to understand how.

Emma sat with that for a long time.

She'd been thinking of herself as the one who needed to learn. As the American lineage that had nearly died and was recovering. As the custodian who was reaching out to more established families to fill the gaps in her knowledge.

And here was one of those families telling her that what she'd done in Montana was remarkable. That they wanted to understand how she'd managed it.

She thought about what she had that they might not. The documents Robert Moore had left. The linguistics expertise Dr. Hanson had brought. The data security background that had given her the analytical framework to hold multiple complex systems in her head simultaneously. The investigation experience that had taught her to work with incomplete information and follow threads to their conclusions.

And the ceremony itself. Performed without transmission, without elder guidance, without the generational chain of knowledge that the other families had maintained. Performed using documents and translation and the particular stubbornness of someone who had decided the work was going to get done regardless of what she had to work with.

Maybe that was worth something. Maybe partial knowledge approached with the right methodology produced something that continuous transmission didn't, some quality of having had to reconstruct the understanding from its foundations rather than inheriting it whole.

She wrote back.

I sealed it because the alternative was unacceptable. Nine people had died and one was barely surviving and the contamination was spreading. I had seventeen sequences, a linguist's pronunciation guide, and medicine harvested according to the documented protocol. I had preparation but not transmission. I had knowledge but not lineage. And I stood in the circle and it was enough.

She paused. Then added:

I would like to understand how you've maintained yours. I think we have things to teach each other.

She sent it and closed her laptop and sat at the kitchen table in the house where her mother had kept sixteen journals in the attic and her grandmother had passed the custodian responsibility forward without knowing its full name and Emma had decoded a cipher at two in the morning and changed everything.

Outside the window, Carnegie Hall's bell tower stood against the afternoon sky.

Rufus put his head on her knee.

Emma put her hand on his head.

"We're just getting started," she said.

His tail wagged once. Agreement, or something close enough to it.

Emma opened her custodian notebook to a fresh page and began to write.

The knowledge was alive. The network was waking. The transmission had resumed after a hundred and eighteen years of silence.

She had work to do.

EPILOGUE

Three Months Later

The Montana site had been quiet since March.

Emma checked it weekly, not from any technical necessity but from the habit of someone who understood that the work of a custodian was ongoing rather than episodic. She had access to the Forest Service incident reports through Reeves's contacts. She tracked the missing persons databases that covered the Flathead National Forest region. She maintained a correspondence with the Flathead Valley Medical Center about Timothy Walsh, who had been discharged in April and was living with his family in Kalispell and was, by the doctor's careful assessment, making progress.

No new disappearances in the sector. No temperature anomalies reported by the Forest Service field teams who had resumed operations in the area after the advisories were lifted in late April. The wilderness was what it should be.

The Carnegie Hall site was quiet in the way it had been quiet since 1907. The chamber undisturbed. The ash circle sealed. The Werner appeals working through the county system with the grinding patience of legal processes that everyone involved understood would ultimately resolve in Carnegie Hall's favor. The Safety Coalition's operational capacity in the region had not recovered. Their two arrested operatives had pled to reduced charges in exchange for cooperation. Their cooperation had not yet produced anything actionable regarding the organization's larger structure but Reeves was patient and the DA was interested and James documented everything.

The network was waking.

Emma had been corresponding with two custodian families for three months. She had not yet learned their locations, which they maintained with a careful privacy she respected and understood. What she had learned was significant. Their knowledge was deeper than hers and more direct, passed through generations of transmission rather than reconstructed from documents, but her methodology was something they found genuinely useful, the way of approaching the sites with analytical rigor, of building documentation, of creating the academic record that existed outside any single family's custody. Three months of correspondence had produced more mutual understanding than Emma had expected and less than she needed. That was the nature of it. The work was slow and careful and built on trust that accumulated over time rather than arriving all at once.

The Ashcraft thread was moving. Emma had had three conversations with Mayor Patricia Ashcraft since March, none of which had touched on ash circles or ceremonial sites directly, but all of which had moved incrementally toward the conversation Emma believed was coming. Patricia Ashcraft was a careful woman who had been carrying something for a long time and was deciding whether Emma was the right person to show it to.

Emma was willing to wait.

Owen's book was taking shape. He called on Tuesdays with specific questions about sequence and told her on a Thursday in May that he'd found a publisher interested in the proposal, a significant independent press that had done well with narrative nonfiction about indigenous knowledge systems. He didn't tell Emma what he'd said in the proposal about the mushrooms and Emma didn't ask. She trusted him. The outer space thing was probably in there. She'd made her peace with that.

James ran Clue-Minati with the focused intensity of someone who had found the work that fit him and intended to keep doing it for a long time. Three investigations in the three months since Montana, none of them involving ash circles or ancient ceremonies or the Safety Coalition, all of them the ordinary difficult work of finding things that people needed found. He came to Carnegie Hall three times a week to check the security systems and walk the building and sit in the basement security office for an hour being the person who was watching.

Sarah McClanahan served food to everyone who came through the diner door and knew everything that happened in Moores Hill before it officially happened and was the most reliable source of ground-level community intelligence Emma had ever encountered and had never charged anyone for any of it.

Rufus was permanent. That had been settled without discussion. He was simply there, across the doorway at night and at Emma's feet during the day and beside her in the car and present at Clue-Minati in a supervisory capacity that James had stopped commenting on. Whatever he was, whatever had sent him, he had not left and Emma had stopped expecting him to.

It was a Tuesday in June when Emma found it.

She was running the missing persons cross-reference that she'd been running weekly since Montana, the search that looked for clustering patterns in disappearances near the seven site coordinates. It was the same search Owen had been running when he found Walsh's beacon, now refined and systematized and set to alert her to any pattern that fit the contamination profile.

The search came back clean, as it had every week since March.

But something else came back with it.

A ghost pattern in the database metadata. Not a result. A trace. The kind of digital artifact left behind when someone has run a very similar search before you, using slightly different parameters, through a different access point, and the database has cached a fragment of the query structure without fully purging it.

Emma almost dismissed it. Database artifacts were common and usually meaningless.

But she was a data security analyst. Had been a data security analyst for a decade before Clue-Minati. She knew what ghost patterns looked like and she knew when one was worth following.

She followed it.

It took her four hours and three different analytical approaches and two phone calls to Owen, who had kept his database access current in a way that Emma appreciated without commenting on. What she found at the end of four hours was a search pattern. Someone else had been running missing persons cross-references keyed to the seven site coordinates. Not the same search. Slightly different parameters, a different geographic radius, a different weighting for the clustering algorithm. But the same essential question: where are people disappearing near these specific locations.

The pattern was not new.

Emma traced it back as far as the databases allowed, through archived queries and cached fragments and the digital archaeology of fifteen years of database infrastructure. The earliest trace she could find was from 2003.

She sat with that for a long time.

2003.

The year Mark Caldwell killed his first victim.

The year after he'd written in his February journal entry that he'd been fighting for ten years and understood now that he wasn't going to win.

Someone had been running searches keyed to the seven sites since 2003. Not the Safety Coalition. She'd seen their methodology in the laptop Owen had accessed in Carnegie Hall's basement, and this wasn't it. Different approach. Different tools. Different questions being asked.

Someone who had known about the seven sites since at least 2003 and had been quietly monitoring them ever since.

Emma pulled up everything she could find about the search pattern's access points. The traces were deliberately obscured, the kind of careful digital hygiene that someone with serious technical capability had applied systematically over fifteen years. Not perfect. Nothing was perfect. But good enough that she couldn't identify who was running the searches, only that they were being run, and had been run consistently, for two decades.

She thought about Werner's last words to her, relayed through James. Tell her she made the right choice. The sites can't be safely managed. They can only be destroyed.

She thought about the response from the custodian family. That you came back intact is more remarkable. We would like to understand how.

She thought about the network. Five out of seven. Two sites destroyed. Four families maintaining their knowledge in silence and privacy, waiting.

She thought about who would have known about all seven sites since 2003. Who would have had the technical capability to run these searches undetected for two decades. Who would have had a reason to monitor the sites quietly without ever taking any action that showed up in any record she'd found.

She went back to the access point traces one more time.

She had been looking at them as a data security analyst, trying to identify the infrastructure. But she looked at them now as something else. As a daughter.

The earliest trace, from 2003, had been routed through a commercial VPN service that no longer existed. Standard practice for someone who knew what they were doing. But the routing node it had passed through before the VPN was a server cluster in Lima, Peru.

Not Cincinnati. Not Indianapolis. Not anywhere in the American Midwest.

Lima, Peru.

Emma sat very still.

She thought about her father.

Robert Caldwell. Who had died in a car accident when Emma was eight. Whose estate had been handled so efficiently she had never questioned it. Whose absence had shaped everything -- Linda's grief, Mark's role, Emma's particular self-sufficiency that she had always believed was just who she was.

She tried to follow the logic forward.

It wouldn't hold.

Because if it was true -- if her father had known about the seven sites since 2003 and had been quietly monitoring them for two decades -- then everything she understood about her own life had a different shape than she thought.

Not a story about loss.

Something else entirely.

She sat with that for a long moment. Not processing. Not connecting dots. Just sitting with the weight of it the way you sit with something that is too large to think around.

Then she picked up her phone and called James.

It rang.

And rang.

Outside the window, Carnegie Hall's bell tower stood against the June evening sky, red brick and white trim, 118 years of standing watch over ground that had been sacred for three thousand years before the first stone was laid.

The phone kept ringing.

Emma waited.

EXPLORE THE WORLD OF MOORES HILL

If you've made it this far, you've experienced the mystery, the darkness, and perhaps caught a glimpse of something deeper in that epilogue... something that suggests Moores Hill holds secrets that go far beyond one man's crimes.

You're not wrong.

I've built something for readers like you. An interactive companion to this series that lets you explore Moores Hill the way Emma does... methodically, curiously, with the understanding that some towns have histories that don't stay buried.

Visit www.MooresHillThrillers.com to explore:

- **An Interactive Map**: Click through locations from the books. See where Emma lives, where Carnegie Hall stands, where the ash circles might be hidden.
- **Character Database**: Deep dives into Emma, Owen, James, Sarah, and the others who make Moores Hill real.
- **The Timeline**: 5,000 years of history, from indigenous settlements to modern crimes. The pieces are all there. Some of them connect in ways you might not expect.
- **Town Records**: Documents, histories, and the kind of details that reward careful readers.

This isn't just a website. It's the other half of the story... the parts Emma discovers between the cases, the history she pieces together late at night when she can't sleep.

Book 4 — *The Marked* — arrives early Summer 2026.

Until then, there's a lot to discover.

MooresHillThrillers.com

See you in the archives.

~ Ray

ABOUT THE AUTHOR

Ray Brown is the founder of SentriPup Labs, a maker of anti-behavioral surveillance technology, and the founder of Human Perimeter Press.

Before turning to fiction writing, he spent decades as a technology and security executive. He served as Chief Information Security Officer for a high-growth technology startup he joined early in its development, helping guide the company through expansion to a successful acquisition exceeding $350 million. Earlier in his career, he held executive leadership roles in enterprise infrastructure, including Vice President of Global Data Center Operations at a Fortune 500 organization. Those experiences inform the technology themes and procedural authenticity throughout his fiction.

A native of Bright, Indiana, Ray grew up with deep family roots in southeastern Indiana and the communities surrounding Moores Hill. Ray's mother, Donna McClanahan was a Moores Hill native. The Moores Hill Thriller Series draws on that connection: the real roads, real buildings, and the community memory of a part of Indiana most people pass through without ever truly seeing.

Ray lives and writes in Okeana, Ohio. His partner, Karen Fox (a St. Leon, Indiana native) serves as editor and primary manuscript reviewer. Beyond local accuracy, she performs full editorial passes, catching continuity breaks, logical errors, and story inconsistencies before publication. Her attention to detail helps ensure each book meets professional editorial standards while keeping Dearborn County authentically grounded in place.

MORE BY RAY BROWN

Human Perimeter Press™

THE MOORES HILL THRILLER SERIES

The Keeper

Book 1 - Available Now

She kept the truth for twenty years. Her daughter will keep it no longer.

The Benefactor

Book 2 - Available Now

Every town has a founding family. Not every family deserves to be found.

The Custodian

Book 3 – Available Now

Some ground was never meant to be built on.

The Marked

Book 4 – Summer 2026

Some inheritances you don't discover. They discover you.

***

If you enjoyed The Custodian, please consider leaving a review on Amazon. Reviews help readers find this series and make a real difference for independent publishers.

Follow Ray Brown and Human Perimeter Press for updates on The Custodian and The Moores Hill Thriller Series.

www.ingramcontent.com/pod-product-compliance
Lightning Source LLC
LaVergne TN
LVHW100516110826
845146LV00002B/660

* 9 7 9 8 9 9 3 9 7 7 6 5 2 *